THE CASSEROLE LADIES

The Casserole Ladies

Zany Misadventures in the Quest for Postmortem Romance

BILLY AND LINDA JOHNSON

Bill Johnson Consulting

THE CASSEROLE LADIES
Zany Misadventures in the Quest for Postmortem Romance

To Craig, the real author in the family

Casserole Ladies: Older unmarried women in towns throughout the South who appear on doorsteps of recently widowed or divorced males. These women bring casseroles and other homemade dishes, such beneficence occurring when these men are most vulnerable to feminine sympathy. Potential companionship and/or matrimony often are motivating factors.

Chapter 1

Sunset Memorial Cemetery occupies seventeen acres of barren land not far from downtown Thomasville. Although South Georgia weather in September is typically mild, an unseasonable chill pervaded the pitch-black midnight air, the kind of chill that sends shivers down your spine. Cold gravestones on which they sat intensified the three ladies' shivering. Daffy and Babs, nervously fidgeting on the edge of one marble slab, were separated by two feet of damp centipede grass from Gidget, anxiously squirming on another. All wore expensive designer stilettos, heel-deep in red Georgia clay. Thirteen lit candles encircled them. Creepiness enveloped them. Some people will do anything for postmortem romance.

"Where the hell are they?" asked Daffy, alpha-dog of this group of Casserole Ladies. She wore her mean face—one that would have frightened Hannibal Lecter. "I just knew those two would get lost. Fort Knox my ass! They should have been here by now."

"You know Lilly and Lizzie," Gidget said. Many in Thomasville regard her as the intellectual of the group, but this is a relative assessment. "Besides, they probably had to stop at Dillard's in Tallahassee on the way back. Lilly ain't bought any shoes this week, so she may be going into withdrawal."

"Well, I say we get on with this... uh, what'd we decide to call it? Oh yeah... this ceremony without 'em. It's already midnight, and my butt's getting cold. Three of us are enough anyway," Babs said. This 'ceremony' was her brainchild and latest of her many harebrained schemes.

"Suits me. My butt's getting' sore." Daffy wiggled her rear end which had little fat to cushion it. "It's late, and I got a nine o'clock appointment at the hair salon."

"Getting your hair colored?" Babs asked.

Daffy, Daphne Belvedere, covers up her grey with a tasteful shade of auburn, reminiscent of the school color of her *alma mater*, Florida State University. Her response quoted a line from an old Clairol TV commercial. "Only my hairdresser knows for sure."

"Your hairdresser and everybody else in Thomasville. You are female and over fifty, aren't you?" Gidget's question evinced a phenomenon regarding females, aging, and hair coloring.

At sixty-nine, the oldest, tallest, and most slim of these Casserole Ladies is holding up pretty well despite some sagging and wrinkles. The lines around Daffy's dark, piercing eyes merely accent strength of character. Overall, she's not an unattractive package, which many acknowledge was wasted on her late husband, whom her reply referenced. "Not everybody knows. Royce didn't."

Forty-seven years ago, Daffy married a man more than ten years her senior—a consequence of small-town mainline family interbreeding. Until he died five years ago, Royce Belvedere owned one of Thomasville's local banks, which explains her enormous wealth. The old boy was known for being a stickler for propriety. Daffy never shies away from talking about his lack of carnal imagination and how she intends to make up for it. Take the conversation she had with Lilly after death of the latter's husband less than a year ago.

"How... how did you manage after Royce died? I... I mean with having to adjust to... to no sex? Wasn't it tough?"

"Hmph! Adjusting to no sex after Royce died was like an accountant being told he doesn't have to be exciting anymore. Don't take this wrong, but my goal after Royce died was to find a boy toy that I could have sex and carry on an intelligent conversation with. Unfortunately, that's easier said than done... and not because of a shortage of boy toys willing to have sex."

Many older Southern women traditionally keep a Bible on their nightstand and read a passage every night. Not Daffy. Her nightstand prominently displays a dog-eared copy of *Fifty Shades of Grey*. Help with finding postmortem sex strongly influenced Daffy's decision to attend tonight's ceremony. Another influence was desire to support Babs, who has a fetish for offbeat things.

"Ladies, I repeat, this cold gravestone ain't helping my scrawny butt. Let's get Babs' show on the road," Daffy said.

Babs began fumbling inside an expensive leather Bottega Veneta satchel big enough to park a Volkswagen Beetle in, but came up short. She anxiously looked around. "Who's got the doll?"

In addition to coming up short, Barbara Neauxgeaux (pronounced 'No Go') is short—five feet, six inches tall when wearing four-inch heels. She decided last year to resume using her maiden name, an odd decision given her advanced age. When asked why, she replies that Madame Cassandra, a spiritual advisor just outside Thomasville city limits, advised it.

"Your doll's probably scared and hiding in that circus tent you call a handbag. Where'd you get that thing from? Ringling Brothers?" Daffy asked.

"Ho, ho, ho. Excuse me if I forget to laugh. I just wish this satchel had only cost me as much as a circus tent. That's the last time I carry my credit card when I go shopping with Lilly and Lizzie."

Babs has no worry about money. She married a Griner. Avery was younger, which appealed to her strong maternal instinct. The fact that he hailed from one of the richest families in Thomasville appealed to her pecuniary instinct. As she likes to say, "The silver spoon in baby Avery's mouth was made by Tiffany." He died four years ago, leaving Babs a lot of money but no man to take care of, a shortfall tonight's ceremony will hopefully aid in rectifying.

"Can we please find Babs' doll..." Daffy put on a different mean face this time—one that would have frightened Norman Bates. "It's cold, and my butt's uncomfortable."

Babs was not that uncomfortable sitting on hard marble due to ample padding in her rear end. Like many sixty-three-year-old women, she has a weight problem. It shows in butt, breasts, and cheeks so cute you want to grab one between your thumb and forefinger and squeeze with delight. Her cheeks, that is. At 5' 2", Babs' petite stature makes hiding excess weight a problem, but one solvable with $950 for a loose Milano silk blouse and Lafayette 148 wide-leg pants. Her hairstyle, a neck length bob colored light brown, completes the camouflage.

"Ohhhh, shoot! Where is that doll?" Exasperated, Babs upended her satchel onto the gravestone and began frantically rummaging its contents. "No wonder Avery never wanted to be my partner when we played scavenger hunt."

Some women, Lord knows why, enjoy taking care of men. Such it is with Babs. She pampered Avery the same as she did their kids and grandkids. A need to spoil another man motivates her pursuit of another husband. Psychological testing prior to her 1974 admission to FSU revealed high levels of connubial altruism and an inclination to pursue bizarre schemes like tonight's voodoo ritual. If it's weird or zany, count Babs in.

"Don't panic. I got the doll right here," Gidget said as she extracted the ugly little spud from her Dolce & Gabbana shoulder bag. The little fellow had been previously consecrated in Haiti by a local practitioner of the occult arts.

High school friends nicknamed Gloria Smurfitt after the Gidget character in the 1959 surf movie because of similarities in height and personality. That character was short and defied conventional wisdom. Gidget displays this last characteristic most in her libertarianism. This thoughtful Casserole Lady is quiet except when discussion turns to politics, social mores, religion, or any topic considered off limits in polite conversation by all except libertarians.

"This doll don't look nothing like Bo." Gidget held the doll up for inspection. It was about seven inches in length, crudely made of burlap stuffed with straw, and had two amber glass bead eyes. "I gotta wonder about his political affiliation. I mean... this brown outfit says 'fascist' to me."

"Looks kinda like a Dawg to me," Daffy said.

Gidget graduated from UGA Pharmacy School despite receiving a dubious honor her junior year. Her award, Best Explosion in Chemistry Lab, won out of a competition of thirteen explosions. She held the doll close to her face. "This ugly thing's too cute to be a Dawg. Probably from one of them radical colleges below the border that has an Indian mascot. When are y'all gonna get politically correct anyway?"

"FSU will get politically correct when I quit dying my hair red," Daffy replied.

It could be said sixty-two-year old Gidget's dark brown hair *sans* grey comes from good genes, but it does not. It comes from a bottle of Wella Koleston Perfect. She procures it from her late husband's drug store, which she inherited. Sam insisted that the Smurfitt Phamily Pharmacy should forever remain locally owned. Her reply to Daffy's quip alluded to this. "Sam Smurfitt will come back and sell out to CVS before you quit dying your hair."

Sam died three years ago after being Gidget's closest companion for thirty-six years. They worked together, traveled together, and played tennis and golf together. Saturdays in the fall never failed to find Gidget and Sam watching Dawg football together, wearing matching red Georgia football jerseys imprinted with the face of the team's bulldog mascot.

Gidget sometimes admits, after a few too many at happy hour, that she misses her "best friend" and wishes for another Sam. One suspects a stray irrational hope, such as tonight's voodoo ritual magically bringing her another male companion, as being the impetus behind this logical libertarian's attendance. If Gidget was totally rational, she probably would not be one of these Casserole Ladies.

Daffy leaned in for a closer look at the doll. "I swear to God... He looks like a clone of Royce Belvedere—"

"Daffy! We're in a cemetery. Royce may be listening," Babs said in all earnestness.

"No! I swear to God. He looks just like Royce... dull... lifeless. I remember when Royce and I would go to Christmas parties. I would decorate him with Christmas tree lights just so people would notice him."

"How about we get on with this ceremony?" Gidget asked.

"I agree. Hand me the doll." As Babs accepted the doll from Gidget, she realized something was missing. "Oh, oh... first hand me the photo of Bo."

"Oh yeah!" Daffy fumbled inside a Prada Daino Shopper. Oddly enough, the expensive handbag contained only nineteen dollars in fives and ones. A dreamy look glowed in her eyes as she extracted an 8"x10" photo and passed it to Gidget. She in turn accepted then ogled the image so long that she had to be prompted to relinquish it to Babs.

Babs placed the photo and doll next to a collection of occult oddities lying in front of her on the gravestone. Most notable among them was an old book, crudely bound in material made of stiff Haitian bunchgrass making it cumbersome to open—a process Babs carefully performed. Daffy held a flashlight overhead as Babs located the correct page.

Sitting on a cold gravestone in a deserted cemetery at midnight likely contributed to Babs' bumbling recitation of the Haitian voodoo love spell. "*Stepi... Stepitali...* uhhhh... *Me...* uh... *Melutasi...* uh... uh... *Rabubo... Ro Ro...* uh... Bo."

"Y'all sure y'all got that right? Or did y'all screw it up? I hope this don't turn out to be another German pipeline thing." Daffy seldom minces words.

"Well, that's what it says right here," Babs said. She gingerly positioned the book for Daffy's viewing.

After a minute of silent reading, Daffy asked, "What language is this anyway? It don't look very much like French to me."

"I'm... I'm not sure. Miss Monique told me they speak French down there as well as a couple other things."

Gidget leaned over and likewise silently read before commenting. "It don't look like French to me either... but I don't speak French."

"Neither apparently does Babs," Daffy said.

"Ho, ho, ho. Excuse me if I forget to laugh. I told y'all I only took one semester of French my freshman year."

"Did you pass?" Gidget asked.

"Don't ask. Don't matter anyhow. We don't need to understand the words... just say 'em. Now, we need the ointment... the red one."

Gidget reached into her handbag, extracted a jar, opened it, and added it to the pile of oddities.

"Okay..." Babs moved the book back and forth in front of her like a trombone slide, struggling without her reading glasses under Daffy's flashlight. "Says here we each put a dab of this ointment on our index finger, rub it into the doll's genital area, and pass it to the next one. Which finger is the index finger?"

"This one." Daffy held up her hand, middle finger extended.

"Why do we have to rub it into the genital area? Sounds kind of gross." Gidget picked up the little fellow, delicately patted some red goo on its head, and laid it down.

"Don't ask me. That's what it says right here in this here book. Oh, oh! After you rub it in, then you got to kiss it," Babs said.

Daffy said, "This gets kinkier by the minute. Kissing a voodoo doll's crotch while sitting on a gravestone. I could get into this."

"Restrain yourself, Daff. There's got to be a psychological name for doing something like kissing dolls' crotches. It sounds like some sort of weird sexual fetish. Dollyphobia?"

"No. That sounds like a fear of Dollywood," Daffy said.

As always, Gidget provided an answer. "Agalmatophilia is a fetish where you get aroused by things like mannequins and dolls."

"I don't wanna know how you know that." Daffy moved her hands to cover her ears in a 'happy place' gesture.

"My grandmother's brother got caught having sex late one night with one of the mannequins in the store window at Mansour's. Spent three months in LaGrange City Jail."

"Tell me that at least it was a female mannequin."

"Okay, Gidg. Pick him back up, rub the goo on his crotch, then kiss him. Go ahead. We ain't got all night," Babs said. Gidget obeyed, except she kissed the doll's face, eliciting Babs' rebuke. "Not there. Down there... on his little crotch."

"You're kiddin'! I ain't kissin' down there where we put all that goo. Besides, that sounds... kinda sick."

"Y'all don't have to if y'all don't want to. It just means more of Bo for those of us that do."

Gidget quickly bussed the little fellow as directed and handed him to Daffy. After she and Babs completed their assignments, a noise sounded nearby.

"What's that?!" Daffy asked.

"Where?"

"Over there. That way. Over there." Daffy pointed to a nearby headstone.

"What if it's a cop? I saw headlights go by the cemetery a while ago," Babs said.

"What if they wanna see our IDs? My driver's license picture looks awful." Daffy had requested the DMV clerk to reshoot her photo one more time, but the woman balked after the eleventh attempt.

"If they ask for my driver's license, I'm not gonna give it to them unless they promise not to look at the picture." As she spoke, Babs put on her mean face. Hers would have frightened Winnie The Pooh.

"I'm gonna give them my Social Security card instead! Thank God that don't have my picture on it," Gidget said. One for the books—a libertarian with a Social Security card.

"Y'all just keep your cool. I don't see anything," Daffy said.

"Me neither."

More noise, this time closer.

"Sounds like footsteps." Gidget's head rotated back and forth. "I still don't see anything. What if it's one of them homeless men we see downtown? I bet they come here to sleep."

"What if it's a rapist?" Babs asked. "Or worse."

"What could be worse than being raped?" Daffy likes sex, but only the consensual kind.

Babs had the answer. "A ghost. I used to hear all sorts of stories about ghosts in this cemetery when I was a kid."

"Don't be silly. There's no such thing as ghosts."

"No ghosts in this here cemetery. Just zombies." Gidget ended her tease with stiff Frankenstein shoulder movements.

"Why did you have to say that?!" Babs asked. "Ghosts, okay. Zombies, not okay."

"Be quiet. Listen," Daffy said.

Ominous footstep-like sounds very near their location pierced the darkness, growing louder as seconds passed.

Gidget moaned. "I knew coming here was a stupid idea." Talk about stating the obvious.

"Quiet! Sounds like it's real close. Anyone remember to bring a pistol?" Daffy asked. Silence provided an answer. "I should've known. The one night we need a gun, everyone forgets to bring theirs."

Something close by snapped.

"Where did that come from?"

"Right there!!!"

At that point, a scary-looking small shape bounded from behind a nearby headstone and darted straight between the ladies' marble slabs.

"Aiiiiiiiiieeeeeeeeeeeeeeeeee!!!!!!!!!!"

"A 'possum!!"

"A racoon!!"

"SHIT!!!!!"

The terrified little creature minimized travel time between the ladies' feet and disappeared. Babs fell sideways on the slab in her effort to escape. Daffy collided with Gidget, causing both to fall backwards. Daffy then collided with Babs as she completed her fall. Gidget finished with a butt-over-head somersault. In the end, three women lay in a heap, on and beside the gravestone slabs. Four of six stiletto heels were destroyed. Simultaneous with this pile up, a sudden explosion of blinding light detonated—a light so bright that it pained everyone's optic nerve.

"Don't move! Stay right where you are!" The booming voice came from somewhere within the blinding light. A creature seemed to materialize through the light in a manner similar to the way Star Fleet personnel materialized during teleportation in *Star Trek*. The being was very large, over six feet tall, and clad entirely in black. Darth Vader on steroids.

As her eyes began to adjust, Daffy addressed the being. "Darrell? Darrell Mundell? It's me... Daffy."

"Mzz Belvedere? Daffy? Is that you?"

The being became recognizable as a Thomasville City Police Officer. The source of the blinding light was his police cruiser's headlights. Officer Darrell walked over to the pile of women and began helping them stand up.

"Mzz Gidget, Mzz Babs, Mzz Daffy." After Officer Darrell took Daffy's hand and assisted her, he stood back and surveyed the scene. "Y'all know what my first question is."

Three heads furiously rotated, each looking at the others for some sort of bogus but plausible answer, as well as someone to deliver it. It was up to Daffy. "Well... uh... we... uh, we were just about to uh uh—"

Babs took over. "To celebrate a... uh, religious festival..."

"A religious festival? Here, in Sunset Memorial Cemetery? At midnight?" asked Officer Darrell.

"Yeah, it's one of our church's time-honored festivals," Daffy said.

"What kind of church festival?"

"Yeah, it's called the Festival of the uh..." Gidget's attempt quickly aborted itself.

"The Festival of the Departed," Babs said. After that, she experienced lockjaw of the brain. "uh... uh... uh..."

Daffy took over, each phrase embellishing on the previous. "The Festival of the Dearly Departed... no, no... the Loving Festival of the Dearly Departed... the Loving Festival of the Dearly Departed Souls. Yeah, that's it."

Casserole Lady teamwork at its finest.

Officer Darrell silently looked at each of the three women nervously fidgeting in front of him and rolled his eyes upward. "The Loving Festival of the Dearly Departed Souls. I don't believe I've ever heard of that one before."

"It's one of them Episcopal things... always at midnight on September 5th. That's why all them candles. You know how Episcopalians like their fancy ceremonies," Babs said.

"All y'all ain't Episcopalian, are y'all?" Officer Darrell must have known the answer as he attended Sawgrass Baptist Church with Babs.

She quickly realized this and offered an explanation. "Oh, I'm... I'm just here to support Daffy and Gidget... and for the festival wine."

"Y'all know this place is closed after 6 pm. Loving Festival or no Loving Festival..." Officer Darrell paused in a failed attempt to stifle a chuckle. "Lord God... This is gonna get a lot of laughs at shift change... How am I gonna explain this one? I get a call at midnight about some sort of goin's on at the cemetery, slip in with headlights off, pop my headlights on, and find what looks like a bunch of Kardashians in a pile up on the Montrose family's plot."

"You ain't gonna tell anyone about this, are you?!" Gidget asked.

"Ain't no way I ain't telling the other officers about this one... This is way too good. But don't y'all worry, everyone knows y'all. They'll understand. Y'all should consider yourselves lucky that I ain't arresting y'all for trespassing. Are y'all about finished with your 'festival'?"

"Oh yeah, we don't have that much more to do," Babs said.

"Well, I'll let y'all get back to it. Just be careful and be quick. I gotta go see about a rogue squirrel on South College Street." With that, he got into his cruiser and drove off.

"Let's take Darrell's advice and get this thing finished quick. Where the hell are Lilly and Lizzie anyway? They missed all the fun," Daffy said, sarcastically referring to this kind of nonsense as fun. Lilly and Lizzie's fun came earlier in the day in their own quest for postmortem romance.

Chapter 2

Lilly's Mercedes GLC sped along a four-lane U.S. highway in northern Florida. If stopped, it would not be the first time her lead foot, clad in an expensive Manolo Blahnik sandal, garnered a speeding ticket. No matter, they must complete their mission by nightfall in order to be back in Thomasville by midnight for Babs' voodoo ritual. Lizzie, mastermind of the mission, sat beside her in the front passenger seat, impatiently looking for road signs. A blonde and a redhead in a fast SUV on a balmy September morning.

Lilly's foot eased up ever so slightly on the gas pedal. "Oh, fudge! I think we should've taken Route 27."

"I think we should've taken Uber," Lizzie said.

This operation arose from a conversation two hours earlier while Lilly and Lizzie had breakfast with Daffy, Babs, and Gidget at Henderson's, a restaurant frequented by the well-to-do in Thomasville. Only Lilly seemed to appreciate Lizzie's idea of a 'prospecting trip' to the Active Adult Retirement Community in sunny central Florida known as The Villages. No surprise there. Despite stark differences in their looks and personalities, these two always jell. Lizzie explained the trip's rationale to the other four ladies.

"Y'alls' 'ceremony' tonight sounds peachy, except for being at midnight in a cemetery, but I'm thinking that a little prospecting trip might be more productive."

"Huh?"

"What I'm talking about is going to where the widowers are and bringing 'em back here."

"Huh?"

"Look, what I'm talking about is going to the Fort Knox of Old Widowers and bringing back a truckload of gold."

"Huh?"

"Where is this gold mine of old widowers?" Lilly asked, then enthusiastically volunteered, "I'd love to go with you!"

"Where else... The Villages. But don't worry. We'll be back in time for the 'ceremony' tonight."

This is how Lilly, a genteel widow, and Lizzie, a lowbrow, four-time divorcee, left right after breakfast in Lilly's Mercedes to go look for old men. Unfortunately, finding postmortem romance in contemporary Thomasville, Georgia, has come down to this kind of nonsense. Like the rest of the country, this small town lacks sufficient male suitors for older women, such as our ditsy heroines who find life without male companionship unbearable.

The ladies' travel quandary, two hours into their trip, results from a heated argument but not with each other. Shortly after departure, Lizzie got into a dispute with the Mercedes' voice-enabled GPS—the newest one with the latest artificial intelligence technology.

"We should've brought my TomTom," Lilly said as the Thomasville City Limits sign grew smaller in her rearview mirror. "I've never used the GPS in this Mercedes."

"How'd you learn to use your TomTom?"

"One of my younger grandkids... I forget which one... showed me when I got it ten years ago. But they've all been too busy to show me how this one works."

Lilly traded in her two-year-old Mercedes SUV for the new one six months ago. Reading the GPS technical manual is something she would never attempt. A delicate Southern lady never stoops to reading technical manuals.

"You gotta get with the twenty-first century," Lizzie chided. "Nobody uses them old-style GPSs anymore. Don't worry. We can figure this Mercedes out. It's no different than the voice navigation on my Lincoln. Just push your talk button, and let me take over."

"Where's that?"

Lizzie's intense search for the correct button resulted in the activation of both heads-up display and active lane keeping assist, deactivation of parking assist, and Bluetooth connectivity to Lilly's iPhone before striking pay dirt.

"How may I help you?"

Lizzie smiled confidently. "Umm... we need y'all's help with goin' to... uh, that there Villages... uhh..."

Unfortunately, written words fail to convey the sometimes-complex nature of a Southern accent, especially one as thick as Lizzie's. Some, actually a lot, of people in Thomasville characterize this Casserole Lady as crass, but this should not be construed as indicating she cannot communicate adequately. Suffice it to say that her accent probably accounted in no small part for subsequent responses by Lilly's voice navigation system.

"I am sorry, but I do not understand. Do you want to start route guidance?"

"No, we wanna go to that there Villages. That place in Fluerder where all the old people live."

"I am sorry, but I do not understand. Here is a list of navigation categories from which you may select."

The GPS' screen next displayed a menu.

"I don't see no Villages on y'all's list. I don't even see no cities on it." Lizzie turned to Lilly and whispered, "This thing don't work nothing like my Lincoln's voice navigation."

Unfortunately, the Mercedes heard her comment.

"You are using Mercedes voice navigation, not Lincoln voice navigation. Navigation commands may differ. Please refer to your owner's manual."

"Don't y'all think I know that I'm in a Mercedes and not my own Lincoln?! I ain't that senile," Lizzie whispered the next word to no one in particular, "yet."

"Lizzie! Calm down."

"Please do."

"Did y'all's GPS just say that? My Lincoln's a hell of a lot easier to use than this damn thing. What a piece of shit."

"Please refrain from using profanity when interacting with Mercedes voice navigation."

"Don't y'all tell me what to do!"

"Lizzie! Calm down. You're only making her madder."

"Me calm down?! This damn bitch is s'pposed to be working for us."

"Please refrain from using profanity when interacting with Mercedes voice navigation."

"I'LL SAY WHATEVER I WANT TO Y'ALL, AND Y'ALL CAN'T DO NOTHING ABOUT IT! STUPID BITCH!"

"Please refrain from using profanity when interacting with Mercedes voice navigation."

"WHY DON'T YOU JUST GO TO HELL?!" Lizzie looked at Lilly. "I'm telling you... I could've done a better job finding the Villages using a paper map."

"If you think you're so damn smart, find the Villages yourself, [inaudible]."

It was at this point that Lilly's entire GPS system abruptly shut down, displaying a 'system temporarily unavailable' message. Lizzie swears she heard the voice navigation system add the word "bitch" at the end of her last statement. An hour and a half into system unavailability, they still discussed the episode.

"Maybe next time you'll treat my GPS with a little more respect," Lilly said.

"Next time, let's bring your TomTom..." Lizzie hesitated. "We... I... I can't believe I'm saying this... We may just have to stop at a convenience store and ask for directions."

"We can't do that. Wendell would rollover in his grave if I stopped on the road to ask for directions. He always said asking for directions was a sign of low IQ."

Wendell, Lilly's deceased husband, died almost a year ago, shortly after she turned fifty-four. Both hailed from Thomasville gentry, his being the White family. It was love at first sight for both, and they experienced thirty-one years of marital bliss that she desperately misses. Finding true love once again motivates her in this Florida excursion as well as most of her Casserole Ladies misadventures.

Lilly then revealed the real reason why she never likes to stop at convenience stores to ask for directions. "Besides, they's so nasty. I have to Purell myself after I walk out. You never know who's touched what in convenience stores... people that ride motorcycles, hippies, you name it."

An obsession with cleanliness accords with Lilly's most notable personality characteristic—pure naïveté, unblemished by multifaceted thinking. That kind of thinking can get too messy. Friends sometimes comment that the name, Lilly White, perfectly matches the slim blonde's alabaster complexion and flaxen hair. She began coloring it during her freshman year at the University of Florida and has since forgotten the original color.

"Have it your way," Lizzie said, "but at least we got some pretty scenery to look at as we wander through Florida... At least I think we do. It's hard to tell when things go by so fast. You ever think about driving in NASCAR?"

"Ho, ho, ho. Excuse me if I forget to laugh. Besides, you ain't missin' nothing anyway. This part of Florida ain't nothing but pine trees and palmetto bushes. Limiting people to sixty-five miles an hour on a four-lane road is ridiculous—" Intense screams from her passenger suddenly interrupted Lilly's travelogue.

"HEY! HEY! What's that?! Slow down! SLOW DOWN!" Lizzie yelled.

Lilly's lead foot immediately lifted off the gas pedal. The windshield turned black as dozens of very small creatures smashed into it.

"Love bugs. It *is* that time of year in Florida. This is when they swarm, making love. I don't know why Florida DMV don't issue travel advisories this time of year about these gross things." Lilly's disgust with the nasty situation registered on her face.

"That's right! I'd forgotten. The nice thing about love bugs is once they smash into your car, they don't come off easily."

"I'd forgotten that this is the time of year they mate, or I'd have suggested we take your Lincoln."

"At least someone has found sex in Florida," Lizzie said.

Sex, but more importantly the money that married sex potentially yields, has been a lifelong quest for Elizabeth Sherbert. Finding another meal ticket spurred her into making this Florida trip. Thomasville locals debate as to which spouse's infidelity was the reason for her latest divorce. No matter, as he agreed to a generous settlement. Despite this, Lizzie complains that sixty-five-year-old women should get more alimony because they have more needs. Her needs result from spending money faster than it comes in.

After the Mercedes' wipers had sufficiently cleansed its windshield of one of Florida's most famous sex shows, Lilly participated in one of her town's oldest institutions—the Thomasville rumor mill. It is also the fastest and most accurate source of local gossip. She said, "Speakin' of sex, one of the ladies in the garden club forwarded me a text the other day from one of her friends who got the text from her cousin that said that her mother texted her that she saw one of the other garden club ladies having lunch with Sonny Biskit."

"Sonny Biskit... All *that* man wants is food and sex." Many would say Lizzie's comment applies to *all* men.

"Speaking of Sonny, I think Daffy is planning on giving in to him again."

"Oh?"

"Yeah, she mentioned last night that he asked her to go to a tractor pull in Waycross," Lilly said.

"I like tractor pulls myself, but the location of that one alone should be enough to make that decision. Tell me that she said 'not only no, but hell no'."

"She said she hasn't decided which is worse... a tractor pull, Waycross, or being with Sonny Biskit."

"But you think she just might take him up on it, don't you?"

Lilly nodded. "Yep."

"I'd have to be a lot more desperate for sex than I am right now to consider a tractor pull in Waycross with Sonny Biskit. If he, at least, had money, I might reconsider." Lizzie's compulsive spending is widely known. Case in point, she has the local plastic surgeon on retainer and eyelids tighter than Nancy Pelosi's to prove it. Lizzie is presently debating between lip implants or a Caribbean cruise.

"Even considering going with him says just how pitiful the eligible bachelor situation is in Thomasville."

"Daffy must need sex more than I need a meal ticket that is probably playing golf right now in The Villages," Lizzie said.

She often says what's on her mind before her brain can judiciously filter its content. Her mind was not her main attraction during her younger days, especially as a college freshman when she weighed significantly less than she does now. Lizzie was quite popular with the boys that year. Maybe it was the green eyes and red hair, which is still red, although the roots are not. There was no sophomore, or any other subsequent academic year at the University of Georgia (hereafter referred to as either UGA, Bulldogs, or simply Dawgs). Rumors insinuate that the Dean of Women advised her not to return in September 1970. They also insinuated that some sort of sexual misadventure with a faculty member provoked this advice. Lizzie remains uncharacteristically untalkative about it to this day.

"Daffy's getting on up there in age... she's looking at seventy, ain't she? She's been widowed for what, five years now?" Lilly asked.

"She ain't the only one looking at seventy. I'm looking at it right now on your speedometer. Slow down. Looks like a sign coming up anyway. What's it say? I forgot my glasses."

"Me too."

"I do declare Lilly. Y'all would forget your nose if it weren't stuck on your face, but I guess that's not too bad for a blonde who thinks that if you cut a snake in half, you get two snakes."

"Ho, ho, ho. Excuse me, but I forgot to laugh. Make fun if you want, but snakes do refresh themselves. Each half grows the part they's missing." Lilly slowed the SUV to a crawl and leaned over to better read the sign. "Looks like 'something Villages,' and there's an arrow pointing to the right."

A smile of smug satisfaction appeared on Lizzie's face. "And the other ladies this morning all said we'd probably get lost. Here's the turn."

Two more signs and three more turns later, they drove down a gravel road.

"It just dawned on me," Lilly said, "you never mentioned exactly what we're gonna do at The Villages. We can't very well hogtie five men and make'em ride back to Thomasville with us."

"Y'all just let me do the talking. We're a couple of mature, hot chicks looking for a more relaxed lifestyle—"

"More relaxed than in Thomasville?"

Not realizing Lilly was serious, Lizzie smiled at what she assumed to be a feeble attempt at humor. She said, "We're gonna hang out around a couple of the common facilities. Like the recreation center, pool, and so forth, and we're gonna check out the male population and extend some invitations... as appropriate, of course. My only worry is that there might not be much in the way of a male population. This is an over fifty-five development and may be overflowing with old women like us."

"There ain't much on this road either. Wait... I think I see some-thing up ahead on the left." Lilly slowed to a stop in front of an asphalt-paved driveway with an arched entrance and began reading the sign on top of the arch, "Suwanee Village—"

"Must be a section of The Villages." Lizzie squinted. "What's it say below that? I can't read the smaller lettering without my glasses. Before I forget, remind me after we stop to show you the pictures my daughter just texted me of her youngest child's third birthday. She was naked, running through the backyard sprinklers—"

"Your daughter or granddaughter?" Lilly asked.

"Ho, ho, ho. Excuse me if I forget to laugh."

"Just kidding. Which of your daughters sent the pix?"

"The one by my first or second husband," Lizzie said.

"I thought you had daughters by both of 'em?"

"Yeah, but who can keep track with four ex-husbands?"

"Hold on a minute..." Lilly leaned out her window. "It says, 'A Naturist Community for Alternative-Lifestyle Adults'. What's 'A Naturist Community'?"

"I think it just means that it's one of them planned developments where they don't tear out all the trees and put up a bunch of asphalt parking lots and high-rise concrete condos," Lizzie said. "I've heard The Villages is real big on keeping its landscaping kind of natural."

"Yeah." Lilly scanned the area. "They do have lots of plants and trees around here. What about 'Alternative-Lifestyle Adults'? What does that mean?"

"Oh, they're just trying to be polite and not hurt the old farts' feelings. They just don't wanna say 'for Old Retired Folks.' 'Alternative-Lifestyle Adults' is just another way of saying old retirees that don't have to get up at seven o'clock to go to work and can wear their lounge pants until one o'clock in the afternoon. Go ahead... follow the driveway on down to the office."

Chapter 3

Morning drive to Suwanee Village and midnight voodoo ritual both arose from the previously mentioned breakfast meeting that morning at Henderson's. That gathering began with a classic example of Babs' wackiness.

"Huh?!" Their young waitress' face revealed disbelief more than inquisitiveness. The girl's exclamation was in response to Bab's assertion that the Earth has seven moons.

Daffy stared daggers at Lilly. "You know never to bring up the subject of the moon in front of Babs."

"But... but it's such a lovely pin. I was just complementing this sweet young thing on it," Lilly said. She had noticed a brooch depicting a smiling moon pinned on their waitress' blouse as she took their orders.

Babs immediately commented that it was "a Full Moon, one of Earth's seven moons." As a child, her family often sat on their front porch at night. Babs' father occasionally pointed out a Quarter Moon in the night sky or a Half Moon or a Waxing Moon and so on. Babs childishly understood each of the seven phase designations to be a different physical moon and never abandoned this belief, even in adulthood.

After orders were taken and their puzzled young waitress departed for the kitchen via the bar, they turned their attention elsewhere.

"So, continue with your story." Daffy, the group's leader, typically guides their conversations. She looked at Babs. "Did you meet anyone?"

By 'anyone', these Casserole Ladies knew she meant single men, usually of advanced age and often widowed, deemed suitable as potential mates.

"Ain't that the purpose of going on a cruise?" Lizzie asked.

"There was a very nice gentleman from Charleston," Babs said. "He was a widower in his mid-60s. We hit it off right away... a very good conversationalist, excellent at shuffleboard, loves gin rummy, not too overweight—"

"Get to the good part." Lizzie interrupted because she knew Babs was beginning what was sure to be a long-winded account of her interactions with the gentleman from Charleston. Interruptions tend to be commonplace among these Casserole Ladies as they tend to ramble.

"I'm getting there. And he was a great dancer. I haven't danced that much since high school... except for the time Avery drank too many Singapore Slings at the Country Club—"

"When are you gonna get to the good part?" Gidget asked, reinforcing Lizzie's request for pithiness. "The part where y'all got together—"

"I'm getting there. Anyway, we started discussing things on the way to my cabin... I used getting him some BenGay as an excuse to swing by my room... By the way, that's the last time I'm staying in a cabin with a balcony on one of those cruises."

Daffy's exasperation finally bubbled over after two minutes of Babs' balcony story, resulting in an outburst. "We don't need to hear no more about getting seasick on your balcony! When ARE you gonna get to the good part? What did y'all do on your bed?"

"As I was about to say before being so rudely interrupted, he's lying face down on my bed, and I'm rubbing BenGay on his lower back... kind of reminded me of how I used to rub it on Avery's back, and he'd snooze off on me—"

"We're not talking about Avery! We're talking about the man from Charleston, please!"

"Oh yeah... anyway... did I mention he'd pulled a lower back muscle doing the limbo? Can you believe it? A sixty-six-year-old man should never attempt limbo. When I tried it, they had to peel me off the floor—"

"I know there's gonna be a payoff somewhere in this story—"

"I'm getting there. Just be patient. Y'all know that when I got a story in my brain, I got to tell it exactly like it is in my brain. If I take short cuts, it don't come out right. Anyway, so I'm really enjoying slowly rubbing the BenGay into his lower back when I make my move. That's when he tells me that all he's looking for is some sort of platonic love—"

"Oh, how sad!" A look of sorrow spread over Lizzie's face as she tsk-tsked. "And he wasn't even too overweight! How often do you find an older man that ain't grossly overweight? What did you say?"

"I said, 'Sounds pretty good to me. I'm game'—"

"Pretty good?! You gotta be kidding? You're game for a relationship with a man that involves no sex?!" Gidget rolled her eyes.

"I didn't realize that's what he was talking about until he explained it to me! I assumed platonic meant some sort of kinky sex thing. It don't mean that at all. It's like you said... It means no sex, just talking. Who the hell wants just that?! Ain't sex why God invented Viagra? Poor old guy... He's apparently still got this thing going for his deceased wife."

"Sounds like pickins on that boat were mighty slim..." Lizzie shook her head. "Which pretty much describes the situation right here. Suitable men in Thomasville are scarcer than deviled eggs after a church picnic. Seems like the ones we run across are only after a nurse and a purse. Where did your boat stop? Meet anyone in port?"

Before a reply could be offered, their waitress approached with three Mimosas and two Bloody Mary's. After a toast, Babs continued.

"Mmmm... Hope I can remember all of 'em. They stop at so many places on these cruises. Uh... Nassau, Saint Thomas, Port-au-Prince, Martinique... goodness gracious, I can't remember 'em all, it was so many. It was a wonderful cruise. Two weeks' worth of the unholy trinity—buffet, booze, and blather. Worst of all, they had the best-lookin' pool boys, and none of my bathin' suits fit right. But at least they had a pretty good hairstylist on board. I always worry about getting a bad hairdo on these cruises."

"You know what they say when you get a bad 'doo, don't you?" Lizzie asked.

"No, what?"

"Wait long enough, and it'll grow on you."

After a round of groans, Babs said, "I just wish Avery could've been there with me."

"He would have loved being there, having you look after him. Maybe next cruise, you'll find someone." Gidget's *faux* consolation ended with a tease. "Or, maybe take Sonny next time. You could look after him."

"Please!" Daffy's screech resulted in a spray of Bloody Mary from her mouth. "Why do you have to remind us? Talk about slim pickins. Sonny Biskit has the personality of a dishrag and is almost as smart as one. He's what's wrong with this town."

"Then why do we put up with him?" Lilly asked.

"Because there ain't enough acceptable, older single men. Way too difficult around here for us lonely uh... mature women. Isn't this just the best Bloody Mary ever? It restores my faith in alcohol consumption... not that my faith in alcohol consumption has ever wavered. I say we have our waitress bring out another round when she brings our food."

"I agree on all y'all's points, especially the rounds. I'm not going to the pharmacy this morning, so another glass or two shouldn't be a problem..." Gidget paused, carefully selecting her words as well as enjoying another sip of Mimosa. "The supply of single men... uh... supply of single men compatible with our chronological situations..."

Daffy deliberately lowered her glass in order to emphasize a point she was going to make about Gidget's verbal pussyfooting. "If you mean our old age, just say it."

Gidget seemed heedless of Daffy's comment and continued her lecture. "It's like in economics... supply and demand imbalance... too many of us, too little of them. We need more of them—"

"Or less of us," Lilly said. She noticed the others looking at her and asked, "What?"

"You might want to think about that a little," Lizzie said.

Gidget forged on. "The point I was going to make is that the limited supply of acceptable men facing women in our chronological situations results in loneliness—"

"And sexual frustration," Daffy said.

"As I was about to say, it would be so nice to have someone that could be as good a companion as Sam was. Even watching football without him ain't the same. Georgia scores a touchdown, I'm sittin' there in my red Georgia jersey, I unconsciously do a high-five expecting to bump Sam's hand, but my hand touches nothing but air..." Gidget had unconsciously initiated a high-five gesture during her reminiscence. As her voice trailed off, she found herself looking up at her hand. Self-consciously, she lowered her gaze and ran her hand through her hair.

"I know it's lonely, Gidg, I know, and grandkids ain't the same as men—" Daffy said.

"Except in their emotional quotient levels." After four husbands, Lizzie would know.

Daffy abruptly switched tone. "As long as them damn Mahjong Mammas keep beating us to the punch, we're all gonna stay lonely. Seems like one of 'em snatches up every suitable man just as soon as he comes on the market."

Mahjong Mammas, four other older unmarried women, and our five Casserole Ladies were members of a larger Thomasville women's social organization years ago. That entity engaged in a variety of entertainments, including dice and card games. Unsurprisingly, disagreements arose. Our five ladies wanted to play Bunko exclusively, while the other four preferred Mahjong. In an acrimonious split, two smaller groups emerged. Our five Casserole Ladies began playing Bunko exclusively, while the other four only played Mahjong, accounting for their nickname—Mahjong Mammas. The Mammas are now led by one of the most sneaky, conniving women imaginable. More on her later. As the Mammas and Casserole Ladies contain widows and divorcees, competition for males serves to heighten inter-group hostility.

"Speaking of coming on the market," Lizzie said as she opened her Michael Kors handbag. She extracted her iPhone and read something from the Thomasville rumor mill. "I just remembered. A friend texted me this morning... Where is it? Oh, here it is. A friend of hers forwarded a text from her sister saying that one of George Bentley's neighbors put it on the neighborhood Facebook page that she saw a body being rolled into an ambulance parked in his driveway this morning."

"Beverly Bentley?!"

"Who else? It's been over a year since she was diagnosed with cancer."

"Poor Beverly. Poor George..." All five uttered the lament simultaneously and observed a moment of silence, something that rarely occurs among this group.

"We gotta do something about it!" Lilly's exclamation shattered the silence such that diners at the next table looked over.

"About what? Beverly's death?" An odd look appeared on Gidget's face as she asked her question, voice lowered.

"About everything... Mahjong Mammas always getting to the men first."

Daffy said, "About a beautiful hunk like Bo Thomas still on the market after three years."

"About having to go outside all by yourself on cold early mornings in pajamas to get your newspaper," Gidget said.

Babs frowned. "We need to do something about having to date men like Sonny Biskit."

"I'd like to do something about having to pump my own gas."

Daffy looked at Lizzie. "I hope you're talking about your car."

"But what *do* we do?" Lilly asked.

"I know what." Babs smiled and swallowed the rest of her Mimosa.

"Is it legal?" Daffy asked. "It better be legal! Your last bright idea cost me a fortune in legal fees."

"How was I to know that panel of buttons and switches controlled a pipeline in Germany? Besides, Lilly pushed the button... not me! Ain't these Mimosas tasty?"

"Don't try to change the subject on me, Miss Babsie Neauxgeaux. And Lilly wasn't the one who said, 'They won't have anything important in an unlocked room.' Over 5,000 acres of potatoes in Bavaria ruined…"

The NSA case number is J2I-2017-GER-00135.

"At least our mugshots weren't in color." Daffy had missed her monthly touch up before the German pipeline incident. She said, "And why do they have to include that stupid ruler that shows a person's height in them pictures. At least Royce was long gone when it happened. No telling what he'd have done. Y'all know how he was."

Lizzie nodded. "Royce Belvedere would've had a dying duck fit over that little incident."

"Although… it wouldn't have cost me anything in bed. Anyway, I know I'm gonna regret it, but what is this… this scheme of yours this time?"

"It ain't no scheme! And, it's legal as well. At least, I think it is."

"Are you going to get to the point, or is this going to be another never ending story? What exactly is it?" Lizzie asked.

"Something I picked up on the cruise."

"Picked up?" Lilly asked, eyebrows raised. "Someone other than the gentleman from Charleston? What's his name?"

"His name? Aren't we literal today? Not bad for a blonde that reorganizes her shoe closet every week." Daffy winked at the others.

"Ho, ho, ho. Excuse me if I forget to laugh," Lilly said.

"Is Babs ever gonna tell us who this 'something' is?" Gidget asked.

"Babsie'll get 'round to it… in two or three hours," Lizzie said.

Babs furtively looked around and whispered, "Voodoo. The 'something' is voodoo. I visited the Marche de Fer in Port-au-Prince. The Marche is a market filled with shops selling voodoo stuff."

"They have voodoo in the Bahamas?" Lilly asked.

"Port-au-Prince is in Haiti. Anyway, the owner of one of the voodoo shops was very helpful. Miss Monique. She helped me pick out some stuff… potions, dolls, some books… We can try 'em out. It'd be fun!"

"Voodoo... fun?! You mean like wearing pantyhose to a July wedding on the beach is fun? Please explain." A third of Lizzie's Bloody Mary disappeared in one gulp. "But first, pass me the Tabasco sauce, Babsie. Tabasco has to be one of the best inventions in history... even better than the wheel."

"What about the electric hairdryer?" Lilly asked.

"I'll concede the point," Lizzie said, "or it'll be an hour before I get my Tabasco."

As she passed it to Lizzie, Babs' eyes focused on the bottle. "This stuff reminds me. We could use one of Miss Monique's love potions on whomever we want as our 'intended'."

Everyone at the table knew the identity of the 'intended'.

"And! We could use one of Miss Monique's wrath ointments on the Mahjong Mammas!"

"Bless your heart," Daffy said, "but this is about as crazy as anything you've ever come up with."

"What's wrong with it? Let her continue, Daff. What else we got to talk about? Besides, maybe she could hex you-know-who." The other ladies knew Lizzie referred to the leader of the Mahjong Mammas. "Now that I think about it, maybe we could hex all my exes as well."

"Does Babs have enough ointment for that?" Gidget asked, only somewhat facetiously.

"Probably not, but I'm all in for this voodoo if it'll conjure up a new meal ticket for me." Lizzie's gaze moved from Gidget down to her own stomach. "This body ain't gettin' any younger or thinner... except for the hair on top of it. Thank God for Clairol Age Defy and loose-fitting blouses."

Daffy quickly followed with something else for which to be thankful. "Don't forget Spanx."

"Or Neutrogena," Lilly said.

Lizzie said, "Or Botox..."

Gidget offered her own prayer. "I'm thankful for leggings."

"What about clothes with vertical stripes?" Babs asked.

"That's an old-wives' tale... that vertical lines are slimming. Two British psychologists proved in 2009 that horizontal lines actually make y'all look thinner," Gidget said.

"What do I do with all my clothes with vertical lines?"

"Before this continues to deteriorate into some sort of body shaming discussion," Daffy said, "let's get back to this voodoo stuff."

"Yeah... let's use Babs' wrath ointment on the Mammas. Give them all more wrinkles," Lizzie said, "and saggier breasts—"

"Especially on you-know-who," Lilly said.

"Especially on Stoney Lee," Daffy concluded. Stoney was the Mahjong Mammas' leader.

Daffy and Stoney had joined Kappa Delta the same year at FSU, and animosities remained long after their bitter contest for the presidency. Stoney's leadership of the Mahjong Mammas only heightened their bad blood. The Daffy-Stoney rivalry is particularly acute vis-à-vis Thomasville's most eligible widower, Bo Thomas.

"How exactly would your love potion work on, let's say... Bo?" Daffy asked.

"I'd have to look in Miss Monique's book, but we could figure it out. We could try it out on George Bentley first if you want. Sounds like he is on the market now, and tonight's a Full Moon."

"I vote we go for the 'Holy Grail' himself." Lilly used their pet name for Bo. The Ladies sometimes jokingly spoke of their desire to 'sip from the Holy Grail of bachelorhood.'

"Why not both?" Lizzie asked. "I'm not on a diet when it comes to men."

"Ladies, voodoo does nothing to address the real problem," Gidget said.

"What do you mean?" Daffy asked.

"Casting spells, even if they work, does nothing to increase the supply of widowers. A shortage of widowers is our real problem."

The other Ladies looked at Daffy.

"If we can't do anything about the shortage, I guess we have to work with what we do have." Daffy turned to Babs. "You say we can also do something about the Mahjong Mammas?"

"Yep."

"Nothing serious. Just something to slow them up a little."

"One of the ointments I bought can give an intended victim a pretty good tummy ache... several days' worth. I bought it with the Mammas in mind. We could even time it to work during Beverly's viewing, so we would have George all to ourselves."

"Speaking of which, what casseroles are y'all gonna take to her viewing?" Lilly asked.

"We can talk about that later," Daffy said as she looked at Babs. "When could we do this... what'cha call it?"

"It's called a voodoo... uh... ceremony..." One suspects Babs called it a ceremony instead of a ritual in order to make it less off-putting to the other Ladies.

"When and where?"

"Tonight... during the Full Moon... midnight... Sunset Memorial Cemetery."

At this point in the conversation, Lizzie announced her 'prospecting' trip to sunny Florida. "Y'alls' 'ceremony' tonight sounds peachy, except for being at midnight in a cemetery, but I'm thinking that a little prospecting trip might be more productive."

Chapter 4

Advertised *ad nauseam* on TV, The Villages is a fifty-five plus planned community in the middle of Florida. Suwanee Village is only about fifteen miles from the Gulf of Mexico, nowhere near the famous destination. As the Lilly and Lizzie slowly cruise to the office, they pass live oaks dripping with Spanish moss, palmetto bushes, and a variety of subtropical and tropical plants.

"It's real pretty here. Look at these beautiful plants. Look at them orchids," Lilly said.

Lizzie pointed a blacktopped area lined with live oaks dripping with Spanish moss. "There's the parking lot."

"Ooohhh! Look at all them expensive cars. Must be a lot of money around here."

"You mean meal tickets around here but don't be too sure. You can't judge a book by its cover. How many trailers you drive by where there's Cadillacs parked in front?" Lizzie asked. "That looks like the office. Park over there."

Once inside, Lilly immediately noticed something unusual about the man standing behind the chest-high registration desk across the room. She whispered, "Lizzie, that man don't have a shirt on."

"Yeah, but that's probably not that odd around here. This is Florida, and it's still warm in September. Follow me."

"Hellooow, ladies! Welcome to Suwanee Village. I'm Kim." He eyed Lilly up and down. "Oh, Honey! I love that outfit. Hot pink is my favorite color. And those sandals. Are they Manolo Blahniks?"

"Yes... yes, they are. You know about Manolo Blahniks?" Lilly asked.

"Heavens, yes! I bought a second pair just last month."

Lilly and Lizzie looked at each other and shrugged.

"Ladies, is this your first visit?"

"Yeah, we've never been here before..." Lizzie struggled to remember the spiel they rehearsed on the walk from the Mercedes to the office. "I'm... I'm Ms. Sherbert, and this is Ms. White, and uh... we've heard about your place here and just wanted to check it out. We've uh... been looking for a place like this for some time... A place where a couple of mature women like ourselves can uh... well, can just be ourselves and enjoy the company of others uh... you know, in situations similar to ours."

"Hon, I know just what you mean. We get Saturday night slacks stopping by all the time to be themselves. You've arrived at absolutely the right place for someone with a fluid lifestyle like yours. I know you'll just fit right in. The girls will just love you. Planning on staying overnight? We have some vacant cabins."

"No. We're not planning on staying overnight. We're from Thomasville, and we have to get back there tonight for a uh..." Lizzie wisely did not want to admit they needed to return to Thomasville for a bizarre ritual at midnight and instead made something up. "A movie! Yeah, it's one of them new Minions movies. I gotta take my grandson to it. Anyway, we thought we'd just hang out awhile... Meet some of your folks... Kind of get a feel for the place before we head back. Where should we go around here to meet some other people?"

"The best place would be the pool. This time of day, that's where most of our members are. You can just pay for two $25 day-passes, hang out at the pool, and see if you like our place. It's got a great bar, perfect for those who prefer a 'liquid lunch.' They make a really mean Cosmo. There's patio chairs, chaise lounges, and tables with umbrellas. You can stay there all day if you like. Sweetie, trust me... the other members are going to gobble you two up."

"That sounds perfect." Lizzie turned to Lilly. "You got a Ulysses S. Grant on you?"

"Oh yeah." Lilly began fumbling in her handbag.

"Is that a Dooney & Bourke?" Kim's eyes popped. "I don't think I've ever seen one that big before."

"It doubles as a sleeping bag when she goes camping," Lizzie said.

"Ohhh, you are a hoot. I'll have to remember that one." Kim paused his laughter. "Seriously, that is one fierce handbag."

Lilly returned a quizzical look as she handed him a fifty-dollar bill.

"Babygirls, to get to the pool, go out that side-door." Kim raised his hand and pointed. Lilly leaned in toward him.

She asked, "I hadn't noticed your nail polish before. What a lovely shade. What color is it?"

"Coral. It's one of Pantone's new shades. You like it?"

"Coral is my favorite color. I just bought two new pairs of coral shoes last week. These sandals and a pair of Gucci Mules."

Kim leaned forward, his eyes looking over the desk at Lilly's shoes. "I think coral and hot pink make a divine color combination."

"That's what I told my hairstylist, but she looked at me like I's from Mars."

"I get into arguments all the time about color combos with my stylist. He's so dense sometimes. Don't you worry gurlfriend, coral and hot pink are close enough on the color wheel to be a fabulous color combo."

"Ladies..." Lizzie nodded at the side-door.

A chastened Kim hung his head. "I'm sorry. It's easy for me to get carried away when I get to talking colors."

"Same with me and shoes," Lilly said.

"Don't get me going on shoes. Anyway, you two go out that door and follow the pathway. The pool is about seventy-five yards behind this building. You'll come up on the pool house, and the pool is behind that. There's showers, lockers, toilets, and everything you'll need inside. Don't forget your suntan oil. I don't want to see you burn that gorgeous skin."

"We won't need it. We didn't bring our bathing suits," Lilly said as she and Lizzie walked toward the door.

"Ohhh... You two are so lit... The others are going to enjoy your sense of humor." Kim fluffed his hand at them as they exited. "Ciao!"

As soon as the door closed behind them, Lilly looked at Lizzie and said, "That was no normal guy."

"You think?"

"How could a registration clerk afford two pairs of Manolo Blahniks for his wife? No, if he can afford these shoes, he's got to be the owner of this place."

They walked down a pathway beautifully landscaped with a variety of exotic plants that included Pitcher-Plants and Banana Flowers. Approaching the pool house, they heard music.

"Disco! Alright! That's a good sign. Takes me back," Lizzie said.

"Me too! First time I ever had sex, I was listening to 'How Deep Is Your Love?' at a drive-in."

Lizzie nodded. "You and every other teenager in the late 70s."

"Look, there's a door for the Men's Showers and one for the Women's Showers."

"I say we go in the Women's Showers," Lizzie said, drawing a laugh.

The duo stepped inside to find a deserted room. Halfway through the room, a toilet flushed, and a naked woman emerged, headed for one of the sinks. The ladies glanced at one another with eyebrows raised but kept going toward the door labeled 'Pool Entrance.'

The woman glanced at them as she washed her hands and asked, "Aren't you two gonna get undressed?"

"Oh no, we didn't bring our bathing suits." Lilly flashed a classic Southern belle smile, the one showing a lot of white teeth.

"So? That's the whole point around here."

"But we didn't plan on going swimming. We just wanted to meet folks," Lilly said, still smiling.

"That's fine, but you can't wear clothes by the pool."

"But, like I said, we didn't bring our bathing suits." Lilly's smile disappeared.

"Honey, not only do you not need bathing suits by the pool, you can't wear *anything* by the pool. That's the rules." The naked lady dried her hands and calmly walked to the 'Pool Entrance' door, which she opened and stepped through. Lilly and Lizzie stood speechless for a full minute, a record.

"Lizzie... this must be one of them nudist clubs."

"You think? I didn't even know The Villages *had* a nudist club."

"I bet that man at the registration desk didn't have any pants on either."

Lizzie walked to an empty locker and began unbuttoning her blouse.

"What're you doin'?" Lilly asked.

"What do you think? I'm gettin' nekkid." Lizzie affected a casual manner which, given her unrefined personality required little effort and seemed a small price to pay for a meal ticket.

"You gotta be kidding. You can't do that. You saw the other door for men. There might be men out there!"

"I hope so. Come on girl. Get nekkid with me."

"I... I don't know. I've... I've never been nude in public... except the times a bunch of us streaked the Kappa Alpha house..." Lilly neglected to include the Library, Administration Building, and Gator Football Locker Room. Even the most genteel of Southern women let go during their college years.

"Who *hasn't* streaked a KA house? Come on."

"I don't know... What if some of them got cameras?"

Lizzie looked at Lilly as if she had two heads. "Lilly, no one out there will have any pockets to put a camera in."

"My body ain't much to look at anymore..."

"Do you think that woman washing her hands had a body worth lookin' at? Come on. Don't let me go out there nekkid by myself."

Lilly stood perfectly still, wrestling with her brain. Public nudity in light of her nature and background would require a tremendous leap. But skeptics forget that age often lessens inhibitions, especially when one's children no longer live at home. Add to that Lilly's inclination to follow others, more so when it offers possibility of true love, and what happened next becomes understandable. Hesitantly, she walked over to the lockers and began undressing.

After several agonizing minutes, Lilly stood naked, excepting one item of apparel, her shoes. Not only her fetish, shoes are also her security blanket, something much needed in her current state. Another moment of indecision surfaced as she turned and noticed her reflection in a mirror. "Oh shoot! I can't go out there!"

"Why? What is it?"

"They're gonna know I'm not really a blonde."

Lizzie harrumphed, shook her head, and gave Lilly a stern look. "You won't see one woman out there who has her natural hair color. Just check things out. Now get out there. We're all adults here. Remember?"

Reluctantly stepping through the doorway with her slim waist wrapped in a towel, Lilly said, "Wish we would've brought some suntan oil."

"Act nonchalant. If you act nervous, everyone's gonna pick up on it and stare."

"I can't imagine why anyone would stare at a fifty-five-year old woman with no clothes on." Sometimes Lilly's sarcasm is spot on.

"Put on your happy face and act normal," Lizzie said. These Casserole Ladies acting normal in a nudist camp sounds like a stretch.

Lilly said, "I'd feel better if I could at least wear a bra. There's something about being naked without a bra."

"Being naked and braless seem to go together to me, but look... just think of all these folks as... as just a bunch of gynecologists. Think of this as a gynecologist convention."

Lilly remained silent, deep in thought for a few seconds before responding. "That don't work."

"Why?"

"Because it reminds me of that joke about the gynecologist and the cold speculum. Wish I could remember the punch line."

A look of disgust crossed Lizzie's face. "Walk over to that table, sit down, and ditch your towel."

Lilly complied and sat down. "Good God! Why are chairs so cold when you're naked?"

"Maybe it's because you ain't got no clothes on when you're nekkid."

As they settled down, a naked waiter approached and delivered his greeting wearing a big smile and nothing else. "What can I get you girls?"

"Something tasty." Lizzie nodded in the direction of several people lounging in the pool. "Like one of those young studs."

Their waiter made a face and pouted his lower lip. "What we got here... Doris Day? Those boys are already taken, sweetie, but don't worry. There's plenty of material here for a couple of Saturday Night Slacks like you two."

"Oh, I'm just kidding. What do you recommend for a liquid lunch?"

"Cosmopolitan, Manhattan, Mojito... They're very popular with this crowd. Appletini is getting popular. Most boys here favor Mojitos, girls like Appletinis."

"Let's be different. Bring us two Mojito's," Lizzie said.

"Honey, different is why you're here. Back in a poof."

After their waiter left, Lizzie leaned in close and whispered, "See. Nothing to worry about being nekkid. When everyone's nekkid all the time, you don't even notice it. Our waiter never even looked at our tits."

"Thank God he didn't have an erection. I'd a died if he did. What do we do next?"

"We sit here and pretend like we do this all the time. As men come up, we'll chat, then decide if we want to see them some more. If we do, we get their phone numbers."

"What are we gonna write them on?" Lilly asked. She looked around and changed the subject. "I see a mix of both old and young people here. I thought The Villages was an old folks only community?"

"The younger ones here are probably visiting their parents."

"I think that woman with the tattoo over there is staring at us. The one sitting at that table with the woman that has pink and purple hair."

Lizzie casually swiveled her head in the other table's direction. "That's interesting... Usually women stare at other women because they're checking out each other's clothes or hairdo. I guess when they're nekkid, they're checking out each other's stretch marks."

"Or out-of-the-way tattoos."

"I didn't notice it till you mentioned it. Good catch. That is an interesting looking tattoo... right above her coochie. That's what I call making a statement."

"That tattoo reminds me of an old Willie Nelson joke Wendell told me."

"If you can remember it, don't bother telling me." Lizzie looked back at Lilly. "Weirdhair looks like an airhead, but Mzz Tattoo looks kind've tough to me. Good boob job though. She has that calculating look on her face... probably knows we're her competition for what few men are here."

"Now that y'all mention it, only about thirty people here... half of 'em men, half women. Don't look good for us."

"None of these studs hit on a couple of good-looking cougars like us?" Lizzie asked. "Only way that happens is if they're all gay."

Both shared a laugh until their waiter dropped off their drinks and departed. Lilly, who normally sips her drinks politely, took several gulps in rapid succession.

"I swear... we've been here... what, about fifteen minutes, and no men have flirted with us. By now, back at the Country Club pool, I'd have already gotten at least two or three flirts," Lilly said.

"If that's the case, what're you doing here? You should be back there, picking up men."

"I'd feel weird doing that. All of 'em know I been married to Wendell. Besides, they're all married anyway."

"Just because they's married, don't mean they's off limits. Your hunting license don't restrict you to single men only."

A disgusted look crossed Lilly's face. "You're missing the point. We're not even getting any nibbles here."

Lizzie nodded her agreement that things were not going right. She said, "Let's try something I've used in the past to attract men... although it's usually in a bathing suit. Let's lean back... Go ahead... that's good. Now, let's lean our heads back so our boobs stick out... Go on, don't be shy. Quit trying to cover 'em up and let your arms fall to your side... That's it. Now, we close our eyes like we're sitting here, getting some sun, and wait a few minutes. Trust me. This never fails to draw a couple of lusty gents."

Two minutes into their faux sunbathing, a voice spoke from above. "Hello girls."

They opened their eyes to see Mzz Tattoo and Weirdhair standing over them. Mzz Tattoo said, "Haven't seen you two around here before. Thought we'd come over and introduce ourselves. I'm Nikki, and this is Vikki."

"Hey Nikki. Hey Vikki. I'm Lizzie, and this here's Lilly."

"Lilly and Lizzie. I like it... Has a nice sound to it, don't it Vik?"

Vikki vigorously nodded in an explosion of pink and purple bouncing hair. "Yeah, it's got alliteration, rhythm, symbiosis."

"You guys make a good pair. Where you from?" Nikki asked.

"Thomasville. Thought we'd like to come down and check out y'alls' club. Seems nice."

Nikki stood straight and leaned back, almost as if wanting to display her augmented breasts.

"Well, we're so glad you're here. Vik and I are having our weekly get together later this evening in my cabin and would love to have you two drop in. Should be fun, if you know what I mean."

"Ohhh, we'd love to, but we're not staying overnight." Lilly made no attempt to conceal her disappointment. "We've got a... an engagement tonight back in Florence that we got to go to. We'd love to stay. I know your party will be a blast."

"Maybe next time we're here," Lizzie said.

"Yeah, maybe next time. Too bad. I'm sure we'll miss having you tonight. Vik, let's head on back to our table before our Appletinis get warm."

"See ya, Lilly and Lizzie," Vikki said as she turned to follow her companion.

As they left, Lizzie whispered, "Nikki sounded pissed. I hope she didn't think we were making excuses 'cause we really didn't want to go. I'd love to go to their party. I bet a bunch of these nekkid studs will be there just ripe for the plucking. I'm almost tempted to skip Babs' ceremony."

"I'd really love to go to their party too, but Babs really needs us tonight. I just wish it wasn't at midnight."

"I just wish it wasn't in a cemetery. Anyway, Nikki's party sounds like a weekly event, and we can always go the next time we're here. Say! This is one of the best Mojitos I've ever drank. I can see why the waiter said it's so popular. I'm almost finished with this one." Lizzie signaled the bartender, holding up two fingers, then scanned the pool. "We still ain't had any men come over."

"I'm telling you, at the Club I'd have had at least one or two older guys hitting on me by now. And that's in my bathing suit."

"Check out those two guys sitting on the edge of the pool."

"They are cute. Not too young."

"More importantly, not too old. Check it out. One of 'em has an erection."

"We need to get their attention somehow."

The waiter interrupted with their second round of Mojitos. After he departed, Lizzie finished off her first Mojito and purposefully nudged the empty plastic cup off the table so that it landed next to Lilly's chair.

"Stand up and bend over to pick up my cup... but don't do it too fast," Lizzie said.

"But I can just reach down and pick it up."

"The object is not to pick it up. The object is to bend over, and show the guy with the erection your butt."

"No way!" Lilly apparently still maintained a façade of modesty.

"Why not? He's seen it and everything else you got since you been out here."

Lilly pondered that thought for ten seconds, then did as told. That often happens with Lilly. When she had completed the assignment, she asked, "Did he look over?"

"No. Apparently he's too busy talking to that guy sitting beside him. Let's take the bull by the horns. No pun intended."

Lizzie stood and began walking toward the pool. Lilly reluctantly followed.

"Hey y'all," Lizzie said as she slid into the water close to their targets. "Mind if we join y'all?"

"Goodness gracious no. We always enjoy talking to a couple of todger dodgers," the man with the erection replied.

Lilly and Lizzie exchanged puzzled looks as Lilly sat next to the edge of the pool.

"Thank you. I'm Lizzie, and this here's Lilly."

"Lizzie and Lilly... Sounds nice... Good alliteration and rhythm... Real symbiotic. I'm Arty, and this is my friend Marty. Marty here was just commenting on how divine you two look. Aren't those Manolo Blahnik's, Marty?"

"Yes, they are," Marty replied.

"I'm surprised you noticed," Lilly said.

"How could we not? Marty just bought himself a pair two months ago. They're my favorite!"

Marty looked at Lilly. "And you look soooo cute in them. If you two girls have nothing to do tonight, the Tit Queen at the table over there is having her weekly party tonight. I'm sure she wouldn't mind a couple of extra bodies."

"Oh yeah," Lizzie said. Emphasizing her disappointment, she frowned. "She asked us over, but unfortunately, we have to get back to Thomasville tonight. I'm taking my grandson to see that new Minions movie."

"You have a grandson?" Marty asked, surprise evident in his voice. "You must have adopted."

"Nope. Y'all see all of these stretch marks?' Lizzie pointed to her stomach. 'Weldon made most of 'em, and Weldon wasn't adopted."

"Who's Weldon?" Arty asked.

"He's the father of the grandson we're talking about. The one I gotta take to the Minions movie."

Marty asked, "And Weldon was your son by your husband?"

"Yeah, either my second or third husband."

"Fluid, eh?" As he spoke, Arty exchanged glances with Marty, then both silkily slid into the water. Arty said goodbye as they swam off, "We need to finish our laps. It has been soooo nice talking to you two lovely gals. By-eee."

Back at their table, Lilly took a long pull off her Mojito. "Looks like we ain't finding much gold on our prospecting trip."

"Calm down, sweetie. You're just upset because that didn't work out too well."

"Before we came to this pool, I didn't think I was in that bad a shape."

"Me neither... you that is... I don't think you're in bad shape. Me, I'm another story. Let's get some more Mojitos." Lizzie waved to their waiter and held up two fingers as she gulped.

Lilly looked around. "We're not so bad looking compared to these other women. Look at that woman at the bar. Talk about saggy breasts—"

"If her tits get any lower, she's gonna have to put curb feelers on 'em."

"And that woman on the chaise lounge by the pool. She's definitely been in the sun way too long."

Lizzie nodded. "Her skin reminds me of one of my old hand bags... the alligator one I got rid of two years ago."

"So, why ain't any of these men making moves on us?" Lilly asked.

"Because what's going on at this pool ain't normal."

"Whadda you mean?"

"It's because of what you said a while ago. You said that it's half men and half women around this pool. That ain't normal. What's normal is usually more women than men. When you go to the five-dollar movie on Tuesday, what do you see? More women than men. That's why it's so hard for older, single women like us to find romance."

"But that don't explain why the men here haven't flirted with us. You think all these men might be married?"

"No, odds are against all them being married. Besides, most married men look worn out and pissed off. All these guys, even the older ones, look like they're in reasonable shape and pretty happy. I think it all goes back to what Gidget said at breakfast about supply and demand."

"What was that?" Lilly asked.

"Too many single older women, too few eligible men. When a couple of hot cougars like us can't draw attention among all this testosterone, what's wrong is there's too much estrogen in the environment. These guys know they don't have to work for it."

"Well, I'd say The Villages ain't no Fort Knox."

Chapter 5

The full moon had noticeably traversed a dark sky above Sunset Memorial Cemetery since Daffy, Gidget, and Babs anointed 'Bo' doll. With Officer Darrell's admonition in mind, all were anxious to perform the remaining voodoo ritual and leave. They purposefully sat back down on their marble gravestones just as another set of headlights turned into the cemetery.

"I hope that ain't Officer Darrell coming back," Gidget said.

"Why would he be coming back?" Babs asked.

Daffy quipped, "Forgot to arrest us?"

The trio sat frozen as the headlights made several turns, clearly heading their way.

"That ain't Darrell's Crown Vic. That's Lilly's Mercedes," Daffy said.

Lilly's SUV slowly turned onto the gravel lane that bordered the Montrose family's plot and stopped nearby. The vehicle's engine and lights turned off, but its doors remained closed. Although two heads could be seen through the windshield, they remained eerily still. A minute passed with no activity inside the Mercedes. Daffy finally stood, cautiously approached, and opened the driver-side door only to see its occupants fast asleep.

"Lilly! Lizzie! Wake up! WAKE UP!" Daffy shouted.

It took ten minutes before the two sleepers were sufficiently roused and able to relate the gist of their story. Lilly finished with a prayer, sort of. "We almost didn't make it back here. It was dark before we left Suwanee Village. Thank God my GPS decided to start talking to us again."

"We were so buzzed that she probably took pity on us. She could tell we were in no condition to navigate ourselves back to Thomasville." Lizzie's comments and slurred words prompted an exchange of puzzled looks among Daffy, Gidget, and Babs. Lizzie said, "It's a long story and involves an uppity German lady."

"Thank God my Mercedes has that autonomous driving stuff. Neither of us was in any shape to drive back. We were so—"

"Lilly," Gidget said, "your Mercedes don't have autonomous driving."

"Who drove?" Lilly looked at Lizzie. "It wasn't me."

"Me neither." Lizzie shrugged. Some things in life are simply unexplainable.

Daffy explained they had completed the first love spell on Bo before being interrupted by the police. She concluded by saying, "I suggest we skip doing a love potion on George and go straight to the Mahjong Mammas wrath thing. I don't want Officer Darrell to come back checking and find us still here. Hand Babs Miss Monique's book and the flashlight, and let's get this show on the road. Who's got the flashlight?"

A few minutes later, the wrath ritual began.

"Okay. If I read this right, each of us holds one of these five dolls and rubs a little of this ointment on its tummy." Babs distributed four small cloth dolls and kept one for herself. "There's one doll for each of the four Mahjong Mammas, except Stoney. We'll do two dolls for her. Double coverage. I'll pass this jar of green paste around."

As each woman dabbed a finger into the ointment, Lizzie said, "This stuff smells worse than a McDonald's dumpster."

"Please! Just hold your nose and dab it on. We need to get outta here." Daffy subsequently smeared the ointment as directed.

Once all had completed the task, Babs squinted at the book and said, "Now, repeat three times after me... *Hammuta Sadika Re Re...*"

This was quickly followed by the Ladies' chorus.

"*Hammuta Sadika Re Re*"

"Hammuta Sadika Re Re"

"Hammuta Sadika Re Re"

"Okay, now... uh... hold on. Let me check something." Babs picked up the book, furiously turned pages, and squinted at the words. "Okay... I forgot. You're supposed to hold the doll next to your tummy when you repeat that phrase."

"What was the phrase?"

"Hamm... uh... *Hammota Satika Re.* Now, we all say it again three times like we did before, but y'all hold your dolls next to your tummies while y'all repeat it. Everyone ready?" Babs surveyed the nodding heads, then began. *"Hamm...* uh... *Hammoda Saluta Re."*

The Ladies quickly mimicked Babs

"Hammuh Hammoda Saluta Re"

"Hammuh Hammoda Saluta Re"

"Hammuh Hammoda Saluta Re"

Gidget cynically shook her head. "Good enough for government work."

"My sentiments exactly." Daffy nodded. "How soon will this start working?"

"I think early this morning... probably sometime shortly after sunrise."

"And it'll last long enough to keep the Mahjong Mammas' tummies nauseous through Beverly's viewing and funeral?" Lizzie asked.

"Should."

"Good. Let's pack things up and get outta here." Daffy stood and briskly rubbed her behind. "That's the coldest marble gravestone I've ever sat on."

Daffy sent the first text message to Babs shortly after sunrise.

Daffy Belvedere: How U feel? I've been puking for 15 minutes. :-(

Babs Neauxgeaux: Me 2!

Daffy Belvedere: Any word from others?

Babs Neauxgeaux: Nope!

Daffy Belvedere: Let me text them and get back 2 U.

After five minutes, Daffy sent Babs another text.

Daffy Belvedere: Others throwing up as well. Gidget tried several nausea meds, even Rx stuff. Nothing works.

Babs' reply was typed on the run, so to speak.

Babs Neauxgeaux: Talk 2 U later. Got 2 make sacrifice 2 porcelain god. :-(

The five days following their voodoo ritual did not go well for the Casserole Ladies. Waves of nausea confined all to their houses, except for visits to Dr. Fischel, whom all used as their family physician. He gave similar advice to each. "There's nothing you can do except take over-the-counter medications and take it easy."

"Take it easy! I don't wanna miss Beverly's viewing. Cain't you give me something?"

"The only thing I can give you is some advice. Quit eating at Cootie's Carryouts." Stores in the chain of regional convenience stores frequently received scores in the seventy to seventy-nine range on state food service inspections.

Tummy aches kept our Casserole Ladies from attending Beverly Bentley's viewing and funeral. The Mahjong Mammas missed neither event, a topic that came up five days after the Sunset Memorial voodoo ritual. They lunched at SASS, another toney Thomasville restaurant.

Lizzie began the conversation after they were seated. "Today's the first day I've felt semi-human. 'Rode hard and put up wet' don't even come close to how bad I been feeling."

"Leona came in to clean the morning after our 'ceremony,' took one look at me, and told me I looked like I'd drove through a car wash without a car," Daffy said. "I haven't been able to eat anything. Lost seven pounds."

"Me too!" Babs nodded. "Six pounds."

"Looks like we all lost weight. At least we got a good excuse to go clothes shopping this week." Lilly patted her stomach.

Lizzie looked at Lilly as if she had suggested they stop using lipstick. "Who needs an excuse to go clothes shopping?"

Gidget looked up from her phone, raised her head. "Ladies, Suwanee Village isn't part of The Villages. It's nowhere near The Villages. You two were in a gay and lesbian nudist club. It says so right here."

"And to think that we thought it was kind of a 'clothes optional' part of The Villages." Lilly shook her head while grabbing the iPhone. After confirming Gidget's revelation, she said, "I can't believe we were that stupid."

"I can, and I know one thing. I'm off Mojitos... at least for a couple of days," Lizzie said.

"I just can't believe all them people were... were..." Unable to finish, Lilly laid the phone on the table in silence. Gidget picked it up and began typing again.

"All those terms y'all mentioned, 'Saturday Night Slacks,' 'fierce,' 'todger dodger,' all of 'em are terms used by the gay and lesbian community. Take a look."

"How naïve could we be?" Lizzie glanced at the phone. "Don't answer that."

"Worse of all..." Lilly looked down at her shoulders and chest. "I'm burned to a crisp. My skin's peeling worse than Frankenstein's mummy."

"Frankenstein didn't have a mummy," Gidget said.

"Yes, he did. I saw the movie."

"I knew Gidget or I..." Daffy hesitated then looked at Babs. "Or Babs should've gone along to keep y'all out of trouble."

"Why? Staying outta trouble is no fun," Babs said, confirming the wisdom of Daffy's hesitancy.

"Your trip and our voodoo ritual show that what we've been doing ain't working. Once again, the Mammas got the jump on us." Daffy turned to Babs. "And how about explaining what went wrong with that voodoo ritual."

"Why all y'all looking at me? It ain't my fault we all got sick. Don't blame it on me—"

"Who else should we blame it on?" Gidget asked. "All of us getting sick right after that voodoo stuff is awful coincidental—"

"Emphasis on the word awful," Lizzie said.

"It's like they say." Babs shrugged her shoulders. "Poop happens. Oh! Here comes our waitress. Let's order an appetizer. How about some fried jalapeño dill pickles?"

"You have got to be kidding! Why not fill up on fried chitlins instead if you want to go back to bed for another week?" Lizzie asked.

After orders were taken, Gidget turned on Babs. "Them words didn't look too French to me. You must've screwed up the words to your hex."

"I think we *all* screwed up... more than just the words." Daffy's statement exemplifies her leadership qualities—promoting team spirit and sharing responsibility. As with most long-lived female klatches, these women have endured a lot together. Piling on Babs would only strain their cohesion. Instead, Daffy tried to focus their ire on the Mammas by retelling the latest from the Thomasville rumor mill. This rumor contained a bombshell. "All four Mammas were on George's doorstep at least an hour before Beverly's viewing began. They had so many casseroles, they had to make three trips from Stoney's Escalade to haul 'em all in."

A clown could have driven a red fire engine through the restaurant at that point with less shock effect upon the ladies. Babs vigorously piled on. She said, "I also heard about the Mammas' showboating at Beverly's viewing. Not one, but *two*, different asparagus casseroles."

"Two?!" Lilly shrieked.

"Yeah. Two asparagus casseroles! A fancy one in a creamy Alfredo sauce, topped with parmesan cheese. I think it might've been an Ina Garten recipe. The other one was that tired, old recipe with Campbell's cream of mushroom soup and Ritz crackers."

Lizzie's eyes rolled as she rendered an opinion regarding post-mortem casserole etiquette. "I can't think of how many funerals I've seen that cheap, worn-out recipe at."

The other Ladies chimed in, setting standards higher than a Michelin Guide.

"I'd be embarrassed to take that casserole to dog's funeral," Lilly said.

"There's always plenty of that casserole left over," Daffy responded.

"Hope it didn't clog up George's garbage disposal," Lizzie said.

"Too many Ritz crackers'll do that sometimes," Gidget responded.

Babs' next comment floored her companions. "Penny even brought homemade lasagna. Can y'all image?"

Daffy shook her head. "What gall!"

Lizzie agreed. "Some people have no sense of propriety!"

"Talk about lack of decorum!" Lilly said.

"What kind of person would bring lasagna to a dead woman's viewing?! Unbelievable! Talk about lack of couth..." Lizzie paused mid-sentence as two new patrons entered. All five Ladies turned to watch the hostess greet George Bentley and a woman and escort them to a table on the other side of the restaurant. As they sat down, the woman ostentatiously waived to the Ladies.

"Penny Perdoo! Poor George is scraping the bottom of the barrel," Lilly whispered as she put on her best smile and returned Penny's wave.

Lizzie looked back at her companions and shrugged. "I may have to rethink my stance on lasagna."

Penny is distantly related to the chicken fortune. Her branch changed spelling of its surname a long time ago after a dispute arose within the clan. Perdoo is her maiden name, which she recently resumed after her last divorce. Thomasville residents generally consider her one of the least impressive members of the Mahjong Mammas.

"George would be Penny's husband number what... three or four?" Gidget asked.

Penny got the short end of the stick from her last husband and is in a situation similar to Lizzie's; i.e., looking for a meal ticket. Unlike Lizzie, she refuses to go to a hairstylist and has a do-it-yourself dye job.

"Four," Lizzie said. "Trying to catch up with me. You'd think she'd spend a little cash and get that hair in better shape if she's going bear hunting. What could George possibly see in a wrinkled old bag with jet-black hair?"

Daffy turned back to the others, her resting bitch face (RBF) amped up like a neon sign in Vegas. "Men are such shallow creatures. That half-wit never noticed her mangy hair because she probably wore the same cheap, low-cut dress she wears to all the viewings. His eyes never got above her cleavage."

"Don't forget her lasagna," Babs said. "She probably spoon-fed it to him. Best way to a man's heart is through his stomach."

"Speaking of stomach." A smile suddenly replaced Daffy's RBF as their waitress approached. "Here comes the appetizers and drinks. Let's talk about something else. Enough of this depressing lasagna crap."

After food and drinks were dispensed, the conversation turned to a subject near and dear to hearts in the region.

"Who's gonna win the Georgia-Florida game this year?" Babs mischievously asked. The early October football game between the two colleges always generated a lot of passion throughout the region. As an FSU graduate, Babs could afford to inflame rivalry among her companions.

"Y'all mean the Florida-Georgia game," Lilly said.

"I just wish I could watch it with Sam. It would be nice to have male companionship..." Gidget noticed the others looking past her and turned around. George and Penny stood close to their table.

"Hey Ladies," George said. "We saw y'all and wanted to stop by and say hey. Heard about y'alls' virus. Dr. Fischel was at the viewing and mentioned all y'all must have all got the same bug. I know Beverly missed y'all. She loved all y'all so much."

Hypocrisy oozing from her words, Penny said, "We were *soooo* sorry y'all couldn't make it. Beverly was *soooo* beautiful."

"We loved her as well. It was heartbreaking not being there. I heard her viewing and funeral were... were..." Daffy tried to think of something to say besides 'the same old thing.'

"They were wonderful. The food was great." George turned his gaze lovingly to his companion. "Penny brought the best lasagna... first time I've ever had lasagna at a viewing."

Penny put on her best 'ain't I wonderful' face and said, "Sometimes, one has to think outside the box. It was the least I could do to comfort George in his hour of grief."

George looked at Gidget. "By the way, I didn't get a chance to thank you for visiting Beverly last week. Just before she died, she told me how happy she was to have seen you."

The other Ladies' looked at Gidget.

"You didn't mention you'd seen Beverly before she died. The day she died?" asked Babs.

"Uh... oh yeah," Gidget stammered. "I stopped by early in the morning to bring her some medication... and to see how she was doing."

"It must've helped. She died not too long after you left with a real peaceful smile on her face," George said.

"The funeral home did such a good job on her. They were able to keep that same smile on her face." Penny smiled.

"Maybe they'll do as good a job on you," Daffy said.

"Penny let's let these folks get back to their food, and go order our own," George said. "That dip does look good. Y'all should try some of their fried jalapeño dill pickles."

"They are *theee* best. It's *soooo* good to see y'all again. Toodles." Penny pretentiously blew a kiss over her shoulder as she followed George.

Once George and Penny were out of earshot, Daffy said, "Y'all watch. That bitch will even make homemade treats for Bruno if that's what it takes for her to get a seat up front."

Bruno is George's eight-year old boxer and best friend. George's age and excessive weight make walking Bruno difficult. As a substitute, every morning at 8:30 Bruno jumps up into the front passenger seat of George's black Cadillac SUV, and the two take a half-hour ride. For six years, Thomasville residents have been treated to the sight of them slowly driving around town.

"Let's talk about something else besides a disgusting gold-digger like Penny. How about we finish these drinks and order a bottle of wine?" Lilly asked. Hearing no response, she noticed the others staring past her. She looked over her shoulder. A hostess led Bo Thomas and his seventy-nine-year-old mother to a corner table.

Beauregarde Thomas, Thomasville's most eligible widower. Most people think the fifty-seven-year-old resembles a middle-aged Dean Martin. Tanned, lanky, and good looking. His dark-brown hair normally shows a few streaks of gray at the temples, but not today.

En route to his table, Bo noticed the Ladies and signaled for the hostess and his mother to continue without him. He turned and headed their way. "Good morning, Ladies. I hope y'all are feeling better."

All five women sat in stone cold silence, staring at Bo's hair.

"What did you do to your hair?!" Lizzie asked. Another thought that bypassed her brain's filter.

"Lizzie! Don't be rude!" Daffy said.

"I know... I know. Y'all should've heard Momma when she first saw it." Bo's hair was strawberry red. He laughed and shook his head. "It's weird. Something just hit me about five days ago. I woke up, went to my barber as soon as he opened, and told him to dye it. He tried to talk me out of it. It was just something... I don't know... something I just *had* to do. Probably some sort of mid-life crisis, I guess. Funny thing. Sales this week have skyrocketed."

Bo owns an equipment rental business. It does quite well, which is another thing besides his good looks that women find appealing.

"Sounds like your red hair helped your business. Better than advertising on a billboard," Gidget said. Talk about understatement. People often fail to notice billboards. No way Bo's hair could go unnoticed.

"I must say Miss Lilly and Miss Lizzie, y'all look as if y'all have had some sun. Did y'all go to Seaside recently? Is the water there still warm?" Bo asked.

"Uh... uh... why no... uh..." Staring at Bo's hair, Lilly was dumbstruck.

Daffy helped her out. "Oh, they've just been enjoying the outdoors lately. It's nice on my back patio. We must have you over soon."

Bo nodded. "Anyway, I just wanted to stop by and say 'hey' and make sure y'all are feelin' better. I'll let y'all get back to your lunch. Nice seeing y'all."

As Bo made his way to his table, Daffy looked at Babs. "What do you have to say about that?"

"At least we know voodoo works?" she asked in reply.

"Just not the way you intended."

"You can't blame Bo's hair on me."

"Red goo! How else could that have happened?"

"You mean *where* else could that have happened?" Lizzie asked. "Someone must've put some red ointment on the doll's head instead of his crotch."

All eyes focused on Gidget, who sheepishly lowered her head. "It... it just seemed so... so wrong to put it down there. I only had a little dab on my finger anyway..."

"A little dab'll do ya." Lizzie recycled a tag line from an old Brylcreem commercial. "Now, Bo's a redhead."

"I wonder what color Bo's bush is now?" Daffy asked.

Lizzie smiled. "I wonder something even more interesting. Who performed that dye job?"

Chapter 6

The Ladies sat in silence, contemplating Lizzie's question. Eventually, their alcohol appetites overwhelmed their imaginations.

"What about that bottle of wine Lilly suggested? Where's our waitress?" Babs asked.

"I don't know if wine is gonna be strong enough for me after seeing Penny slobbering all over George like that. We may have to upgrade to hard liquor," Daffy said.

Lizzie immediately took advantage of Daffy's mood. "Might I suggest bourbon?"

Gidget asked, "What next?"

"What do you mean?" Lilly asked

"What are we gonna do next?"

"What I'm gonna do next is have the last of this pimento cheese dip if no one else wants it," Lizzie said.

"That's not what I'm talking about. It goes back to what I was saying about supply and demand." Gidget glanced at George Bentley's table. "When a goober like George gets snapped up as soon as he comes on the market by a nitwit like Penny, something's wrong. Not enough supply, too much demand."

"I thought your degree was in Pharmacy, not Economics," Lizzie said.

"Don't matter. Gidget is spot-on about opportunities for romance around here. Losing a goober like George to a doofus like Penny makes me want to..." Daffy closed her eyes, covered her ears, and began repeating, "Happy place, happy place, happy place--"

As Daffy chanted, Lilly looked at her companions and whispered, "She just needs to chill out for a while. Let's let her be."

After finishing her mantra, Daffy resumed. "Ladies, I have a vision. A vision of rolling over Sunday mornings to find a man's face resting on the pillow next to mine... a reasonable-looking face—I won't be too greedy. A head full of hair would be great, but not a deal breaker. A face with teeth that were brushed before bedtime. A face with a clean body below it that took care of me before bedtime."

"Just Sundays?" Lilly asked.

"Only Sundays. Men get sloppy if things become too routine."

"Bo's face, right? You're worried that Stoney Lee is gonna get him before you do. Aren't you?" Babs asked.

As previously mentioned, the Daffy-Stoney feud is bitter and long standing, going back to their college days at FSU. A series of harmless pranks—short-sheeting each other's beds, Saran Wrapping toilet seats, and so forth—followed loss of Kappa Delta presidency. Things turned bitter after Roberta Lee got caught on campus smoking marijuana. Daffy subsequently coined the nickname 'Stoney.' It stuck, and Stoney never forgave Daffy.

"That ain't ever gonna happen. At least, not as long as Clairol and Revlon stay in business," Daffy said.

"Oh! Oh! Speaking of Clairol, I heard Stoney invited Bo to be on the Tourism Bureau's Board..." Lilly paused, noticing the others' stares. "What?"

"Just trying to figure out the connection between haircoloring and Stoney's invitation... Bo's hair dye job?" Gidget's logical brain at work, which is counterproductive when dealing with Lilly.

"No. I heard about the invitation while I was at the beauty parlor this morning," Lilly said. Beauty parlors and nail salons are important components of the Thomasville rumor mill. "My stylist said one of her customer's told her that one of her friends who works at the Tourism Bureau texted her about Stoney bringing Bo onto the Board."

Daffy rolled her eyes. "Okay. Now I understand. That is bad news. The Board's Chairwoman working closely with Bo. Makes me even more pissed off... and determined."

"Supply. We need more widowers," Gidget said.

"What're you suggesting?" Lizzie asked.

Gidget recoiled, a worried look flashing across her face. "Nothing... nothing except now we got a smaller supply facing us."

"Gidg," Daffy said. "Don't stop thinking. No one's discouraging you. We need good ideas like yours right now."

"This here Lockwood Chardonnay sounds like a good idea." Lilly looked up from the wine list.

"Gidget's right. We need more widowers." Lizzie flagged their waitress and proceeded to order the wine Lilly requested.

"Marketing," Gidget said.

"Marketing? What do you mean?" Babs asked.

Daffy picked up on the idea. "Marketing ourselves? Gidg's right that the supply of older single men is low. We have to compete in the market for what few men there are."

Lizzie looked down and grabbed a handful of stomach. "Marketing with this body only works if I'm a Lane Bryant model."

"How about marketing Thomasville as a great place for widowers? How about 'Widow Capital of the World?' Sounds catchy, don't it?" Gidget asked.

"I like it!" Babs enthused, but she likes any offbeat idea.

"We need a marketing expert," Gidget said.

"What about that new Tourism Director that Stoney just brought on board." Lizzie's face scrunched as she tried to remember. "What's her name... Stacie something—"

"Stacie Goodie. They had an article in the paper about her. Has a degree in marketing from Georgia," Daffy said.

"I don't know." Lilly shook her head.

"What do you mean?"

"She's a Yankee."

"A Yankee?"

"Yep. From Atlanta."

Many people native to south Alabama, north Florida, and south Georgia consider anything north of Montgomery Alabama and Columbus Georgia to be Yankee-land.

"How old is this new director?" Lizzie asked.

"The newspaper said thirty-eight," Daffy replied.

This news brought a collective sigh from the four other Casserole Ladies, followed by an earnest desire voiced by all five in unison. "Oh, to be thirty-eight again!"

"So, how would we use her?" Daffy asked to no one in particular then turned to Gidget. "You've been awful quiet. What do you think?"

"With all this talk about marketing, I'm thinking we're too focused on the demand side of our problem. Oh, here comes our wine."

After the waitress poured the wine and departed, Daffy took a taste. "This Lockwood Chardonnay is yummy."

"Speakin' of Lockwood Chardonnay," Lizzie said. "I hear that Stacie Goodie is divorced."

"Okay, I'll bite... even though I'll probably regret it. What's the connection between this here Chardonnay and Stacie Goodie being divorced?" Daffy asked.

"Easy. I came home early from shopping one afternoon. I think it was about ten, fifteen years ago when you and I went to Dillard's in Tallahassee." Lizzie looked at Daffy. "You bought that gorgeous dress by…what was that designer that was so in style back then... it was either a Dolce and Gabbana or a—"

"It was a Badgley Mischka. They were on sale, but what does this have to do with wine and the new Yankee Director's divorce? Lockwood Chardonnay don't even come close to sounding like Dolce and Gabbana."

"I'm gettin' there. Anyway, we got back from shopping, and you were driving, so you dropped me off at my house. Remember? We got back early because you remembered while we were shopping that you had a pedicure that afternoon—"

"Chardonnay... Stacie Goodie's divorce... please—"

"I'm gettin' there... Anyway, you asked me if I needed help carrying my packages in, and I said something like 'No, you go on to your pedicure. Your toenails look awful!' I was just kidding of course, and we had a good laugh—"

"I know this is going somewhere." Gidget rolled her eyes.

"Anyway, so I haul my packages out of Daffy's Lincoln, and she leaves. Then, I open the door, throw my packages on the bench in the foyer, and head for the family room, straight to the bar to get myself a gin and tonic. Remember, Daffy? It was summer and real hot that day, and I love a gin and tonic on a hot afternoon—"

"Lizzie, you gotta speed this up." Daffy squirmed in her chair. "I gotta go pee sometime."

"Okay, okay... as I was saying, I walk into the family room, and there's my second... or was it my third? Anyway, it don't really matter... second or third husband on the couch all tangled up with his secretary... that bitch. I'm so pissed, all I want to do is throw something, so I pick up the nearest thing which is a half-drunk bottle of Lockwood Chardonnay sitting out in the open on the bar. Those slobs hadn't even bothered to put it back in the wine cooler! Missed both of 'em and broke the picture window behind the couch. I've never seen a woman put on clothes that fast. Needless to say, we got divorced right after that—"

"My hairstylist also told me this morning that her customer also said that Stacie Goodie said she was through with men. Said she'd never make that mistake again," Lilly said.

"This sounds like one Yankee I could learn to like." A smile spread over Lizzie's face.

Chapter 7

Later in the week, the Ladies lunched, this time at SoHo, another upscale Thomasville restaurant.

"Things are getting worse. On the way to work this morning, I saw Penny Perdoo riding around Thomasville in George Bentley's SUV," Gidget said, so disgusted that her visage could have graced Mount Rushmore.

"Who was sitting up front with George—Penny or Bruno?" Lizzie asked.

"Who else? Bruno."

"Yeah, but it's still not a good omen for that dog. Bruno better watch his flanks, or he'll be sitting in the back before he knows it," Daffy said.

Lilly erupted. "That gold digger! Couple of months from now, she'll probably be sleeping in George's bed—"

"Already is," Gidget said.

"How you know?"

"One of my pharmacy techs told me that the evening tech said she saw Penny come in the other night and buy some K-Y jelly."

"That just means she's having sex with him... not sleeping overnight in his bed," Daffy said.

"She also bought a toothbrush, Skinmedica Dermal Repair Cream—"

"Skinmedica? Wow, that's expensive stuff."

"$103 a bottle at my drug store. You ever see her without her makeup? Yuck! I checked the sales receipt info on the point of sale terminal that she used. She loaded up on overnight travel toiletries."

"Such as?" Lilly asked.

"Deodorant, shampoo, toothpaste, Chanel bath soap—"

Lizzie, skeptical of Gidget's assertion, shook her head. "That still don't mean anything. She could've just been buying replacements."

"Yeah, *but*... she also bought a Revlon Compact Travel Hair Dryer."

Babs, Lilly, Lizzie, and Daffy nodded. The latter said, "You're right. She would've a bought a full-size blow dryer if she was replacing a burnt-out one. Nope, that blow dryer's for temporary overnight sleep overs... certain to become permanent all too soon."

"George must not mind tattoos." Lilly put her wineglass down with a flourish, eager to flout possession of inside information.

"Tattoos?"

"Yeah. Saw her in the pool showers at the Country Club last year. Cute little tat of Tony the Tiger right over one of her butt cheeks."

Daffy and Gidget, squirming in their seats, seemed uncomfortable at Lilly's observation, but said nothing.

"Did we ever decide on whether George would be husband number three or four for Penny?" asked Babs.

"I think we decided on four." Lizzie's smile betrayed a touch of pride. "She's still one behind me."

At that moment, Stoney Lee and Bo walked into the restaurant. A hostess approached, and Stoney scanned the restaurant and pointed to a table. En route, they paused at the Casserole Ladies' booth. Bo leaned in and smiled at them. "Ladies, y'all are certainly looking lovely this morning... the epitome of Thomasville beauty."

In chorus, all simultaneously accepted his compliment with an "Oh Bo!!"

Daffy followed up by saying, "Bo, you do say the sweetest things."

"It's the gospel truth," he replied.

"Ladies," Stoney said, "seems like it's been forever since I've seen y'all. Can't chat long. Just wanted to bring Bo down here for lunch. We've just finished his first meeting as a board member and thought this would be a great way to celebrate. Gotta go. Bye."

Stoney abruptly turned and walked off, Bo in tow.

"No wonder her husband jumped off that bridge in Mississippi," Lizzie said.

Always the libertarian, Gidget tried reasoning. "It never was determined to be suicide. He was a big bourbon drinker. He might've had too much that day."

"I'm a bourbon drinker, but you don't see me jumping off no bridge." Lizzie looked down at her Old Fashioned as she massaged her temples. "Although that sounds like a good idea today. Maybe I'll switch to Mojitos."

"Ladies, we all like bourbon, but none of us jumps off bridges. That's not the point," Daffy said.

Lilly asked, "What is the point?"

"The point is that we're losing. Penny with George, Stoney with Bo. The Mammas are beatin' us to the punch. We gotta do something different... something big."

Babs could not contain herself. "Oooh, oooh! Voodoo... voodoo—"

"Yeah, right," Lizzie said, "and afterward, we join a witches coven."

Daffy continued. "As I was trying to say, we need to do something that will blow the pantyhose off the Mahjong Mammas' behinds."

"We may get an opportunity soon," Gidget said.

"Whadda you mean?"

"Claudia Anderson died late yesterday."

"That's terrible... even if she did cheat at Bunko. How'd you hear about it?" Lizzie asked.

How else except via the Thomasville rumor mill which operates with no regard to Federal patient information privacy regulations. Gidget explained, "One of my pharmacy techs said one of the evening-shift nurses at hospice emailed all the nursing supervisors about it. One of the supervisors forwarded the email to a friend of hers who mentioned it on Facebook. My tech saw it and called me last night."

"Looks like the supply of widowers is increasing." Lizzie nodded at Gidget. "Exactly what you've said we need."

"I never said I wanted more supply that way!" Gidget said, somewhat agitated.

"Calm down," Daffy said. "We need to find out when the viewing is. I don't want to miss this one."

"Day after tomorrow. It was in the Facebook posting."

Daffy took charge. "Okay, Ladies. We need to decide what casseroles to take over."

"You definitely gotta bring your tuna casserole. That's always the first thing to disappear. I'll bring my green bean casserole," Babs said. Daffy nodded her agreement.

Lilly nodded. "Count me in for chicken divan."

"I'll do my baked spaghetti." Unlike lasagna, Lizzie's baked spaghetti apparently does not violate polite society's sense of propriety and decorum.

"Don't forget dresses with hemlines below the knees..." Daffy's eyes scanned all her comrades, settling on Babs. "And a *reasonable* amount of cleavage."

"Wonder what the Mahjong Mammas will be wearing?" Babs asked.

Chapter 8

Following deep South tradition, Claudia's viewing took place at the Anderson home, an antebellum beauty in the Tockwotton historic district of Thomasville. She and her husband bought and restored the house after he opened his fifteenth 'Cousin Cootie's Carryouts.' This is a chain of thirty-seven convenience stores in southwest Georgia. In addition to the usual gasoline and convenience items, Cootie's is known for its breakfast and lunch carryout buffets. Their turnip greens are excellent. The chain's namesake opened his door to see our ladies on his doorstep, casseroles in hand. "Hey y'all. Miss Daffy, I see you brought your whole crew."

The speaker's given name is Charlie, but everybody calls him Cootie. Don't ask why. Suffice it to say that he is one of those kids who got a nickname in middle school that stuck.

"Oh, Cootie... We're gonna miss her so much. We've all talked about how Bunko won't be the same without her." Claudia's cheating was widely known. A tear trickled down Daffy's cheek as she gave Cootie a hug, forgetting the tuna casserole in her hands.

"That's okay, Sugar..." Cootie stepped back to let Daffy and the other Bunko Babes enter. He picked bits of tuna casserole from his tie and pointed to the formal dining room behind him. "Why don't y'all put your casseroles in there, then come back and give me some hugs. Claudia's in the parlor. Mmmm...mmmm! This tuna casserole *is* tasty!"

"We'll be right back."

As they filed in, Cootie greeted each. "Thank y'all... Miss Babs, Miss Lilly, Miss Gidget, Miss Lizzie."

"We may have to wait a while to speak with Cootie." Lilly nodded at guests queued up in the foyer as she placed her chicken divan on an antique dining room table. "Let's go look at Claudia while he's busy. I wanna see if they got her roots covered up right."

"Lilly! Have some respect," said Gidget.

"Well... Claudia would be horrified if her roots weren't covered up right. You know how she was about her roots."

"But the poor woman is dead!"

"It's not me! They need to hire some women in these funeral homes. Male morticians never think of that stuff."

Daffy tried to rescue her teammate. "What was the true color of her roots?"

"Brown... I think."

"I'm pretty sure she was a red head," Babs said.

"Them roots been grey for the last ten years." Lizzie looked around, then whispered, "She used the same hairstylist as me."

"She was always a blonde ever since I can remember," Daffy said.

"We may find out pretty soon. Let's go take a peak." Lilly began leading the pack across the hallway.

"Don't y'all just hate yourselves for talking about the dead this way?" Babs asked, unable to suppress her grin.

Lizzie, brain unchained, verbalized her thoughts. "Not really. Besides, I couldn't help myself even if I did."

"Me too," Daffy said.

They soon congregated around Claudia's casket. Daffy scanned the crowded room and whispered, "Claudia can rest easy. Them roots got covered up just fine. They did a pretty good job."

"What happened to her face?" Lilly asked. "All the wrinkles are gone."

"It's called embalming," Gidget said.

"Maybe I should try it." Lizzie leaned in for a closer look. "Look at that smile on her face. What shade of lipstick is that? She must've been happy at the end—"

Cootie stepped between Lizzie and Lilly, draping an arm over each of their shoulders. "She does look real peaceful. They did a real good job on her. Don't her smile seem natural? And thank God I still had one of her wigs to give the mortician."

"Uh... She looks beautiful... especially her hair," Babs said.

"Miss Gidget. Thank you for stopping by hospice on her last day. I know she appreciated seeing you."

Gidget fidgeted before replying. "Oh... uh... it was nothing. I had to say goodbye one last time."

"And which of you brought that baked spaghetti?"

"Oh! It's mine... Momma's recipe," Lizzie said. As others crowded around the casket, it left little room to maneuver. Accordingly, Cootie's weight problem became his asset. Lizzie felt his thigh pressing against hers and responded in kind. She smiled at him. "I hope y'all like it."

"Like it? I love it. I've got to get that recipe from you. I want to add it to the Carryouts' buffet."

"Maybe we should move on and give others a chance to say good-bye," Daffy said.

"What's the rush?" Cootie looked over at the casket. "Claudia ain't going nowhere."

Five minutes later, the Casserole Ladies milled about in the foyer by themselves.

"Cootie's been eatin' too much of his Carryout buffets," Babs said.

Lizzie nodded. "A lot of it's going to his thighs."

"What's with Cootie's sidewalls?" Gidget asked. "When I saw him the other day, they were grey."

"I never knew Claudia wore a wig," Lilly said.

"Her hair was almost totally grey the day I saw her at hospice."

Daffy instantly reacted. "You didn't tell us you saw Claudia the day she died."

Gidget was uneasy again. "I forgot to mention it. Uh... I saw they ordered a prescription for her and wanted to make sure she got it that day."

"Look... here come the Mammas," Babs said.

Six people stepped inside the foyer. Stoney held onto Bo's arm, followed by Penny and two other Mahjong Mammas. All four women toted casseroles. A fifth woman seemed to tag along behind them—a stranger, carrying no casserole. As the entourage headed toward Cootie, Lilly whispered to Lizzie, "Probably that Yankee-Lady."

"Bo, Stoney, Ladies." Cootie rushed to greet them. "Just put your stuff on the table in there so y'all can come back and give me some hugs. Mzz Stoney, I see you brought your asparagus casserole! I can't wait! Might be a candidate for the Carryouts' buffet."

Approaching the Casserole Ladies, Stoney squeezed Bo's arm. "Sugar, hold up a second. We need to say hey to these... ladies. It's so nice to see all y'all here. Daffy! That has got to be the prettiest dress ever! I love it more every time you wear it."

"Bless your heart," Daffy replied. "You may need to get those eyes checked again. Age does take a toll on one's eyesight, you know. Or, it just might even be your memory. That happens sometimes when you get old... I hear. I bought this little ole dress yesterday at Dillard's just for Claudia's viewing. By the way, those shoes you're wearing are the cutest ever! I think it's great Walmart has finally started carrying leather shoes."

Stoney's subsequent retort unnerved all five Casserole Ladies. Lilly and Lizzie's Florida misadventure must have become grist for the Thomasville rumor mill. She said, "Speaking of leather, it might be too hot to wear your leather costumes to the Suwanee Village Halloween Fantasy Fest. If you try body painting your costume, you might want to have the painter give you some boobs."

"Body painting might not be a bad idea for you as well, but you better go to one of them outdoor billboard sign painters for your costume. They might have enough paint."

"Speaking of enough paint, I hear the Clinique counter at Dillard's sold out last time you were there."

Bo tactfully ended the slugfest. "Stoney, shouldn't we put all the casseroles on the table and go see Claudia?"

"That does it!" Daffy wore her George S. Patton face five minutes later on Cootie's veranda.

"All right! What you got in mind?" asked Babs.

Daffy scowled at her companions. "Before we discuss that, how did Stoney find out about Suwanee Village? It's probably all over Thomasville by now. Which of you leaked?"

Two women lowered their gaze.

"I only briefly mentioned it to Skylar at the beauty salon. She was saying how she's going to the Fantasy Fest in Key West, so I told her there was a closer one," Lilly said.

Lizzie shrugged. "One of the checkout clerks at Harvey's asked me what I was gonna do for Halloween—"

"Don't tell me," Daffy said, caught herself mid-sentence, and lowered her voice, "that you're actually thinking about going there!"

"Might be kinda fun," Lizzie said.

"Let's get back on task. Daff, what do you mean 'that does it?'" Gidget asked.

"Oh, I don't know. I don't know." Daffy shook her head. "We gotta up our game... now."

"How?"

"I wanna do something dramatic. Any ideas?"

"Oh! Oh! Let's make a checklist. Wendell always loved checklists," Lilly said.

"A checklist?"

"What kind of checklist?" Gidget asked.

"Something that we can use whenever a wife dies," Lilly said.

Daffy said, "Go on." But her tone said, 'Please don't.'

"Things... rules... standards..."

"Such as?" Lizzie asked.

"Okay, how about rules on what to wear when visiting the widower? Like, tight blouses and low cleavages only after first visit."

"Never take refried bean and guacamole dip. Too gassy."

Babs nodded. "Yeah, only tasteful casseroles like broccoli and rice."

"No salads... unless the widower is bisexual," Lizzie joked.

Daffy shook her head. "Ladies, while I appreciate your ideas, I'm looking for something more dramatic. What we've been doing ain't working. A checklist ain't radical enough. Look inside that window. See how Stoney's all over Bo. I'm gonna... we're gonna lose him unless we come up with something big. We need to go rogue!"

Gidget finally joined the discussion. "I still say we need to increase the supply of widowers."

"How? Start poisoning old wives?" Lizzie asked facetiously.

"No, of course not! We need to get more widowers to come here... to Thomasville."

Daffy agreed, "It's like we were saying the other day. Better marketing. Marketing Thomasville... and us... to widowers. Maybe use that Yankee-Lady? I think that was her trailing the Mammas. Maybe we can use her to help us find the right kind of male companionship."

"What about voodoo?" Babs asked. Reacting to a collective groan at her suggestion, she said, "No, seriously. I've done more reading. We could—"

"I know something we could do that'd be radical, really rogue..." Lizzie deliberately neglected to elaborate, purposefully building her companions' curiosity.

"Okay, out with it. What?" asked Daffy.

"A calendar."

Chapter 9

Five multi-colored beachballs lie on a linoleum tile floor around three nude Casserole Ladies who stand in front of a canvas backdrop. The backdrop depicts a beach scene and hangs inside Phrank's Photography. Frank is noted for his 'boudoir' photography.

"Daffyyyyy... Gidgeeeet, y'all come on out," Babs said, voice elevated.

Lizzie ridiculed their modesty. "It ain't nothin' we ain't seen before."

"Hurry up!" Lilly pleaded. "I'm gettin' cold."

This scenario may not make sense unless we recap everything since Claudia's viewing yesterday. It may not make sense even after the recap.

The Casserole Ladies, unable to agree on a single course of action, decided to pursue two as they steamed on Cootie's veranda.

"I say we should try voodoo one more time. The other book I been reading has some great spells and chants," Babs said.

Lizzie shook her head. "Not that again."

"Marketing! We need to try some serious marketing." Gidget continued to push her idea. Libertarians can be pushy at times.

"What do we market?" Babs asked. "My calendar idea is the way to go."

"No way am I posing nude," Lilly said.

"Why not?" Lizzie asked. "All your vital areas will be discretely... behind something."

"What will our kids say? And the grandkids! They'll put me in a nursing home for sure."

"Maybe Lizzie's calendar would be a good marketing gimmick," Gidget said.

"Let's at least try one of the voodoo spells. How about a 'Good Luck Floor Wash'?" Babs asked.

The floor wash caught their attention.

"Go on," Daffy said.

"It's a common spell in voodoo intended to bring good fortune, which I figure we could use right now."

"How's it work?" Lilly asked.

After Babs explained, they agreed to try it, starting in Babs' kitchen.

"If it don't work, at least we'll all have clean floors," Daffy said.

By 8:45 pm that night, all had been on their knees for fifteen minutes, wiping Babs' kitchen tile floor with sponges, soaked with a slimy liquid dipped from a bucket.

"What's in this stuff?" Gidget asked.

"Van Van oil."

"I know that, but what's *in* Van Van oil? It stinks."

"Let me get my list." Babs extracted it from her pocket. "Lemongrass oil, citronella oil, vetivert oil, Palmarosa oil, pyrite—"

"Pyrite! That's Fool's Gold. Where did you get that?" Gidget asked.

"Well..." A sheepish look spread across Babs' face. "I wasn't sure what pyrite was, so I asked the checkout girl at Harvey's, and she didn't know what it was either, so I just picked up some Purex instead. I figured something else that started with a 'P' would be okay."

"What about vetivert oil? What's that?"

"The checkout girl didn't know what that was either..."

"So, what'd you buy instead?"

"Windex."

"Closest you could get to something starting with 'V' that sounded cleaning related... right?" Gidget asked.

"Yeah."

"At least your kitchen floor looks pretty good now," Daffy said. "What next?"

"Well, that's pretty much it, according to this spell, but I thought we'd combine it with another good luck spell."

"We've gone this far, and your floor does look pretty good. Go for it."

"Okay, let me get them notes." Babs pulled another piece of paper from her pocket. "Okay, repeat after me. *Nwa Majik Fanm.*"

"*Nwa Majik Fanm.*" The other Ladies repeated in unison.

"Super... next. *Eklate Vwazen Mwen Koule.*"

"*Eklate Vwazen Mwen Koule.*"

As soon as they finished saying the word '*Koule*', an explosion occurred.

"WHAT WAS THAT!" Lilly shouted.

"I don't know." Babs jumped up and ran to her back door, the others not far behind. "Sounded like it came from next door, in the Richardson's backyard."

From Babs' patio, they witnessed a blaze in her neighbor's yard.

"It's their garden shed. It's on fire!"

An hour later, the Thomasville Fire Department had extinguished the fire. Unfortunately, the garden shed was a total loss. Daffy called an after-action meeting inside Bab's house.

"Did you copy that chant correctly?" Gidget asked.

"I'm pretty sure I did." Babs handed her the paper.

"What language is this?"

"Some sort of Haitian stuff, I think."

"It's probably a version of *Three Stoogeese*," Lizzie said.

The final result was not a tragedy. Babs wound up with a pretty clean floor, and the Richardson's insurance adjuster assured them their garden shed was covered. Perhaps this incident could have been avoided had Daffy overseen Babs' transcription efforts that afternoon. Instead, she stayed on Cootie's veranda while Babs went shopping at Harvey's, and Lilly and Lizzie went to Phrank's to set up their photography appointment.

Daffy spied the Yankee-Lady as she milled about by herself in the parlor, obviously too new to mingle effectively. Daffy waved for her to come outside, and after introductions and small talk, they got down to business.

"My girlfriends and I are thinking of something that might be right up your alley," Daffy said. "A calendar that might get Thomasville a lot of attention."

"Oh? Calendars don't typically bring that much attention... unless they're really spectacular."

"The calendar we have in mind fits that bill. Ever hear of the Rylstone Ladies?"

"No... not that I can recall. Wait! Wasn't there a movie about them?"

"Bingo. Starred Helen Mirren. About a bunch of older women in England that made a calendar."

"Yeah. I remember it now."

"They were nekkid. Didn't really show anything, but you could tell they were nekkid. Was great publicity for Rylstone Women's Institute. We thought if we did something like that, it might be good for Thomasville... call it 'Widows of Thomasville'." Daffy neglected to add that expectations were that it would also be good for Casserole Lady romance.

"How did you come up with this idea?"

"One of my girlfriend's boyfriends suggested it."

Lizzie had explained that Sonny Biskit suggested it one night when he was "trying to get into my britches."

As their conversation drifted, Daffy became more at ease with Stacie Goodie. The topic of Bo came up.

"I almost didn't get the job because of him," she said.

"Oh?"

"One of the hostesses at the Visitors Center told me that her pedicurist was doing a pedicure on one of the members of the Board of Tourism who told her that the Board hired me over Stoney's objections. She said Stoney thought I might be competition for her with Bo after he came on board."

Daffy nodded. "Sounds just like her."

"I probably wouldn't have taken the job anyway if he'd been on the Board when I interviewed."

"How so?"

"Well, I've been divorced for about a year now. Bo reminds me too much of my ex. Good looking guy, knows the right things to say to a girl, but..."

"But?"

"My ex was a cheat. Followed him after work one day and caught him screwing one of my girlfriends. Those idiots forgot to lock the door to her apartment. The pictures I took are on my Facebook page."

"I don't think you have to worry about Bo. He's too faithful to his wife's memory. Refuses to get involved with any woman. Thinks he would be unfaithful to his dead wife."

"Doesn't matter to me. I'm off of men for a long time. Bo seems to be getting friendly with Stoney."

Observing their conversation through Cootie's window, Stoney nervously tapped her foot as she chatted with Bo. Outside, both women seemed to be enjoying each other's company. They parted, Stacie agreeing to use the calendar should it appear marketable.

"I take it back!" Lizzie exclaimed as Daffy and Gidget stepped from behind the changing screen. "Y'all do have something we ain't seen before! What is that? Turn around."

Daffy hesitatingly turned so the lower part of left butt-cheek was more viewable. "It's a tattoo of Willie Nelson."

"How come I never saw that while we were clothes shopping?"

Daffy shrugged.

"Sonny never mentioned you had a tattoo." Lizzie's brain again neglected to filter its thoughts. "When'd you get it?"

"FSU sorority initiation."

"Why Willie Nelson?"

"There was a popular joke going around at the time about a woman with a Willie Nelson tattoo."

"Looks more like a birthmark now. Maybe that's why I missed it. Let's see what Gidget's hiding. Drop the towel, girl. Go ahead. You got to sooner or later."

Gidget lowered her towel.

"Isn't that Ron Paul!?" Babs asked.

Gidget looked down at a small tattoo of the politician's face on her right breast. "Yes, it is."

"When did you get that?" Lizzie asked. "Looks like someone did pretty good work."

"1988, when I attended the Libertarian National Convention. I was a little high and excited after his nomination." As Gidget looked up, her eyes widened. "Lizzie! When did you get that Brazilian bikini wax?"

"A remnant of my Seaside trip last month. Worried I might get lucky and didn't want whomever to find out I wasn't a true redhead." Lizzie inadvertently glimpsed herself in a full-length mirror. "Oh God! I never realized the human body could accommodate that much cellulite."

"Or so much flab." Babs grabbed a handful of her own belly. "Maybe we should try voodoo on our bodies."

"Or not!" Gidget said.

"Why not?" Lizzie asked. "What could be worse than what I'm looking at in this mirror?"

"I Googled that chant we recited last night." Gidget walked over to her clothes and extracted a piece of paper. "This is Haitian Creole. Do you know what 'Nwa Majik Fanm, Eklate Vwazen Mwen Koule' actually means?"

"No, what?" Babs asked.

"Black Magic Woman, blow up my neighbor's shed."

Chapter 10

Some think Liam's the best place to be in Thomasville at happy hour. No surprise our Casserole Ladies are there. Daffy leaned closer to Stacie and raised her voice several decibels in order to be heard. "I'm not surprised no one at the Tourism Bureau has taken you here yet. Those goobers never wanna go anywhere that's fun."

Daffy subsequently finished her second Mexican Firing Squad in one gulp and signaled their waiter.

"I've been here almost a month," Stacie said, "and the only place we've gone for lunch is Subway."

"The real reason Jared lost all that weight was he got sick of nothing but Subway and quit eating," Lizzie said.

"The only place my grandkids ever holler for is Chick-fil-A. Chicken nuggets! Chicken nuggets! God, how I dread seeing them things on the tray." Babs turned to the waiter as he leaned in to take their orders. She batted her eyelashes. "Could I have another one of these Cosmos, Stefan? Pretty please."

"Yes'm."

Daffy hiccupped. "Another Mexi, Mexi... another one of these whatevers."

"It's called a Mexican Firing Squad, Ma'am," Stefan said.

"Yessiree! Good looking and smart..." Daffy flashed her best smile at him, then wrapped an arm around Stacie. "And another whatever our new friend here is having."

"She's a Zombie... I mean she's *having* a Zombie." He looked around. "Anyone else?"

"Another house Chardonnay." Like many intellectuals, Gidget favors wine.

"Hold on the Cosmo. I'm gonna try something different." The bar menu swayed a little as Babs held it close to her glasses. "How about a Corpse Reviver instead? Mine needs reviving right now."

"Another Tell Tale Hearts, please. It sounds so romantic," Lilly said.

"Another Maker's Mark, sweetie." Lizzie looked over her shoulder at their waiter, already walking toward the bar. "Ain't that a cute little butt! Looks good enough to take home to momma."

Daffy's eyes also followed the young man's progress. "I would indeed love to take him home with this momma. I wouldn't get greedy. Just a night of good, hot sex. That's all. Just some hot sex for a night... or maybe two."

"Good luck." Gidget hiccupped. "He's gay."

"No way! How do you know?" Lilly asked.

"The Thomasville rumor mill," Gidget said."

Lilly shook her head. "What a shame for us... what a *terrible* shame."

After a moment of silence, Daffy said, "I'd love to take a run at him anyway."

"Me too," Gidget slurred.

"Which brings me to the subject of our calendar." Daffy hiccupped, then looked at Stacie. "What's the latest?"

"The galleys look great. Printer says he'll have two hundred copies ready to go for initial distribution by next week."

"That's only a week after we took the pictures. Wow."

"Having a relationship with a gay man would probably be advantageous." Babs stared glassy-eyed at their waiter as he maneuvered through the crowd toward them. "They're caring people by their nature."

"They are." Gidget nodded, drained the last of her wine, and second-guessed herself. "Aren't they?"

Babs drained the remnants of her Cosmopolitan. "I need someone I can take care of. Taking care of a gay man would be fun."

"Not nearly as much maintenance as a straight man," Lizzie said. "Think of all the money you'd save on Febreze."

"He's so cute," Babs said. Her next words were slightly incomprehensible. "I jus' wanna take 'em home and feed 'em. I bett'e neva gets a good, home-cooked meal."

"Hell, the last home-cooked meal I had was at my neighbor's house eight years ago." Lizzie had trouble pronouncing 'last' and 'house.'

Babs' head collapsed into her palms, elbows resting on the table. Her eyes continued to stare at their waiter as he delivered their drinks. All six women stared in silence until he was out of earshot.

"I do have some exciting news about the calendar. I—" Stacie's attempt to upgrade the conversation was interrupted.

"He don't a home-cooked meal," Daffy said before drinking from her new Mexican Firing Squad. "All he needs is hot sex with a woman... You know, a bar's a lot like a church—"

"Except much better... but not as quiet. What's the exciting news?" Gidget asked, hiccupping in the process. "Since he's gay, I bet he's pretty smart."

"It's about the calendar—" Stacie was again interrupted.

"Which means he'd be a great companion. Good talker. Someone you could spend a lot of time with and never run out of things to talk about." Gidget took a hefty drink of wine then remembered something else. "Wonner if he likes football."

"About the calendar. I got calls from—"

"Fuhget aboud it," Lizzie slurred, then slurped some more Makers. "Havin' or not havin' sex with him ain't the important thing. The important thing is a young millennial like him takes you to a restaurant and probably don't have enough dough to pay for the meal... much less the bar bill."

"A bar is like a church, and happy hour is like a church's Mass—" At this point, it is difficult to tell who is speaking. Probably Daffy.

"I bet he makes pretty good tips. We should give him a calendar. What's the news on it?" Lilly asked.

"I got calls from the producers at—"

"Someone you can have sex with on Saturday night, who don't snore too loudly afterwards, and who leaves right after breakfast on Sunday." Probably Daffy again.

"Even if he don't make good tips. As long as he'd love me. I don't want to love any man that can't love me back," Lilly said. "Mmmm, mmm. This is so good. What is this I'm having? I forget."

"Tell Tale... Farts," Babs said, head still cradled in her palms. "I think."

"Hearts," Stacie said.

"That gets back to what I've been saying about an insufficient supply of men... not enough men to love us back," Gidget hiccupped.

Daffy nodded to no one in particular. "And we're *never* gonna be happy without men to love us back."

"Have y'all thought about using technology?" Stacie asked.

Lizzie perked up. "What do you mean? Like a vibrator?"

"No, no. Things like the Internet, Facebook, the Cloud..."

"What about one of them sex robots?" Babs raised her head slightly. "Now, that's technology!"

"What about the calendar? You mentioned something about producers—" Daffy opened and closed her eyes several times as she attempted to focus.

"I do miss Wendell so much." Lilly teared up. "Just to have someone to love again."

"Does Stoney know about the calendar?" Daffy asked.

Stacie nodded. "Yes. Since it involves the Tourism Bureau, I had to inform her. Suffice it to say, she's not thrilled."

"I bet she's got her panties in a wad. She gonna stop it?"

"No, which brings me back to what I was trying to tell y'all. Both Channel 46 and Channel 49 in Tallahassee heard about it, and both want to do stories on it. There's no way she's gonna spike Tourism Bureau involvement in a calendar getting that kind of publicity for the

'Widow Capital of the World'. How come you two hate each other so much?"

"It goes all the way back to FSU—"

"Actually, I wouldn't mind a little hot sex with a cute gay guy, so long as he'd at least pick up the bar bill." Lizzie held up her empty glass and looked around for the waiter.

"You might not mind," Gidget said, "but he might."

Daffy tried to pick back up on her story about her feud with Stoney. "She stole the sorority presidency from me—"

"More supply... If we could marry gays, it would mean more supply." Babs' head returned to her palms. "Just what Gidget wants."

"But I got back at her. I married the guy she had her sights on. Royce. She's had a case of psychological hemorrhoids about it ever since, but I had Royce." Daffy smiled, then frowned and made a circling motion with her forefinger as she said, "Whoop-de-do."

"Babs is onto something." Gidget raised her voice an octave. "Let's buy one of them male sex robots. They call 'em 'sexbots.' How much does one cost?"

"Why don't y'all try Facebook instead?" Stacie asked.

"It's tough growing old... especially if you're a woman," Daffy said.

"What do you mean?"

"Just look... Men grow older, they get more attractive—"

Lilly said, "We could get one of my grandkids to show us how to use Facebook—"

"You already use Facebook, don't you?" Lizzie asked.

Babs looked at Daffy. "Our waiter's gotta be no more than twenty-two, and he looks pretty attractive to me."

"No, no. That's not what I mean. Look at Bo. Late fifties. No one even notices the grey in his hair or the wrinkles on his face," Daffy said.

"What face? All I see is ass." As soon as she finished, Lizzie realized her mistake. "Oh, I thought you were talking about our waiter."

"But take any woman our age. What does a man see? Wrinkles, stomach, grey hair—"

"He sees blonde hair if she's smart," Lizzie said.

"Lilly's right." By this time, Gidget was buzzed, no two ways about it. She responded to a comment made by Daffy, not Lilly. "Women get older, we get less attractive. A man gets older, he improves with age—"

"He becomes more valuable..." Daffy paused to sip her Firing Squad. "He may still need a little training, but at least not on things like raising the toilet seat."

"Finally has enough money to pay the dinner bill," Lizzie said.

Babs said, "Not always. Look at Sonny Biskit."

"Doesn't overdo it when it comes to sex." Gidget's comment brought stares from all others at the table.

"That's improving with age?" Daffy asked. "Even worse is when he can't do sex period."

"That's why God created Viagra," Lizzie said. "No wait, I forgot. A woman created Viagra."

Daffy put her glass down. "You said the TV channels want to do a story on our calendar? How did they find out?"

"Get real. No way something like this is gonna be kept secret in Thomasville," Stacie said.

"Do they want to interview us? When?" asked Lilly.

"This Tuesday."

Babs raised her head slightly. "I like the Facebook idea."

"TV interview?! Holy Shit! I gotta make an appointment at the beauty salon." Lizzie slammed both hands on the table.

"We should all go together, so we can coordinate hair styles. I'll call tomorrow," Lilly said.

"Wonder if Sonny would do a threesome with our waiter?" Babs asked, raising her head higher.

"Don't be gross. No more Corpse Retrievers for you," Daffy said before hiccupping again.

Stacie shook her head. "I believe she's been having Corpse Revivers, not Retrievers."

"Facials... don't forget facials," Lilly squealed.

"And nails," Lizzie said as her head weaved back and forth. "They're the only part of my body that grows longer and not wider."

"Just proves what I was saying," Gidget said. "A man gets older, he still looks great on TV. Women have to go through beauty salon hell just for a TV interview. Now, if we were males—"

"We'd have no trouble getting a date with Stefan." Babs' head retreated to her palms.

Chapter 11

Four heads leaned in close to Lilly who sat at her computer the next day. She had finished setting up a Facebook page titled 'Widows of Thomasville' and attempted to customize it when her computer screen began displaying unusual things.

"What happened!?" Lilly's head swiveled in search of an answer. Answers came, none helpful.

"Your computer looks like it's got a worse hangover than I got," Babs said.

Daffy's advice followed the same theme. "That computer and Babsie both need a little hair of the dog."

"I tried to get you to stop at the Waffle House on the way home last night," Gidget whined, referring to the Southern chain noted for curing hangovers.

"I knew I should've slept in instead of doing this kind of... nonsense," Lizzie said.

Lilly voiced her priorities. "We had to do it this morning if we're gonna make our appointments at the beauty salon this afternoon."

"Stacie better be right about this Facebook page thing. If I don't get an old rich man contacting me today, then I gave up three hours of beauty sleep for nothing."

Gidget also looked at the computer screen over Lilly's shoulder. "I thought you used Facebook before."

"Not anymore. I started using it last year to keep up with my youngest daughter when she started her freshman year at Florida but had to quit after a month."

"Why?"

"All she ever posted were pictures taken in her sorority house. I quit checking on her for my own peace of mind."

"Okay, so what do we do now? How do we get rid of this crap and get to some place that looks understandable?" Daffy asked.

Her questions were met with shrugged shoulders.

"Mister Factoid." Mister Factoid was Daffy's nineteen-year-old grandson. She nicknamed him in his early teens because he always seemed to know a little something about any subject. She said, "Mister Factoid always says when you screw up on a computer and don't know what to do, just type 'control,' 'something,' 'something.'"

"What?" asked Lilly.

"Just hold that little key that says 'Ctrl' and hit a couple of other keys at the same time."

"But what other keys?"

"Uh... 'Alt!' 'Alt' is one of the other keys. It's 'control,' 'alt,' and some other key."

"But what's the other key?"

"Just try some other key on the keyboard and see what happens."

"Try one of them F keys up top. We use them a lot in the Pharmacy. Go for it," Gidget said.

"Okay." Lilly pressed the control and alt keys with index and fore-finger, closed her eyes, and pressed one of the Function keys with her other forefinger. Her computer screen exploded with an endless stream of unintelligible techno-gibberish.

"Wow! You've definitely gone where no man has gone before."

"Reminds me of what it used to look like when I typed on my old IBM Selectric but wasn't looking at the keys," Lizzie said.

Babs stepped back from the computer. "Kind've looks like it's throwing up.

"What does all that stuff mean? How do we stop it?" Lilly asked.

"Who knows?" Lizzie also stepped back, scratching her head. "My first... maybe it was the second husband used to say 'Don't just stand around. Do something.' Trying hitting some more keys."

Lilly did as instructed, and the screen went blank.

Lizzie scratched her head some more. "Looks like that wasn't the right something. Turn the damn thing off and start over."

Lilly complied, Windows came back up normally, but when she tried to access Facebook, the following message appeared:

We are sorry, but Facebook is temporarily out of service. Please try again later.

"Wonder what's going on?" Lilly asked.

"Go back and try again," Daffy said.

Lilly repeated the process with similar results. "Technology. No wonder I hate it. What now?"

"Let's have some refreshments on your porch and try again in thirty minutes."

Fifteen minutes later while sipping Mimosas on Lilly's front porch, her phone rang, displaying an unknown number.

"Don't answer. It's probably a robocall," Lizzie said.

"No, answer it. It might be one of them phone psychics." Babs relies on phone psychics for help with picking her lottery numbers. Lilly ignored her advice.

"This is Lilly White. How may I help y'all?" Lilly sat, phone in ear, while the other Ladies looked on and listened. Over the next three minutes, they heard her intermittently say: "Yes... Yes... Nothing, just trying to customize a page we just created... No... No... Yes... No... I don't know... No... I don't know... We've never done that before... Yes... How dare you talk to me like that... Same to you... I've never known... No... Same to you... I'll have you know my tax dollars pay for your salary... You just try it... I'm warnin' you, I keep a loaded pistol in my purse and one in my nightstand... Well, we'll just see about that!"

Lilly slammed the phone down, her alabaster face glowing red.

"What was that?!" asked Daffy.

"Some jerk accusing me of crashing Facebook."

"Jerk?"

"Yeah. From Facebook."

"Lilly, your tax dollars don't pay any salaries at Facebook..." Gidget paused a few seconds. "At least as far as I know."

"We'd better have some more Mimosas," Lizzie said.

"Is it still down?" asked Daffy.

Lilly retrieved her laptop, checked, and got the same out-of-service message. "That couldn't have been us... could it?"

"No way," Gidget said. "At least as far as I know."

"What's that?"

"A siren." Babs pointed. "There's a police car coming up your street. Looks like Chief Mitchell's car."

The police cruiser pulled into Lilly's driveway, and an overweight, uniformed man climbed out. He said, "Hey Lilly."

"Hey Randy. What're y'all doing here?"

"I got a call from the FBI Office in Atlanta. They want me to bring you down to the Police Station."

"What for?"

"Something about Facebook. They wouldn't tell me anything else except they need to question you."

"When?"

"As soon as they get here. They're driving down now and should be here in about two hours."

"I can't go there now. I got a hair appointment this afternoon."

Gidget looked at the others. "All of us were helping Lilly with Facebook."

"You ain't going there by yourself," Daffy said.

"Do you mean the beauty salon or jail?" Babs asked. "I may have to think about it if it's the latter."

The look of determination on Daffy's face would have put Rambo to shame. "Randy, one of us goes to jail, we all go."

"We got a half-drunk pitcher of Mimosas here." Lizzie got in Chief Mitchell's face. "Damn it, Randy. At least let us finish it."

"Throwing out that much Mimosa would be a crime itself, wouldn't it?" Gidget asked.

"Sorry Ladies. Everybody into the cruiser. I got my orders. The Feds can sort this out at the jail." Chief Mitchell walked to the police car and held the door open. The Ladies dutifully followed, but their resistance stiffened once they saw the inside of the cruiser.

"I'm not gettin' into that filthy thing." Lilly looked as if she had been told there was a shortage of hand sanitizer.

"This thing smells, but I'm afraid to ask why," Gidget said.

"How long is this gonna take?" Lizzie asked. *"Bold and the Beautiful* comes on at one-thirty."

Betraying second thoughts all of them going to jail together, Daffy asked, "They ain't gonna be takin' mugshots, are they?"

"Can they at least wait and take 'em after we can get our hair done?" Lilly asked.

Chapter 12

Located close to downtown Thomasville, the city's police station is not far from Lilly's house. Chief Mitchell soon relocated the ladies as requested, and two hours later a man knocked, then walked into his office. He wore a black suit, white shirt, and black tie and flashed a badge. "Chief Mitchell? I'm Special Agent Sternik. Did you do what I told you to?"

"Yessir, take a seat." Chief Mitchell nodded at a chair. "They been isolated in an interrogation room ever since they arrived."

"No one's talked to them?"

"Yessir, just like you told me."

"The interrogation room—is the room's audio and video recorded?"

"Yessir. And monitored the entire time by one of my detectives, just as you requested. Isn't all this a bit too much for a couple of little old ladies?"

Agent Sternik looked around the room, apparently surveilling its security. As his gaze returned to the Chief, his face displayed a stern expression. "Everything we discuss is confidential, and you will be held accountable if any of it goes beyond this room. Understand?"

"Yessir."

"We found after Oklahoma City and 9-11 that we can't afford not to take everything seriously. Terrorists, especially these cyberterrorists, come in all sizes, sexes, and ages. Terrorists like out-of-the-way, low observation places like Thomasville."

"But I've known these ladies all my life. They're crazy but harmless."

"These five showed up in our database... regarding a German pipeline incident several years ago."

"But—"

"Save it for the CIA."

"CIA?"

"Yeah. They'll be here shortly. You need to understand that these cyberterrorists somehow crashed Facebook. That's no small matter."

"Crashed Facebook! How? For how long?"

"Your first question is what we intend to find out. As to your second question, Facebook estimates it will be down for twenty-four hours." Sternik nodded toward the door. "Bring in the detective that's been monitoring these uh... ladies."

Within a few minutes, a Thomasville police detective stepped into the Chief's office. After introductions, Agent Sternik said, "Start at the beginning... from when they were first left alone. I want a complete synopsis of their conversations from that point until now."

The Detective looked down at several pages of notes. "Well... a lot of bitchin' and moanin' at first about condition of the room... it was either too hot or too cold. One lady found gum and other things stuck to the underside of the table. They talked about the calendar—"

"Calendar?"

"Yeah, they're making a calendar—"

"It's called 'Widows of Thomasville'," Chief Mitchell said. "Everyone's talking about it around here. Apparently, they're photographed semi-nude."

"Go on." Agent Sternik's head nodded as if risqué calendars were accepted tactics used in cyberterrorism.

"Anyway, since they got here, they've been talking non-stop, and I mean non-stop. God! I've had to listen to them for over two hours. I need a break... please!"

Sternik ignored his comments. "Go on. What have they been talking about?"

"Hairdos. They're concerned there'll be mugshots before their hair appointments this afternoon... also talking about their nails, grandkids, something about Mister Factoid—"

"Mister Factoid?"

"Apparently a nickname for Mrs. Belvedere's grandson—"

"Which one is Belvedere?" Sternik asked.

"Daffy Belvedere. The older of the two thin ones," said Chief Mitchell.

The Detective continued. "Anyway, one of the other ladies felt that Mrs. Belvedere's grandson's technical knowledge was somewhat lacking. They all began to argue over this."

"This could be useful. Anything else about this Mister Factoid? That name sounds suspicious."

"Nothing really. Other than he removed a dead possum from Mrs. Belvedere's parlor when he was thirteen." The Detective acknowledged the others' quizzical looks with his own arched eyebrows and shrugged shoulders. "Apparently the possum snuck in one night and OD'd on M&Ms left out in a candy dish."

"What's that got to do with this Facebook crash?"

"Nothing. But Mrs. Belvedere brought it up when Mrs. White... that's Mrs. Lilly White, the other thin one, mentioned that she caught a squirrel chewing a hole through the wooden lap siding of her house."

"Go on."

"Let's see... Mrs. White has a new casserole dish, Tuna and Jell-O Pie..." Agent Sternik looked at Chief Mitchell and both made a face, prompting the Detective to affirm their judgement. He said, "Yeah, me too. Even worse, she plans on taking it to Marjorie Winchell's viewing on Sunday—"

"Please, no more on the tuna casserole. What else?"

"Let's see... Oh! Here's something even I didn't know. George Bentley has been seen riding around with Bruno and Toots Varnell."

A sly, knowing smile spread across Agent Sternik's face. "Tell me more. Bruno's the codename of one of Russia's top spies."

"George Bentley is a fairly recent widower," the Chief said. "Pretty well off. Ever since his wife died, he's been seen mostly with Penny Perdoo, a widow. Bruno is Bentley's dog. A boxer. Bentley takes Bruno for a ride in his Cadillac every morning. He's too fat to walk. Bentley, not Bruno."

"Oh..." Disappointment tinged Sternik's voice. "Go on."

"According to Mrs. Smurfitt, Toots Varnell was seen earlier this week riding with Bentley and Bruno instead of Mrs. Perdoo."

Sternik said, "Tell me more about this Smurfitt. Sounds like an Eastern European name. That could be important."

"Gloria Smurfitt," Chief Mitchell said. "Her deceased husband owned Smurfitt Phamily Pharmacy. The business goes back to the 1930's. She was born and raised in Thomasville."

Agent Sternik frowned. "Yeah, okay. What's all this Toots and Perdoo got to do with hacking Facebook?"

The Detective said, "Nothing... just that it's interesting. Everybody here at the station thought Perdoo had Bentley all wrapped up. Now, it looks like Toots is moving in."

"Who's this Toots?"

"She's one of the ladies in a Mahjong club with Mrs. Perdoo. She attended University of Georgia. That's where she acquired the nickname Toots. You can guess why. Age 71... despite her blonde hair."

"Move this along. Anything about this Toots-Bentley stuff of importance?"

"Nothing really. Except Mrs. Neauxgeaux mentioned that Dean Martin was supposed to have made a fifth Matt Helm movie."

"No-go?"

"Babs Neauxgeaux," Chief Mitchell said. "You can't miss her. When you go into the interrogation room, she's the one almost as wide as she is tall with most of her weight in her breasts."

"I can't wait, but can you tie all this Toots-Bentley-Matt Helm stuff into what we're talking about?"

The Detective took a deep breath. "It's tough, but I'll try. Mrs. Smurfitt said if Toots gets George Bentley, it's less competition for Mrs. Belvedere for Bo."

"Bo?"

"Bo Thomas. One of Thomasville's leading citizens. A widower. Mrs. Belvedere said she thought Bo looks like Dean Martin did in his prime. That's when Mrs. Neauxgeaux mentioned the fifth Matt Helm movie that Dean Martin never made—"

Chief Mitchell said, "If you've ever seen one of the other four Matt Helm movies that Dean Martin did make, you'd know why he didn't want to do a fifth."

"So, if I understand the connection..." Sternik spoke slowly. "Toots Varnell riding with George Bentley means she won't be competing with Daffy Belvedere for Bo Thomas, who looks like Dean Martin did when he made these Matt Helm pictures, which were so bad that he refused to make a fifth one?"

"Exactly!" A broad smile of satisfaction spread across the Detective's face. He looked back down at his notes. "That was about all they said about those folks... other than Mrs. Neauxgeaux gave Mrs. Belvedere some advice about Mr. Thomas."

"What was that?"

"Get him in your bed, then get him in your church." The Detective looked up from his notes. Something, perhaps something reflecting newly acquired wisdom, seemed to sparkle in his eyes. He said, "I thought what she advised was spot on."

"Shit! As much as I hate to ask, what else did they discuss?"

"Mrs. Sherbert, that's Lizzie Sherbert, related the story of an elderly woman in one of the local nursing homes who asked Mrs. Sherbert's daughter who worked there quite a while ago..." The Detective studied his notes and chuckled. "This was Mrs. Sherbert's daughter by either her second or third husband... anyway this elderly woman asked her daughter if her father was a widower or divorced... this was while Mrs. Sherbert's second or third husband was still alive and married to Mrs. Sherbert—"

"Why is that funny?"

"When her daughter told the elderly lady that her mother, Mrs. Sherbert, was indeed still alive and not divorced from her husband, the old woman asked if Mrs. Sherbert and her husband got along very well..." At this point in his story, the Detective was laughing and had to pause.

"Okay, okay, we get the humor. Go on," Agent Sternik said.

Still laughing, the Detective resumed his narration. "Mrs. Sherbert said the old bitch was hoping that they were not... getting along very well, that is."

"Damn! What else?"

"Only that Mrs. Sherbert said something after that about it being too bad that women don't have nuts you could cut off."

"Please, please no more about Sherbert. Anything else?"

"They talked about Stefan—"

"Stefan?" Special Agent Sternik's eyes narrowed. *Another Russian spy codename?!*

"The gay waiter at Liam's," Chief Mitchell said.

"What did they say specifically about him? This could be important."

"One of them, Mrs. Neauxgeaux, was still pissed that he turned her down yesterday—"

"Turned her down?"

"Yeah. She apparently offered him sex and a home-cooked meal."

"Hmmm... Go on. What else?"

"I never knew the Mayor's wife had a facelift last year."

"No, no. I meant what else about Stefan? Besides, what politician's wife hasn't had a facelift?"

"Nothing else about Stefan."

A look of disappointment appeared on Agent Sternik's face. "What else did they talk about?"

"Mrs. Lee. She chairs the Board of Directors for the Tourism Bureau. She swims nude in her pool... every Sunday afternoon... weather permitting—"

"Let's remember," Chief Mitchell said as he looked directly at the Detective, "to send a drone on a routine ISR patrol tomorrow afternoon."

"Maybe have it do a flyaway over Mrs. Lee's house?" the Detective asked.

"Gentlemen, could we please get back to the main point? Finish summarizing."

"Let's see... Mrs. White mentioned something else I didn't know."

"What's that?"

"I didn't know the City Manager is screwing his executive assistant. The others were surprised Mrs. Smurfitt didn't know that." The Detective looked up from his notes at the Chief. "Mrs. Sherbert said that either her third or fourth husband still runs a box truck full of booze up to Effingham County twice a month—"

"So?" Agent Sternik's face displayed irritation.

"It's a dry county."

"Okay. Look, skip all the bullshit talk. Have they said anything about this Facebook episode?"

"Nothing really. Other than they're never gonna follow Mister Factoid's advice when it comes to computers. And, they're gonna have to try another technology besides Facebook to find more eligible men."

Agent Sternik shook his head.

"What now?" Chief Mitchell asked.

"We wait for the CIA."

"The CIA's coming here!? "Why? When?" asked the Detective.

"They're sending an asset from New Orleans. Should be here by two o'clock."

"Those ladies are gonna be pissed about that."

"Oh?" Agent Sternik perked up. "Why you say that?"

"Their appointment at the beauty salon is at two o'clock."

At 1:45 PM, the door to Chief Mitchell's office opened and a geeky-looking older man entered.

"I broke the land speed record getting here." The man flipped open his identification wallet. "Duncan Grooves. CIA. Had to put the blue light on the roof of my Crown Vic."

"Special Agent Sternik, and this is Police Chief Mitchell. I'm gonna ask Chief Mitchell to leave while we discuss this case."

Grooves spoke after the Chief stepped out. "I didn't get much of a briefing before I had to leave. Someone apparently broke into the CIA's backdoor code in Facebook and crashed the entire system for the last..." Grooves looked at his watch. "Six hours."

"How do you fit in?"

"I'm a computer analyst. My boss wants me to find out how these women... It is only women isn't it?"

"Yeah."

"How these women were able to break into program code it took the CIA two years to develop."

"Good God! These women must be computer geniuses."

"Where are they?"

"In one of the Chief's interrogation rooms. Monitored ever since they got here."

"Said anything that might give us a clue as to what they're up to?"

"No, nothing. From what the detective whose been monitoring them told us, they've been putting on a pretty good dumb act, which tells me they're pretty smart."

"Agreed. I want to see just how smart they are. Let's grab the Chief. We may need him."

Shortly thereafter, Grooves stepped inside the interrogation room. He looked around and shouted. "BABS!!! What the hell are y'all doing here?!"

"GROOVIE!!!"

"You two know each other?" Agent Sternik and Chief Mitchell simultaneously asked.

"Know each other?" Grooves looked at Sternik. "We were in freshman English at FSU together. Kappa Sigs and Chi Omegas were like brothers and sisters. Babs was a wild woman at the Kappa Sig house!"

"Groovie was no slow leak himself." A sly grin spread across Babs' face. "Remember the FSU-Florida game our junior year?"

"Remember it? I haven't been able to drink Southern Comfort since."

"Groovie's the only person I ever knew that could drive a car from FSU to the State Capitol, circle it three times, and drive back to FSU without getting caught."

"So?" Agent Sternik asked.

"He drove the whole way in reverse. Others tried but spent a night in the Tallahassee jail."

"At least I never mixed white phosphorus and potassium chlorate in Chemistry class." Grooves and Babs shared a laugh at his comment. He smiled at Chief Mitchell and Agent Sternik, then winked at them. "What in the hell do y'all think you're doing, detaining these nice ladies? This is insane. Anyone that knows Babs knows how these ladies could've crashed Facebook. Let 'em go. I think I can explain things to my boss."

"Thank God!" Lilly said. "If we hurry, we can just make our appointments at the beauty salon."

Chapter 13

Two and a half hours after leaving the police station, four of five Casserole Ladies enjoyed happy hour at The Plaza Restaurant and Oyster Bar. Duncan Grooves wanted someone to walk him through the steps that led up to the Facebook crash. Chief Mitchell, remembering the German pipeline incident two years ago, suggested Gidget stay and perform that task. No hairdo or happy hour for her.

"A dozen raw oysters..." Daffy told their waitress then glanced at her companions. "What?"

"Will a dozen be enough?" Babs asked. "Even without Gidget?"

Lilly shook her head. "I don't think so. I can't never get enough raw oysters."

"Does September end with an R?" Lizzie asked. "Can't eat oysters in a month that don't end with an R."

"You're safe. Besides, after a couple of bottles of that champagne, you won't care what time of day it is, much less what month," Babs said.

Daffy looked at their waitress. "Two dozen raw oysters and a couple of bottles of Moet."

"Nothing like celebrating with Apalachicola oysters." Lilly licked her lips. "Mmmm, mmm! I just love the way they slide down your throat."

"Perfect way to celebrate an end to that ordeal this morning. I was about getting ready to put on my mean face with those men," Daffy said. Her mean face is not a pleasant site, especially if you are a man or a small child. Please refrain from asking if there is any difference.

"Only one of my husbands liked raw oysters... but I can't remember which one... probably the first or third," Lizzie said.

"First or third?" Babs rhetorically asked. "I know all rich men look alike, but come on Lizzie. You were married to him and can't remember."

"None of 'em were that memorable."

"I remember the first time I ate a raw oyster. I was seven years old. Getting that slimy thing in my mouth was like pullin' teeth," Lilly said.

"Yeah," Gidget said. "First time putting a raw oyster in your mouth is like the first time putting a contact lens in your eye."

"Just remember to check your boots when you stand up." Daffy looked down at Lilly's feet. "You don't want to ruin them Salvatore Ferragamo's."

All four ladies wrinkled their noses at the old gross joke about oysters sliding through the digestive tract.

"It's convenient that Gidget had her hair done earlier this week..." Daffy looked around, then lowered her voice. "There's something we need to discuss without her."

"About her hair?!" Lilly's wide eyes suggested intense fear. Nothing worse than a botched coiffure.

"No, no... worse than that."

"What could be worse than bad hair?"

A botched facelift or droopy eyelids from sloppy Botox injections come to mind. The other three ladies leaned in closer.

"It has to do with Marjorie Winchell," Daffy said. Marjorie died on Thursday after a months-long battle with cancer.

"Something about Marjorie's hair?" Lilly asked.

"No... nothing to do with her hair. Gidget visited her right before she died."

Babs asked, "How you know?"

"I was talking with one of my Garden Club friends yesterday, and she mentioned Marjorie's death, which I had already heard about from another woman at the gym. She said—"

"Which one?"

"The lady at the Garden Club... She said it was providential, so to speak, that Gidget was able to at least see her the day she died—"

"See Marjorie?"

"Why providential?" Lilly asked before Daffy could respond to Babs' question.

"Yes, Marjorie. How the hell would I know? I guess because it was the last opportunity to see her before she died," Daffy said, pursing her lips in frustration. "Anyway, I casually asked how'd she find that out, and she said that one of her neighbors was in the pharmacy Thursday—"

"Whose neighbor?"

"The..." Daffy paused, a look of annoyance on her face. "The Garden Club lady... I think. Anyway, one of them asked where Gidget was—"

"Asked who?"

"The clerk at Gidget's pharmacy. Anyway, she mentioned that she had gone over to Mrs. Winchell's house..." Daffy again paused, looked at her companions in anticipation of another interruption, then resumed. "Before any of y'all ask me who went over to Mrs. Winchell's house, it was Gidget. My Garden Club friend figured she must've been taking some medicine to her—"

"When did our oysters and champagne arrive?" Babs asked.

"At least five minutes ago. Look at your plate. You've already ate two oysters. You also need a refill." Daffy picked up the bottle and poured.

"Just how many wives does that make over the past month that she's visited the day they died?"

"Four... I think."

"You sure?" Lilly asked. "I think it's at least six."

"Let's see... Claudia, Marjorie... uhhh..."

"Gidget's been saying we need more supply of widowers. I always worried about her uh... enthusiasm." Lizzie's head drooped as it slowly shook.

"But it's because she's been delivering medications to them. Gidget couldn't be..." Lilly was unable to finish her thought.

"If she did... something," Babs said, "it must have been because she wanted to end their suffering. She's always had a big heart."

"She became a pharmacist to help others," Lizzie said.

"That may be, but I'm worried. What if someone besides us begins to put two-and-two together?" Daffy asked. The others nodded at Daffy's conclusion. She continued. "I'm not justifying what she might have done, but we're a team. We gotta protect each other. We gotta look out for Gidget. We gotta keep her from getting into serious trouble."

"Does that make us accessories?" Babs asked. "If she has..."

"Yep. Yep, it does."

Everyone sat in silence until Babs spoke. "So be it. She's one of us. What do we do next?"

"We'll have to figure that out later. Button it up... here comes our waitress with another bottle," Daffy said.

It was inevitable that the latest hot topic in the Thomasville gossip mill would come up during their happy hour discussion. Halfway through their second bottle, it did. Babs said, "The girl doing my hair this afternoon said she heard a rumor that Stoney and Bo are going on a cruise together."

Daffy's glass froze mid-air. "Over my dead body. I'll call in a bomb threat to the cruise line before that happens."

"You don't believe every rumor you hear, do you?" Lilly asked.

"I only believe the ones I want to," Babs said.

Lizzie smiled. "I enjoy believing the lewd ones. More fun."

"You can believe anything you hear at a barber shop or beauty salon," Daffy said, "but don't believe anything you hear at church or in a bar."

"This is an oyster bar. Does that count?"

"Let me think about that for a while. I'm gonna do something about that bitch, Stoney. Even if this cruise rumor ain't true, she's gone too far."

"You worry me. I hope you don't take this cruise thing too badly," Lilly said.

"It ain't the cruise. Stoney's finally gone too far."

"What you mean?"

"My granddaughter."

Looks of absolute horror appeared on her companions' faces. The biggest mistake anyone can make is getting on the wrong side of a Southern woman vis-à-vis her grandchildren.

"Which one?"

"What'd Stoney do?"

"Tara," Daffy said. "The girl doing my hair told me that Stoney was in the shop earlier in the week, bragging about how Scarlett was gonna win ballet tryouts next weekend. She said Tara didn't have a prayer."

Christmas week every year, Thomasville Tippy Toes Dance Studio puts on its version of *The Nutcracker.* Tryouts are held in September to select an eight-year-old for the part of the Sugar Plum Fairy, considered the plum dance role. Pun intended.

"No!" Three voices echoed in horror.

"Worse... She insulted Tara's Plié. Said it looks like she's trying to pick up marbles with her butt."

"NO!" Another three-voice echo.

"I'm not gonna let that go."

"*We're* not gonna let that go," Lizzie said.

"What're we gonna do?" Lilly asked.

Daffy smiled a Jack Nicholson smile—the one he wore as the Joker in *Batman,* not the one when he broke through the door in *The Shining.* "I even don't know yet, but it's gonna be BIG. REALLY BIG."

Chapter 14

People most notice two things about a woman, hair and mouth. The first thing Lilly noticed Sunday morning as she looked down at Marjorie Winchell was her smile. "It reminds me of the one in that painting."

Babs asked, "What painting?"

"The one where that woman is smiling."

"You mean the Mona Lisa?" Daffy asked.

"Yeah. That's the one. Only Mona looked deader than Marjorie does."

Before anyone could reply, Wesley Winchell leaned in and wrapped one arm around Lilly, the other around Lizzie.

"Thank y'all for coming to her viewing." He looked down at his wife and nodded. "She *was* happy right up to the end."

Daffy surveyed the others, noting a look of apprehension on Gidget's face. Obviously searching for appropriate words, the latter finally spoke with a hint of nervousness in her voice.

"She must've passed enjoying life."

"She did. She was texting her friends up to the end," Wesley said. Five understanding heads nodded up and down as Wesley continued. "Yep. She told me Thursday morning that she was gonna text all her friends before she left this earth. She was addicted to that phone."

"Marjorie had a lot of friends." Daffy nodded.

Babs also nodded. "She was one of my best texting friends."

"I've still got her last text on my iPhone," Gidget said. "Promised her that I'd never delete it."

"Me too." Lilly joined in the head nodding.

"She finished her last text to me with the cutest emoji... an angel-face emoji with little wings sitting on a cloud." This is an instance when it is difficult to tell if Lizzie was trying to be lighthearted.

"I know she's probably texting right now up there in heaven. I'll always remember her walking around the house, that iPhone glued to her fingers," Wesley said. Perhaps this was his attempt at levity. Or not.

"How did we communicate before texting?" Daffy asked.

Four other heads nodded again.

Wesley looked at Gidget and said, "Thank you for stopping by Thursday."

"Oh... oh, I was glad to."

The other ladies shivered.

"And thank all y'all for the casseroles," Wesley said. "What's that one in that blue container? I don't believe I've seen that one before."

"Oh, it's my Tuna and Jell-O Pie." Lilly beamed. "It's a new recipe I got."

Wesley arched his eyebrows. "Uh... sounds interesting. Well ladies, let me circulate. Lot of Marjorie's friends coming in the door."

Lilly had also noticed Marjorie's hair. The topic which came up that afternoon as Stacie and Lilly sat at her computer shortly after the deceased's viewing. Lilly said, "They did a real good job on her hair. Aubergine Red is a tough color to do. I tried it three years ago and gave up."

"Aubergine red *can* look purple if not done right," Stacie replied.

"Tell me about it." Lilly nodded sagely. The voice of experience.

"I'm sure Mrs. Winchell was lovely. Where is the rest of your crew?"

"Babs is going to a tractor pull this afternoon with Sonny Biskit. Lizzie, Gidget, and Daffy are probably still at the viewing. There was a lot of food there."

"I thought you ladies were swearing off Sonny?"

"Yeah, we are, but Babs can never resist a tractor pull."

The look on Stacie's face at that response is difficult to describe—definitely not a look of comprehension. Some find it difficult to understand the appeal of tractor pulls. Stacie changed the subject. "You ready to get started?"

Lilly hesitated. "I don't know. I've never done anything like this before."

"It's done all the time now. Lots of people do it every day. Many women... and men... do it."

"I don't know... After that Facebook stuff, I'm leery."

"Lilly, it's like I said yesterday. Internet dating is no big deal anymore. It's safe. That's why I suggested one of you try it after the Facebook disaster. Can't let one flop ruin technology forever for you."

Daffy had phoned Stacie from The Plaza, after their third bottle of champagne. Using her phone's speakerphone, they discussed what to do next. Stacie suggested another technological tool (i.e., Internet dating). After a lot of hair-pulling, the Ladies agreed and decided Lilly was to be the guinea pig.

"I don't know..." Lilly shook her head.

"Look, let's at least do a Google search to see what's out there. If you don't like it, we'll do something else."

Soon, they scrolled through a list of seniors dating sites.

"This sounds like a good one. 'Sexy Senior Singles'. Let's try it." Lilly clicked on the link. A screen full of nice-looking, older people appeared. "Look at that hunk."

"Lilly, that's just the homepage for the site. That man is probably a model, not a real user. But this site looks as good as any."

After another series of clicks, Lilly was asked to create her profile. The first prompt asked for her age. Lilly typed as Stacie looked on.

"You're not thirty-five!" Stacie said.

"How about forty-five?"

"Lilly, this is a senior dating site. Everyone using it is supposed to be over fifty."

"Get real! No man under eighty is gonna want some fifty-five-year old broad."

"Forty-five... won't work." Stacie shook her head.

Lilly typed '51,' tabbed to the next prompt labeled 'Hobbies,' and paused in thought. She resumed typing.

"I didn't know you fished and hunted," Stacie said, somewhat incredulously.

"I don't, but that's what most men like."

"No, don't put those down. What are your *real* hobbies?"

Lilly paused again. She said, "Cleaning my kitchen, jewelry, indoor herb gardening, shoes, shopping—"

"I'm surprised you didn't include cleaning your bathroom."

"Oh no. The maid does that."

Stacie rolled her eyes. "Just put down tennis and dancing."

After Lilly finished typing, she tabbed to the next prompt and screamed. "OH SHIT! They want a photo!"

"Let me take a picture of you with my phone and upload it for you."

"No way."

"Why not?"

"At my age... with this face. Only a blind man's gonna pick a photo of this wrinkled face."

"Lilly! You look fine. You're only as old as you feel anyway."

"That's a load of crap. I tell myself every night when I go to bed, 'I'm not gonna let the old lady in when I wake up.' Then, I wake up in the morning, look in the mirror, and see an old lady looking back at me."

Stacie bit her lip. "You gotta have a photo of yourself. That's a required part of your profile."

Lilly walked to her bookcase, selected an album, and retrieved an old photograph of herself. "I'll scan this and upload it."

"This looks like a photo taken in your twenties."

"It was."

"You can't use that."

"Why not? I use it every year for the Garden Club's phone directory."

Once that task was completed, Stacie read the next question. "Smoking habits. That should be easy to answer."

Lilly typed 'Never again'.

The process became even more arduous as they got into the Profile's psychological questions. First question: Recently Read Books. Lilly paused in thought. After an extended period, Stacie said. "Just type in a few of the books you've read recently."

"I can't."

"Why not?"

"I don't read books. Only thing I read anymore is magazines like *Southern Living, People, Southern Lady, Garden and Gun...* things like that."

"What was the last book you read?"

"Well... let's see... does the *Cliffs Notes* version count? If so, I read *Wuthering Heights* and *Silas Marner* in freshman English."

"Good enough for government work." Stacie's eyes rolled upward. "Put them down. That's recent enough."

At the next question, Lilly immediately began typing. Stacie commented as she read. "The thing you like most about yourself is how your second toes are longer than your big toes. I don't understand."

Lilly slid her foot out of her shoe.

"See how my second toe is the longest."

"Okay. Why do you like that most about yourself?"

"I can wear pointed-toe shoes easier."

"Look, backup and type 'My honesty,'"

By some act of God, they finished Lilly's Profile, including psychological questions, an hour later.

"I'm glad that's over. What now?" Lilly asked.

"Let's see what's out there. Let's look around."

After searching the site's database, several candidates popped up. Lilly paused scrolling on one. "This one's photo looks interesting. Strong jaw line, full head of dark hair, beautiful eyes, nice lips."

"Ashley Nottamann. Last name sounds like some sort of German ancestry, but that first name is definitely Southern."

"Like Ashley Wilkes in *Gone with the Wind*... my favorite novel. It'd be so nice to fall in love again with a true Southern gentleman... one just like my dear departed Wendell."

"Age 57. Divorced. Ex-spouse's name is Leslie Nottamann. Let's look at his Profile."

As Lilly scrolled through the Profile, both women silently read. Eagerness shown on her face as she looked up at Stacie and said, "What should I do?"

"You can send him a flirt. If he responds, you can email or call him if it sounds promising."

As Lilly went through the flirting process, Stacie murmured, "I hope Mr. Nottamann's profile is more truthful than yours."

Chapter 15

Lilly stood in the foyer of one of Tallahassee's plushest restaurants, A La Provence. Ashley lived in that city, and this seemed a prudent venue for a first meeting. The Maitre d' bowed. "Table?"

"I'm meeting someone, a Mr. Nottamann."

"Oh yes, you must be Mrs. White. Please follow me."

Lilly had dined there before and appreciated the restaurant's ambiance. Creamy ochre-colored walls, gentle-sloping arches framing its windows, and white linen tablecloths reinforced classic French dining. As she approached their table, Ashley stood to greet her. Lilly's eyes roved from top to bottom, taking in a sight for sore feminine eyes. Navy blue blazer cut for a slim athletic build, camel-colored Merino wool slacks, and tasseled loafers—the perfect outfit for a first date.

"Cute as a button. Much better looking than the dating site photo. Drop dead gorgeous. Good enough to eat. Beautiful hair. Not even a touch of grey." Lilly related her Internet date story the next afternoon as the Casserole Ladies sat on Daffy's front porch, enjoying cocktails.

"Probably dyed," Lizzie said.

"That's what I thought. A fifty-seven-year-old with no grey?"

"Maybe just a little touch up?" Babs asked.

Daffy asked, "How tall is he?"

"That don't matter... unless height correlates to penis size," Lizzie said.

Gidget shook her head. "That old saying only applies to a man's shoe size."

"Pretty tall," Lilly said, "close to six feet... real smooth skin, almost no wrinkles."

"What did y'all wear?" Daffy asked.

"The Lyla Sheath Midi Dress."

"The blue one... with no shoulders, just thin straps?" Gidget asked.

"Yeah. That one."

Babs nodded. "Ooooh, girl! You were loaded for bear!"

"I love that one... hemline just below your knees, so it's says 'This here's a refined Southern Lady,' but still showing plenty of calf to draw his eyes downward," Lizzie said.

"And as his eyes are traveling downward, he can't help but notice your cleavage," Daffy said. "That dress's low-cut, V-neck never fails."

"I love its tight fit on you." Lilly sighed.

Lizzie smiled. "I bet he did too..."

Ashley reached out and took Lilly's hand as she neared. "Lilly?"

"Yes. Ashley? It's so nice to meet you. I hope you haven't been waiting long."

"Whatever the wait, it looks to be worth it." Ashley's lips gently touched Lilly's hand.

Lilly beamed. "Y'all do say the sweetest things. I might say the same thing about you."

"Do take a seat." Ashley held her chair. "Did you have any trouble getting here?"

"Oh no. It's not that far from Thomasville. I've been here before." Lilly sat down and looked into her date's handsome face. "It's so nice to have someone hold my chair for me again. Men never do that anymore, you know."

"I believe in the old ways... in polite, genteel Southern society."

"I must admit that I was kinda leery about this Internet dating at first." Lilly did something most Southern women learn to do at an early age—she batted her eyelashes. "But now, I'm glad I did."

"I'm glad you did too."

"I got an impression from your profile... I now see it was correct... You seemed to me to be someone who appreciates femininity... who respects womanhood. Men don't seem to be that way anymore, although I haven't been on many dates since my husband died."

"Same with me. Not a lot of recent dating experience myself."

Their conversation covered a range of topics. Kids, movies, travel, on and on. Both were without mates for over a year—Lilly's from death, Ashley's from divorce. Both were products of the deep South and held many of the same Southern values. Just as Lilly tends to be somewhat shy and reticent in social settings, so is Ashley less inclined to social aggressiveness.

Lilly's description the next day of their dinner conversation was idyllic.

"I'll tell y'all... Y'all couldn't have asked for a more compatible dinner companion. So polite and refined, a great conversationalist. Knew just what to talk about."

"Sounds like you really hit it off," Daffy said.

"We did. I felt a growing attraction as we talked. Ashley's manners reminded me of courtly love... like in medieval times—"

"Next you're gonna say he quoted poetry," Lizzie said.

"How did you know? And, it was English Romantic poetry. Ashley even quoted the first stanza from *She Walks in Beauty*. Y'all know what that poem does to me."

Any suave Southern gentleman knows that mature sophisticated Southern ladies are pushovers for 19th century English Romantic poets, especially Shelley, Keats, and Byron.

"He quoted Byron?" Babs asked.

"Oh, my Lord! Byron is so romantic," Gidget said.

"What'd you do?" Lizzie asked.

"I got so wet that I had to excuse myself and go to the bathroom. I was putty from that point on. You know it's been over a year since I've made love."

"Sounds like quite a catch," Gidget said.

Lizzie asked, "Who paid for dinner?"

"Ashley, although it was supposed to be Dutch treat."

"What happened after dinner?"

Their discussion of poetry led to a romantic conversation. Then, as the dessert dishes were being cleared, Ashley suggested, "Would you care to go to my place for coffee?"

"Oh, I'd love to..." Lilly caught herself. "A cup of coffee before the drive back to Thomasville might help keep me awake. Especially after that delicious Cabernet Sauvignon."

Ashley's house was located just north of Tallahassee in the posh Killarney development, conveniently located off the main road to Thomasville. She parked in the driveway, behind Ashley's Mercedes. Inside the spacious Georgian mini-mansion, Lilly was impressed.

"What a beautiful home!" Lilly said. "You do have excellent taste in furniture and decorating."

"Thank you." Ashley bowed. "But I must share some of the credit with my ex."

Lilly noticed several pictures on a sofa table. "Them must be your kids."

"Yes. Kevin, Paige, and Amanda. They're all grown and gone now."

Lizzie interrupted Lilly's story. "But no pictures of a spouse I bet. I always get rid of them right after the divorce. Either burn 'em or shred 'em... depends on how pissed I am at him."

"Come to think of it, I don't remember seeing any."

Ashley pointed to the sofa.

"Why don't you have a seat while I get some coffee going? I can put a touch of Baileys or Kahlúa in it if you wish."

"Kahlúa sounds yummy."

Ashley brought a bottle of Kahlúa along with coffee and liberally augmented both cups.

"You do make the best coffee." Lilly stared into Ashley's eyes as she sipped. She must have forgotten herself as she spoke her next words. "I could get lost in your blue eyes..."

"I'd love for you to do just that." Ashley sat their coffee cups down, leaned in, and kissed Lilly passionately on her lips. She unhesitatingly returned the kiss. They sat, arms wrapped around each other in this passionate embrace for several minutes as Ashley's hands explored Lilly's body.

"I never intended for things to go this far this soon." Ashley pulled back. "But... it's been so long... I've been divorced for over a year now, with no companionship. I just couldn't help myself. Sorry."

"Oh honey, you don't need to apologize. It's the same with me. I'd forgotten how good it feels to make love."

"Is that what you want to do... make love?"

Lilly had to bite her tongue from screaming 'YES.' Instead, she softly replied, "Yes, yes I do..."

Noticing a pause in her story, Babs exploded. "So, get on with it! Don't tease us! What happened next?!"

"Ashley started unbuttoning my blouse... very slowly... savoring each button. I got so wet! It was excruciating."

"Oh, my God."

"I can just imagine your pain," Daffy said.

Lizzie asked, "Were you wearing a bra?"

Whether or not to wear a bra is a touchy subject with Southern women. Bras are uncomfortable, and September in the deep South is one of the most humid months. But a Southern lady always wears a bra on a first date with a gentleman.

"Hell no." Lilly spat the words out. "I lost my virginity in the backseat of a Ford decades ago. Why y'all think I wore the Lyla Sheath Midi Dress in the first place? So I could wear a bra? No bra, and Ashley's hands took advantage of that."

Lilly leaned back, slipped off one shoulder strap of the dress then the other, and stood, naked from the waist up. Next, she slithered out of it totally. As if teasing, she sat back down on the sofa, displaying her breasts. Ashley reacted expectedly and bent down, kissing her nipples. Lilly lay back on the sofa and wiggled out of her panties. Ashley stood and ogled her with lustful eyes.

"Let me join you."

Ashley's shirt and pants quickly dropped to the floor. At first Lilly was shocked at her date's lack of underwear. She was even more shocked at what was not under Ashley's non-existent underwear.

"Y'all ain't no man! You're a woman!"

"No, my love. I am truly a man."

"No, y'all ain't... You've got a... a—"

"Yes, I do have a vagina and breasts... although they are rather small, but I am really a man."

The other Ladies stared in stunned silence at Lilly.

"If I'm lying, I'm dying. Ashley was really a woman... at least in body," she said.

"No dick?" Daffy asked.

"No balls?" Babs asked, somewhat superfluously.

"Nu-uh... neither. Beautiful little boobs and a nice Brazilian bikini wax job, but no male tools. I finally realized why his voice was so soft and smooth when he spoke... just like his hands."

Ashley kept looking intently into Lilly's eyes. "I really am a man, most of the time. I identify as a man... most days."

"You're not a man all the time?"

"Yes, not all the time. Sometimes my feminine side does bubble up. But that happens less and less as time goes by."

"How long have you, uh, felt like this?"

"I first began to feel like a man years ago, even before the kids were grown and gone. The feeling would hit me at odd times... like when I was in the grocery store. I'd ask myself why the hell am I doing the grocery shopping and not Leslie."

"I used to feel the same way sometimes." Lilly nodded. "That's why I started using Walmart's grocery delivery service..."

"I finally decided to identify as a man a year and a half ago. Leslie just couldn't handle it. He told me he wanted a divorce."

"I bet he did. Are you one of them... What do they call it... transvestites?"

"No. I'm not a transvestite. A transvestite is a cross-dresser. I'm transgender. I have a female body but identify as a male... much of the time... so I guess that technically you could say I'm gender fluid."

Lilly's signature deer-in-the-headlights face always comes quite naturally to her. Especially now. She said, "You got me all confused."

"I know. I don't even try to explain it to my dad anymore." Good luck explaining it to Lilly! "Gender fluid is someone that hasn't gone completely transgender... that is, they don't identify as a member of the opposite sex all the time. Gender fluid means that sometimes I identify as a female, but other times I feel more like a male and identify that way."

"But you don't have male parts."

"That's right. I'm not a transsexual. I haven't decided to undergo medical and surgical treatments to actually transition to the other sex... yet anyway."

"But you like other women? You must be a lesbian."

"As a woman who identifies as a male and likes females, I'm not a lesbian. I'm heterosexual. I love the female body."

"I... I'm so sorry to be asking so many personal questions. I know it must seem rude of me."

"No, it's not. I get asked these sorts of questions all the time. Go on, please."

"I just don't understand how you can call yourself a man," Lilly said, her eyes were wide as saucers, "while having a woman's body."

"Honey, lucky for you I identified as a man today. I feel so masculine at this moment. I want to climb on top of your body right now and—"

Daffy interrupted Lilly's description of the event. "So, let me get this straight. You say this woman is not really a lesbian?"

"I think that's what he... uh she said."

"She said she's as straight as you or me?"

"Yep."

"But she's got a beaver and boobs?"

"Well, it was kinda dark... but yeah, yeah, she had both of 'em."

Babs asked, "And this guy... uh girl checked the box on the dating site that said she's a man?"

"Yep. And with a first name like Ashley... Well, a name like that could go either way. How was I to know?"

"It's too confusing. Women being men when they want to be."

"Men being women when they want to be," Lizzie said.

Daffy shook her head. "My Granny was right."

"How so?" asked Gidget.

"She always said, 'I like my men with a lot of rugged, a little bit of ugly, and just a touch of raunchy,' and my Granny knew what she was talking about."

Gidget looked at Lilly. "What did you do after you found out... found out he wasn't a man?"

Lilly shrugged. "Well, he was feeling like a man yesterday..."

Chapter 16

"So much for Internet dating," Daffy said after Lilly finished. The ladies still sat on Daffy's front porch. She looked at her companions' drinks, now sitting empty on a sterling silver tray on a white wicker coffee table. "Goodness! I was so engrossed in Lilly's story about her date last night that I forgot my manners."

Some might think September a bit too late in the year for Mint Juleps. Not if it is a hot, humid day in the deep South, as so often occurs in that month. Not if you relax on bright floral cushions on white wicker chairs, cooled by gentle breeze from a slowly rotating ceiling fan. Not if you sip them from 10-ounce sterling silver cups, frosted outside from ample crushed ice cooling the smooth bourbon inside.

Daffy stood. "Let me make us up another round."

"What next?" asked Babs.

"Why switch?" Lilly asked.

"No. I'm not talking about switching drinks. What do we do next after Internet dating?"

A car pulled into Daffy's driveway, pre-empting an answer. Stacie emerged. "I hoped I'd find all of you here."

"You must've heard we were drinking Mint Juleps," Daffy said. "I'm gonna make us another batch. Join us?"

Stacie sat down. "Only got time for one. I've heard about your Mint Juleps, but who in Thomasville hasn't?"

Daffy began collecting cups. "I'll be back shortly."

"I'll give you a hand." Gidget picked up the tray.

She was followed by Lizzie who said, "Me too. I'll make sure they don't spill any."

As the trio exited through the front door, Babs turned to Stacie and asked, "What brings you over? Is it about them calendar interviews? Lilly needs something to take her mind off her date last night."

"Yes. I wanted to let you know about the TV interviews. The first is tomorrow with Channel 49, and the second is the next day with Channel 46. They'll both be in Tallahassee at the TV stations during their local morning shows. You'll need to get there no later than 7:00 a.m. Neither station could give me an exact time for your interviews as they kind of get wedged in, depending on how other program segments go. Go to the security desk and tell the person there that you're in the morning show lineup and that the program director is expecting you. Channel 49's program director is Ms. McDougal, and Channel 46's is Ms. McDonald. Funny how close their last names are. Anyway, those are the two people that will take care of you. Got all that?"

"Got it burned into my memory bank." Babs tapped her forehead. "Are you gonna be there?"

"Nope. Gotta go to Albany tomorrow. Meeting with their Tourism Bureau director. I'll probably be at the one on Thursday. This is gonna be great publicity for Thomasville." Stacie looked at Lilly. "Sounds like your date last night wasn't Prince Charming?"

"More like Princess Charmaine," Babs teased.

Stacie searched for words. "It sounds... like he was gay?"

"No, actually she was heterosexual... at least last night," Lilly said.

Before Stacie could ask for clarification, Daffy re-emerged with Lizzie and Gidget, all carrying drinks. After drinks were distributed, Daffy said, "What should we toast?"

"Let's toast your calendars. I have a couple right here. Just got them this morning. They look great. Take a couple with you in the morning. I gave Babs and Lilly info on the interviews." Stacie took a sip. "Mmmm, these are tasty."

Stacie passed out five calendars, and the Ladies frantically turned pages, frowning in the process. Daffy was first to comment. "I look so ugly I'd make a freight train take a dirt road."

Babs shook her head. "I look like I've been chewed up and spit out."

"I look like ten miles of bad road," Lilly said.

Gidget topped Lilly's self-assessment. "I look like I fell out of the ugly tree and hit every branch on the way down."

Best of all was Lizzie's. She said, "I look like Hell with everyone out to lunch."

Stacie vigorously shook her head. "No, no, they look great. This calendar will be a hit."

No one responded. Looks of disgust told Stacie that she needed to change the subject. "Babs, how was your date Sunday with Sonny?"

"The tractor pull was wonderful. Unfortunately, it was in Waycross."

"I've never been there, but it can't be that bad."

"All you kidding? Waycross is so dead that they don't just roll up the sidewalks on Saturday night. They roll up the entire town and take it to Valdosta for something to do."

Never one to pass up a Waycross joke opportunity, Lizzie said, "Waycross was founded on April Fool's Day as a practical joke."

Ditto for Daffy. "Second Street in Waycross is actually in Homerville."

"A night on the town in Waycross only takes eleven minutes," Daffy said.

"You ladies are pretty sharp this morning." Stacie rolled her eyes. "Not."

"It's like my Granddaddy used to say. We slept on the grindstone all night and drank razor soup for breakfast—"

They were interrupted by the sound of a vehicle approaching. Lizzie said, "Looks like George Bentley's SUV pulling onto your street, Daff."

"Who's that with him? It don't look like Toots," Daffy said.

"No, it don't. Wish I had my glasses."

"Looks like Mitzi Merchant," Stacie said.

Mitzi, a Mahjong Mamma, sat in the second row of George's SUV directly behind Bruno who sat up front.

"Looks like she hasn't accumulated enough front seat points yet," Lizzie said.

Babs nodded. "Bruno's very territorial about that front seat. You gotta earn your way up front."

"How many Mammas has George gone through so far?" Gidget asked. "Just about the entire lineup, ain't it?"

"Let's see... Penny, Toots, and now Mitzi. That's a big chunk of 'em."

"I've met her, but I don't know much about her. Who is she?" Stacie asked.

"She married a Merchant. The Merchant family used to own a local pharmacy. CVS bought 'em out about twenty years ago," Gidget said.

"Gidg hates that family, don't you?" Babs asked.

"Yeah. They were the first to bring in big chain competition."

"Mitzi. Unusual name," Stacie said.

"Named after Mitzi Gaynor. Her momma went into labor at the Ritz Theater while watching *South Pacific*."

Daffy said, "Dyes her hair with one of them old-fashioned blue rinses for ladies with grey hair and piles it high up on her head."

"A real big-haired lady," Lizzie said. "She's well off financially but still looking for a meal ticket... like me."

"She told me a long time ago that she thinks she has a twin somewhere in the world who was given away at birth." Daffy rolled her eyes.

The SUV pulled over in front of Daffy's house. George kept the vehicle idling while talking on his phone. He waved perfunctorily toward the Ladies.

"You'd think he'd have at least enough couth to put his damn phone down and say 'hey y'all' to us," Daffy said.

They watched Mitzi's rear door open, and a pile of blue hair peaked out.

"You weren't kidding about her hair," Stacie whispered.

Mitzi's body followed her hair. She said, "Hey, y'all! Bruno's gotta pee!"

She walked around her open door and opened Bruno's. Leaping from the front seat, the big, brown, barking boxer bounded onto the blacktop. *Talk about alliteration! Creative writing teachers everywhere must be pulling out their blue-rinsed hair.*

Bruno ran to the rear of George's SUV and onto Daffy's lawn where he promptly squatted.

"I guess it was a little more than just a pee. When y'all gotta go, y'all gotta go," Mitzi said. A feeble, forced smile accompanied her statement.

Bruno finished his business, and he and Mitzi climbed back into George's Cadillac. The Ladies watched George hang up his phone and put the SUV back in gear. As it drove off, Mitzi's window slid down, and a big blue-rinsed hairdo leaned out. "Sorry 'bout Bruno's poop. Forgot to bring a bag. Bye y'all."

The SUV disappeared around a corner.

"I bet you wanna strangle that woman," Stacie said.

"Is the Pope Catholic?" Daffy scrunched her face, deep in thought. "Although with this one, I sometimes wonder."

"You probably won't even get a thank you note from Bruno," Lilly said in a feeble attempt at humor.

Gidget's attempt also fell short. "Bruno must be a Yankee."

Ditto for Babs' effort. "Mitzi probably thinks Daffy should send a thank you note to Bruno for fertilizing her lawn."

Having realized the inappropriateness of trying to make light of Bruno's bowel movement, Lilly turned solemn. "My momma always said about thank you notes, 'Call within two days and write within three days.' I must've heard that a million times."

Lizzie rescued the scene's comedy with her excellent deadpan humor. She asked, "What about text messages? What's the time frame on them?"

"She was dead by the time they invented texting," Lilly earnestly replied.

Daffy, who had been quiet throughout this exchange, suddenly exploded. "That woman could piss off the Pope! I'm gonna jerk a knot in her tail for letting that dog poop on my lawn! She's lucky I'm too much of a lady to create a fuss in public."

"Did y'all notice how that goofball George was too busy on his damn phone to notice what his dog was doing? Y'all think he was just pretending to be talking to someone? And Mitzi riding around with George now. Wonder what Toots is doing?" Babs asked.

Gidget responded by citing the latest from the Thomasville rumor mill. "One of my neighbors said that her hairdresser's sister texted her that the checkout clerk at Harvey's told her that she has a friend that works at the IHOP that texted her that she saw Toots come in there with Wesley Winchell Monday morning."

"At the IHOP! Monday morning! Y'all all know what that means." Awaiting an answer, Daffy put on her best Veronica Mars sleuthing face.

The others stared in silence. Stacie anxiously looked around, awaiting an answer. She finally asked, "What *does* it mean?"

"Ain't it obvious?! Breakfast early Monday morning at the IHOP! Toots brought her casserole to Marjorie's viewing, hung around all Sunday afternoon, and talked Wesley into a sleep over. They had breakfast after a night of screwing."

"Mahjong Mammas have no sense of decency. She didn't even have the decency to wait to screw Wesley until after Marjorie's funeral on Monday," Lilly said. Notice that Wesley receives no opprobrium.

"Letting dogs crap on my lawn, sluts sleeping with widowers before their wives are cold in the ground, and worst of all..." Daffy's face glowed bright red with anger. "Insulting my granddaughter's plié. Something's gotta be done about these women."

"Who insulted your granddaughter?" Stacie asked. "What did they say?"

"Stoney said Tara's plié looks like she's trying to pick up marbles with her butt."

Trying to stifle a laugh as well as calm Daffy, Stacie committed a *faux pas*. "It probably was just a careless comment. She probably didn't mean anything by it."

"That was no careless comment. You gotta be *reeeal* careful when talking about my granddaughter."

"Grandchildren are part of our continuity with humanity," Gidget said.

Babs nodded. "Concrete evidence for future generations of our existence."

Lizzie said, "How we perpetuate our species."

"They's like lizards' tails." Lilly's observation brought an abrupt end to the chorus. The others stared, trying to make sense of it.

"Like lizards' tails?" Gidget asked.

"Yeah. Y'all know how when a lizard's tail gets cut off, it grows a replacement."

"Okay?"

"Well, our grandchildren are like our replacements."

At a certain level, Lilly's logic sort of makes sense, which is in and of itself, sort of worrying and probably why an extended period of silence ensued.

Lizzie finally exhumed the discussion. "I never miss any of my granddaughter's dance recitals or school plays, and to hear that damn Stoney say Tara's plié looks like she's trying to pick up marbles with her butt is enough to make a preacher cuss."

Oddly, Lizzie's anger had a calming effect upon Daffy, who looked down at the calendar in her hands. When she raised her head to speak, her facial expression was as ruthless as Michael Corelone's. She said, "We're gonna show Stoney Lee and all them Mahjong Mammas."

"How?" Babs asked.

"I got an idea, but it needs more thinking."

Chapter 17

"Get a move on, girl! We're gonna be late!" Babs shouted through the open window of her Cadillac Escalade. The day after Bruno's poop, her vehicle idled in the driveway of Lilly's house as the youngest of these Casserole Ladies scurried toward it.

"So? What's new?" Lizzie asked from the second row.

"Yeah, when are we ever on time?" Daffy sat beside Babs up front.

Gidget rolled her eyes as she moved back into the third row, allowing Lilly to slide in beside Lizzie.

"You'd know the one day I need it most," Lilly breathlessly said as she buckled up, "my facial steamer decides to act up."

Lizzie leaned in close and examined the results. "Shoulda just slathered some Neutrogena on your face and called it good 'nuff for government work."

"Looks like you'll have to use your vagina steamer until you get a replacement," Daffy joked.

"Hold on to your pantyhose." Babs looked down at her backup camera screen and quickly reversed her vehicle out of the driveway. "We're gonna burn rubber to the TV station."

"Oh crap!" Lilly shouted.

"What?"

"I forgot to put on pantyhose. Go back."

Despite a nationwide trend away from wearing pantyhose, Southern ladies still consider them a must with a dress.

"Too late. No way am I gonna try and turn this behemoth around. Hope you shaved."

"Nope. That's why I planned on wearing pantyhose. Problem is, I been wearing 'em three days now."

"Everyone, let Lilly sit behind the coffee table on the morning show's set. We ain't got time to turn this thing around. That'd be worse than turning the battleship *Missouri* around."

"Where exactly are we going anyway?" Gidget asked.

"Today is Channel 46, the CBS station." Babs nervously glanced in the rearview mirror at Lilly, who hesitantly nodded her agreement. "We ask for the morning show program director, Mzz Mc... Mc... What is it?"

"Mc something with a d... McDowell... McDougal... or is it Mzz McDonald? I forget. Just ask for Mc-something," Lilly said.

Her ruling went unquestioned, although Lizzie did have an observation. "Sounds like Mickey D's is running things in Tallahassee."

"Why do they have to have these morning shows so early in the day?" Lilly had opened her Valextra Iside Handle Bag and was touching up her face.

"Because they're in the morning, and the morning is earlier in the day." Babs looked at Lilly in the rearview mirror and grinned.

"Ho, ho, ho... excuse me if I forget to laugh," Lilly said.

"We should've asked for something in the afternoon. I'm missing a big chunk of my beauty sleep," Lizzie said, prompting a comment from Gidget.

"Don't worry... no one will notice."

"Ho, ho, ho. Remind me to laugh later." Lizzie, apparently not wanting to overuse the cliché, modified it.

"Y'all should just sit back and enjoy the scenery," Daffy said.

"Yeah, nothing like looking at pine trees and palmetto bushes at six thirty in the morning."

Thus it went for thirty-six minutes on the thirty-mile drive to the television station. By 7:15 AM, they stood in front of the Security Desk at Channel 46 as a security guard spoke on the phone. The CBS Eye hung on the wall behind his desk.

"I don't like the way that thing stares at us." Lilly made a face.

"I told you that you should've used some Neutrogena," Lizzie said.

The guard hung up his phone and looked up. "How can I help you ladies?"

"We're supposed to be on y'alls' Morning Show. We were told to ask for a Mzz McDonald." Daffy attempted to sound more confident than the faith she had in her guess warranted.

"Hang on a minute." The guard picked up his phone again, dialed an extension, and began a conversation. When he put the phone down, he said, "She'll be right down."

Within minutes, a pert, thirtyish brunette hustled up to them.

"Hi, I'm Karen Lively, Ms. McDonald's assistant. You folks are late. What group are you with?"

"Uh... we're from Thomasville," Daffy said. "We're supposed to be on y'alls' Morning Show."

The Assistant scanned a sheet of paper. "Thomasville... Thomasville... Let's see... I don't see any women's group from Thomasville listed on my lineup. They're always forgetting to update this thing. You're late, but it doesn't matter. There's several groups ahead of you, so they'll add you in last. You know where the Governor's Office is?"

"Governor's Office?" Babs asked. "No one told us it would be at the Governor's Office."

"Oh yeah. That's where they're doing 'em. It's on Capitol Hill. 400 South Monroe Street. You need to hurry. They've already started. I'll phone the Governor's Chief of Staff and tell them you're on your way. When you get to Capitol Hill, look for the Governor's Office signs. Go inside to the Security Desk and tell them who you are. Better hurry up."

Babs broke the land speed record.

"Wonder why they're interviewing us in the Governor's Office?" Gidget asked.

"And what other groups are they interviewing?" Daffy asked. "Other calendars maybe?"

"I just pray they're all a bunch of old bags like us." Lizzie raised her hands in mock prayer. "And not a bunch of millennials."

"What's that called? Age shaming?" Babs asked.

Parking at Capitol Hill was problematic. Babs double-parked behind a big black SUV, hoping to return before its owner did. Check in at the Security Desk resulted in a man wearing a dark blue suit and wire-rimmed glasses appearing before them.

"Hi ladies. I'm the Administrative Assistant to the Chief of Staff. Put these on and follow me." He handed them clip-on badges, turned, and marched in the direction of a massive grand stairway.

Thus began the trek to the Governor's Office. They climbed thirty-plus stairs, turned right, and followed the Administrative Assistant down a never-ending hallway. Midway down the hallway, he turned left and headed down a passageway that terminated at another stairway which they followed down to a lower level.

"Does anyone remember the way back?" Lilly whispered.

"Unfortunately, I forgot my bread crumbs," Daffy said.

Minutes later, the Admin Assistant opened a door and motioned for them to go inside.

"Wait in this room. Someone will come out there when they're ready for you." He pointed to a door on the opposite wall. "What are your names again?"

After writing them on a notecard, he exited via the door through which they had entered. They stood alone.

"That was helpful," Daffy said. "Not. I'm gonna let them know that I don't appreciate being treated like this."

Five minutes passed before the other door opened and a woman leaned in. "Okay we're ready for you. We don't have a certificate for you, so the Governor will hand you a blank one. We'll get you the official one later. Come with me."

With that she held the door open and rapidly motioned them in. Inside, two TV cameras and their crews stood in front of several chairs and a large sofa, located near a massive desk, ostensibly the Governor's.

Another woman walked up and directed them where to sit. They recognized her as Sherise, co-host of Channel 46's Morning Show.

"New York will be jipping in shortly."

"New York? Jipping in?" Daffy asked.

"The network CBS Morning Show... Joining In Progress. Dinah will be interviewing you for their national audience, just like the other groups."

"What do we say?"

"Just answer her questions and tell your story... like the other groups... like they told you to do... Oh, here's the Governor."

The Governor stepped forward and gave compliments as he shook their hands. When he finished, everyone sat down. One of the camera crewmen raised his hand. "Three, two, one, go..."

Sherise said, "We're back with CBS Morning Show. We're still honoring local groups for their civic contributions. Dinah, these ladies are from a civic group from Thomasville, Georgia."

Sherise looked down at her notecard, then back at the camera. "This is Daffy, Gidget, Babs, Lilly, and Lizzie. Love those names."

Daffy noticed Dinah's image on a TV monitor next to one of the camera crews. The anchorwoman's image began talking. "Ladies, we are so honored to be speaking with you. Can you tell us something about what your organization does?"

The five ladies furiously looked at each other, each trying to figure out what organization Dinah referred to as well as what they did, other than make a calendar. Daffy shrugged and said, "We're just a group of widows and otherwise single older women that get together to play Bunko every once in a while."

"Bunko?"

"Yeah. It's a game where you roll three dice—"

Lilly interrupted. "The best thing is that it don't require a lot of thought, which allows us to focus on talking."

"It's mostly a game of luck, which some of us always have." Gidget turned and glared at Lilly. The other Casserole Ladies also turned their heads and glared.

"I can't help it if I win so much."

"We used to play Mahjong, but that was too much work," Babs said. "You couldn't talk very much for having to concentrate on the tiles."

"We started playing it at the Hey Neighbors meetings... That's a social organization in Thomasville," Daffy said.

"We're still in it, but now we also get together on our own with some other ladies that like Bunko and play that game instead."

"We rotate whose house we play it in," Lizzie said.

Gidget nodded. "A different house every week."

"Daffy's house is the best place," Lilly said. "She combined her library with a game room—"

"It has the most beautiful draperies in Thomasville."

"They're a chinoiserie pattern by..." Lizzie looked at Daffy. "I can't remember who made your draperies."

"Brunschwig & Fils."

"The pattern is perfect for fourteen-foot ceilings," Gidget said.

Lilly said, "I've said for years that HGTV should come to Thomasville and do a show just on Daffy's library—"

"No, no... MegaMansions should do it. I can't remember what channel they're on," Lizzie said.

"Travel Channel?" Daffy asked.

"I think it's on AWE channel," Gidget said.

Lilly abruptly changed the topic. "Don't forget the other main reason we like playing at Daffy's house... her maid's apple turnovers."

"And her Long Island Iced Tea—"

"Lizzie!"

"Well, it's true."

"It may be true, but these folks may not want to hear about that," Daffy said.

"Well, what do they want to hear about?" Lizzie asked.

"They probably want to hear about this." Babs held up a calendar and handed it to Sherise.

"What's this?" The local anchor asked.

"It's why we're here. It's called 'Widows of Thomasville'. Or is it 'Thomasville Widows'?" Babs asked. "Anyway, we just got the first copies yesterday."

"This is why you're getting a Governor's Civic Achievement Award?"

"I guess."

"Sherise..." Dinah's voice came over the monitor. "Can you hold that up so we can see it. Maybe the camera can zoom in on it."

Sherise holds the calendar up in front of the camera and displays January as millions of viewers watch. That month depicts our five nude Ladies on a beach, each strategically holding a beach ball. Sherise turns the page to February. Lilly holds a medium sized heart-shaped box of chocolates and nothing else. The Governor, eyes wide, quickly snatches a calendar from Daffy's hands.

"That looks like a calendar. Oh my... I must say..." Dinah turned her head, looked off camera, and whispered, "Was the program director prepared to pixelate things?"

Nothing appeared to happen on camera for fifteen seconds as a frantic discussion took place between Dinah and her producer. Sherise and the Ladies sat silent and immobile as the Governor slowly turned the calendar's pages and smiled. Dinah eventually turned back to the camera and said, "Quite an unusual civic achievement."

"It was for us. Y'all don't know what kind of brain wrestling it took before we all decided on posing nude," Lilly said.

Babs corrected her. "Semi-nude—"

"Which is especially tough for older—" Lizzie said.

Gidget corrected her. "Mature—"

"Mature women like us to do—"

"There's so many things that make life tough for mature women... especially if you're a widow or a divorcee," Lilly said.

Gidget nodded. "You can say that again."

"There's so many things that make life tough for mature women... especially if you're a widow or a divorcee," Lilly repeated. She was not trying to be funny, only do as told. No matter, as it initiated an all-out competition to see who could come up with the toughest thing with which older single women have to deal.

Daffy was first. "Try dealing with a plumber when you're a sixty-nine-year old widow."

"No, no," Babs said, "electricians are worse."

The look of wisdom on Gidget's face would have made the Dalai Lama jealous as she concluded, "Auto mechanics are the worst."

Daffy nodded. "They all pull the wool over widows' eyes."

"Don't forget divorcees," said Lizzie.

Babs said, "Worst is you don't know whether or not they're cheating or not."

"Sounds like all of my ex-husbands."

"And it might be something simple that your dead husband could've fixed in five minutes."

"I don't care what it is," Lilly said, "because it's always $75 minimum when one of them comes out on a service call."

"Worst is being a fifth wheel when you're invited by your neighbor to dinner at the Country Club, and she didn't tell you she was bringing her husband along," Gidget said.

"No, no. Worst is having to deal with money issues all by yourself... with no husband," Daffy said. All females in the room solemnly began nodding including the Governor's secretary, a woman behind one of the Channel 46 TV cameras, and Sherise.

"That is *sooo* true," Lilly said. "Like I always say, your stockbroker is like a cocker spaniel's tail."

Heads immediately ceased nodding. The Casserole Ladies, Sherise, and Dinah stared silently at her. All exchanged perplexed looks. Dinah finally asked, "What do you mean, Lilly?"

"Well, before you dock your cocker spaniel's tail, when she's a puppy, she's just like all puppies... wagging her tail so much you can't help but notice it. Then, after her tail is docked, you never notice it anymore because it ain't there. Same with your stock broker. While your husband is alive, your stockbroker is always calling and checking on you. You can't help but notice him. Your husband's death is like docking your cocker spaniel's tail... afterwards you never notice your stockbroker because he ain't there no more—"

This example of Lilly's wisdom must have struck a chord with the ladies as they immediately began to pile on the stockbroker profession.

"Mine hardly ever calls me," Babs said, "but he used to talk all the time with my husband."

"Mine never waives my account fees like he did with my husband," Daffy said.

"Mine used to send us Omaha Steaks every Christmas. Now, I'm lucky if I get a Hickory Farms box." Disappointment on Babs' face resembled that on Elle Wood's when Warner told her he was breaking up with her in the opening scene of *Legally Blonde*.

Gidget nodded. "We got two things going against us—our age and our sex—"

Dinah finally regained her mental capacities. She said, "Ladies, it sounds like you do have some stories to tell. But tell me... Is the calendar you folks made going to be used for some sort of fundraiser for a local charity?"

"Not that I know of," Daffy said.

Once again, the filter between Lizzie's brain and mouth malfunctioned. "We just thought it might be a way to meet men."

"Governor, how did these Thomasville Ladies manage to win a Governor's Civic Achievement Award?" Dinah asked.

The camera panned to an apparently startled Governor. He quickly looked up from the calendar and placed it on the coffee table. A profile shot of Daffy leaning back *au naturel*, mid-flight on a swing, one arm partially hiding her mammaries, greeted CBS viewers. Mrs. May on full display.

The Governor adopted his best politician's voice. "Dinah, I have to say that it was tough. Many civic associations throughout this region were considered. I wanted to recognize organizations whose members spend their own time, receiving no recompense for their efforts, efforts which benefit others in their communities and make those communities better places to live, better places to raise their children, better places to worship the divine being of their choice............"

This went on for about two minutes until the network had to cut away for a commercial. Initially in a state of shock, Sherise finally recovered during the commercial. She looked at the Ladies.

"Who in the hell are you? How did you manage to get Ms. McDonald to include you in these awards? You're not gonna get away with this."

Sherise's angry outburst horrified the Ladies but elicited a different reaction from the Governor as he leafed through the calendar.

"Calm down Sherise, calm down. I think these calendar ladies deserve some sort of an award myself."

Chapter 18

The Rumor spread like pinkeye in a day care center. Rumors always do in the Thomasville rumor mill. Genesis of The Rumor happened at Ngo's Nails two days prior as Daffy and Gidget enjoyed their regular Thursday afternoon pedicures. The Rumor spread via Ngo and her mother, whose Bingo partner happened to be the mother of the owner of another local Vietnamese nail shop.

"You not on Channel 49 yesterday. You on Channel 46. And you not on Channel 49 or 46 this morning. What happen?" Ngo asked as she exfoliated Gidget's heels while Daffy's feet soaked. Ngo, like everyone else in Thomasville, had eagerly anticipated the Casserole Ladies' television interviews.

"Y'all must've heard the wrong rumor," Daffy said. "Like my daddy used to say, 'Believe half of what you see and nothing you hear.'"

"Calendar look good. You ladies look good. Good looking toenails." Ngo's English is actually better than she lets on with most of her customers. She finds it advantageous to pretend to speak and understand English less than her actual capabilities. Perhaps that is the reason her customers speak freely in her presence.

"I bet everyone in town is talking about that interview and the calendar." Gidget lowered her voice level several decibels, as if that enhanced privacy around Ngo.

"Especially several ladies I can think of whose names I won't mention," Daffy said.

"What you gonna say to 'em next time you see 'em? You know they're gonna rub it in."

"I'm gonna preempt Stoney before she even brings the TV interview up."

"How so?"

"She's gonna regret insulting my granddaughter." The menacing tone in Daffy's next words could have stopped a charging rhino. "Saying Tara's plié looks like she's trying to pick up marbles with her butt."

Neither woman saw the smile that appeared on Ngo's face as she sat on her low stool, looking down while she exfoliated.

"How you gonna do that?" Gidget asked.

"A wager. I'm gonna bet her $10,000 that Tara beats Scarlett in the ballet tryouts this Saturday."

"$10,000? You gotta be kidding. That's a lot of money to bet on Tara's dancing ability."

"She's a cinch. She'll leave Scarlett in her dust."

That is how The Rumor got started.

"I'll have y'alls' Grand Slam," Lilly said.

Their waitress kept her pen still and rolled her eyes.

"Lilly, this is IHOP, not Denny's," Gidget said. "They don't have Grand Slams at IHOP."

"They don't have Grand Slams at IHOP? Shoot!"

The Ladies had decided to do breakfast Saturday morning, and all loved IHOP's pancakes.

Lilly looked back up at their young waitress. "Okay, I'll order your All-Star Breakfast."

"That's Waffle House," the girl replied.

"Heck. What's IHOP famous for anyway?" No comments, please.

"Guess. Look, I'll come back when you're ready to order." Their waitress looked over her shoulder as she walked away. "I'll bring y'all some coffees while y'all decide."

"Well!" Lilly said. "That was about as rude as that man last Wednesday."

That Man was the Governor's Chief of Staff. The cause of his rudeness was a Cadillac Escalade double-parked behind his black SUV, an official vehicle of the State of Florida. Along with his driver, he stood between his vehicle and Babs' Escalade as the Ladies approached.

"I've been waiting here for over fifteen minutes." The Chief of Staff crossed his arms and shook his head. "I should have known this was your vehicle."

It must have been the way he said 'should have known' that set Babs off. "What do y'all mean by that? 'Should have known.' I should have known a tank like this don't belong to no normal jerk. Only a pompous bureaucrat rides around in a tank like this. You must think you're the President of North Korea—"

"Well, this pompous bureaucrat called the police, and a tow truck is on its way—"

"What's your rush? Happy hour's not until 4 o'clock—"

"My rush is my appointment with the Finance Minister of the UAE at his hotel."

And things went downhill from there.

"While we're waiting on our food, I thought I'd fill y'all in on the details of this rumor y'all probably heard about." Daffy scanned the area. Their orders had been taken, and they sat in a large corner booth with a lot of empty tables around them. "I plan on calling Stoney later today and betting her that my Tara can out-dance her Scarlett."

"I know you can afford it, but $10,000 is a lot of money." Lizzie had seen Tara dance many times before at her own granddaughter's recitals.

"She's a cinch. She'll leave Scarlett in her dust." Daffy practiced a unique motivational technique—attempting to make a desired thing come true by saying it over and over.

"What if for some reason, Tara's off her game tonight?"

"I'm her grandmother. I know my granddaughter. No way she'll be off her game tonight." Daffy slowly shifted her gaze from one Casserole Lady to the next. "I hope y'all are all gonna be there tonight to support me."

"Oh shit! I can't make it." Lizzie winced.

"Why? What's up?"

"I gotta go to an AA meeting tonight."

Jaws dropped. Stunned silence gripped the four other Ladies. No one noticed their waitress delivering their food. Finally, Daffy said, "I... I didn't know you had a... a problem. How long have you been going? When did you start... start having problems?"

"Last Saturday night was my first meeting. That's why I had to leave happy hour at the Plaza early last Saturday." Lizzie probably thinks happy hour is good prep for an AA meeting.

"When did you decide to... to take this step? Going to AA, that is?" Gidget asked.

"I been thinking about it for some time now. I've known I have a problem ever since my last divorce, but I kept telling myself 'Lizzie, you can lick this all by yourself.' But you know? You really can't. Everyone needs help."

"Why... why didn't you tell us this before?" Daffy asked.

"I... I don't know... I guess I should have, but this is not something a person necessarily wants to talk about... even with your friends."

The look of agony on Daffy's face is beyond verbal description. She lowered her head and shook it slowly. Blaming herself for not recognizing Lizzie's problem sooner, Daffy's next words were mumbled. "I should have known... one of my best friends... And to think I was serving you Mint Juleps on my front porch on Tuesday. Alcoholics Anonymous. I never knew things were that bad—"

"Oh... it ain't Alcoholics Anonymous—"

"It ain't?" Babs asked.

Lilly's fork froze in mid-air, dripping syrup on her plate. She stared at Lizzie saucer-eyed and asked, "It ain't? What is it?"

"I thought y'all knew. It's Amazon Anonymous."

"Amazon Anonymous!" Daffy said.

"What do they do?" Gidget asked.

"They help over-spenders like me. It's gotten out of hand with me. I need help."

"What do they do?" Gidget asked again.

"Well, a bunch of us meet every Saturday night... That's the heaviest spending time on Amazon... and we go through the AA Twelve Step routine."

Daffy put on her skeptic's expression. Think Kelly McGillis in *Top Gun* when Maverick told her about his inverted maneuver with the MiG-28. Daffy asked, "What do they do in this routine?"

"Well, keep in mind I've only gone once."

"So, what did y'all do at this meeting?!" Gidget asked a third time.

"Well, when it's your turn, you stand up and..."

"Hey y'all. My name is Elizabeth, but y'all can call me Lizzie, and I am a spending addict. I've been a spending addict since 2005 when they started Amazon Prime. At first, I thought I could keep my purchases from my second... or was it my third husband? But I forgot how closely he monitored our credit cards. My purchases kept getting worse. It was a source of conflict with my second or third husband and continued to be so until we divorced in 2009... Or it might've been 2010. I forget the exact year. Anyway, I remember that divorce because we took a wonderful trip to the Dominican Republic to get the divorce. It was one of the best divorces I've ever had, but it was all on my Visa card.

"My spending addiction became even more of a problem for me after I married my next husband in 2014, so I guess he was actually my fourth husband, the one I married after the one I got divorced from in the Dominican Republic. I divorced that one, my fourth husband, in 2017, or maybe it was 2018. Anyway, I've been single and looking for husband number five ever since then.

"I think I can truthfully say that my spending addiction was one of the primary causes of that last divorce. He was a cheap old bastard. But I guess that's why he was a millionaire. Being married to him was three years of hell for me.

"This last year being single has made me realize that I am a spending addict, so I decided to join AA two weeks ago. My last Prime order was a SINGER Quantum Stylist 9960 sewing machine, and I have not ordered anything else for the last three days—"

"Lizzie, you don't even sew," Gidget said.

"I know, but I just couldn't help myself. It was on sale."

"Poor thing. You do need help." Daffy sighed and rolled her eyes. "Just watch out for Wayfair."

Further discussion of Lizzie's addiction was interrupted by a commotion coming toward their booth. Stoney, Penney, Toots, and Mitzi.

"Well, if it ain't the ROLEOs," Stoney said. "Eating their pancakes."

"ROLEOs?" Daffy asked.

"You've heard of the ROMEOs, haven't you?"

"Of course." The ROMEOs consists of a group of older retired men in Thomasville that meet for lunch periodically, hence the acronym Retired Old Men Eating Out.

"Well, y'all are the ROLEOs... Real Old Ladies Eating Out. Emphasis on 'Real Old'."

"Ho, ho, ho. Excuse me if I forget to laugh," Daffy said. "So, what brings y'all ladies... and I use that term loosely, to IHOP? Insufficient limits on your credit cards for Waffle House?"

"We were heading to our booth on the other side of the restaurant and saw y'all over here. We thought we should come over and congratulate y'all on your TV... uh, what's the right word for it? Disaster? Catastrophe? Fiasco? Somehow, none of them quite fits the magnitude of your TV debut, or should I say flop?"

"I thought I's watching a Three Stooges rerun until I realized there was too many of y'all to be the Three Stooges." Toots cackled.

"I thought it was the Marx brothers," Penny said. "They was five of them."

"I thought they was only three Marx brothers?" Mitzi asked.

"They was five, but folks only remember Harpo, Chico, and Groucho—"

"Well that was definitely a Groucho Marx look-alike posing as Mrs. June." As soon as Toots said this, Lizzie bolted from her seat. Daffy and Lilly quickly stood and restrained her. Lizzie had posed for the month of June. The two settled Lizzie back into her seat, but Daffy remained standing.

"Alright, alright," she said. "You've proven you have nothing better to do than watch old movie channels. Now, why did y'all make the trek all the way from the other side of the IHOP? Just to be obnoxious?"

Stoney smirked. "No, we leave that to y'all. We just thought you'd want to hear about our cruise."

Silence.

"Yeah," Stoney said. "Penny, Toots, Mitzi, and me are going on one of them Caribbean cruises with the boys."

"Whoop-de-doo." Daffy shrugged.

"George, Cootie, Wesley, and Bo are going with us."

Lilly said, "That oughta be fun. Shuffleboard on the deck every night until bedtime at 8 PM."

"All four of y'all on the same boat," Lizzie said. "I hope they bring plenty of bran flakes."

"Maybe salmonella will break out on the boat and give y'all something else to talk about besides *Dancing with the Stars*," Babs said.

Gidget said, "I didn't know The Villages operated a cruise line."

Stoney sizzled. She opened her mouth to speak but caught herself before words emerged. She looked directly at Daffy, smiled an evil Maleficent smile, and abruptly changed the subject. Almost casually, she said, "We heard a rumor and came over to find out if you're really foolish enough to bet against my Scarlett."

"It ain't foolish when you're betting on a winner," Daffy said.

"Ha! Your Tara against my Scarlett? You know Tara doesn't have snowball's chance in Hell. I've seen her plié. I just can't believe you want to throw away $10,000 like that."

"$10,000 too rich for you?" Daffy asked.

"No, in fact I thought we should put some real skin in the game."

"You wanna make it $20,000?"

"No, $20,000 is still a drop in the bucket for you, Daffy. I'm talking about real skin."

"More than $20,000? How much do you want to bet?"

"How about this? We all participate in the bet." Stoney's arm swept the area. "Me and my girls against you and your girls. Real skin."

"Go on."

"We got the Georgia-Florida game coming up in a few weeks."

Floridians call it the Florida-Georgia game. Called the World's Largest Outdoor Cocktail Party, this football rivalry between the Universities of Georgia and Florida goes back to 1915. Out-rivals even the FSU-Florida game.

"Okaaay?"

"If your Tara wins the tryouts tonight, me and my girls streak the Georgia-Florida game. My Scarlett wins, y'all do the same."

Many younger people may not be familiar with the term 'streak'. Streaking was a 1970's fad whereby a group of students would run naked across the playing field at college sporting events. Floridians believe it began at FSU.

"You have got to be shittin' me," Daffy said.

"Is the Pope Catholic? No, I ain't shittin' you. I know my Scarlett is gonna win. Her plié alone will wipe Tara's butt off the stage. And my girls back me all the way. What about you and your girls? Or is the prospect of 'real skin' in the game gonna show everyone that you're nothing but an old windbag?"

Daffy looked at her four companions. Their concurrence must be instantaneous. To put this up for discussion and a vote would be to admit in front of the Mahjong Mammas that she was less of a leader than Stoney. Yet, she saw the fear in her companions' eyes. Running across a hundred yards of football field totally naked before a nationally televised audience of millions of viewers? How could anyone survive the ridicule? Certainly, they would have to leave Thomasville forever as a minimum penance.

"What about it, Ladies?" Daffy asked.

Seconds passed before Babs vigorously nodded. Gidget's hesitant nod came next. Lilly looked back and forth between Lizzie and Daffy, then gave the latter a ladylike affirmation. Lizzie's head remained transfixed, looking down at her pancakes, growing colder by the minute. She remembered the last time she had seen Tara's plié.

"Lizzie?" Daffy asked.

Lizzie looked up and smiled. "We always back each other. No matter what."

Daffy turned to Stoney and said, "It's a bet."

Chapter 19

"Bitches." Lilly delivered her invective while staring at four fannies wiggling into a booth far across the dining room. The genteel woman rarely used profanity which was why her companions stared. She noticed and said, "Well, they are."

"It's amazing so much nasty butt can fit into one booth." Gidget shifted her gaze from the wiggling derrières back to her friends. "Houston, we have problem if Tara don't win tonight."

"So, what's new?" Babs asked.

"Don't worry. My Tara's gonna kick Scarlett's butt," Daffy said.

"It never hurts to have a little edge." A mischievous expression spread over Babs' face.

"What do you mean by 'a little edge?'" Daffy asked. "It better not mean what I think it means."

"I bet it starts with v and ends with oodoo," Gidget said.

Babs enthused, "I do have some more of Miss Monique's spells we could use."

"Nope. Absolutely not," Daffy said. "We're not blowing up anymore sheds."

"But, but, but—"

"No, no, no!"

"Hear me out. Just a mild little jinx."

"No! I can't believe you'd even think of putting a hex on a six-year old child, especially the way your spells turn out."

"The way Babs' spells turn out, Scarlett will probably be an exhibit in Ripley's Believe It or Not tomorrow morning," Lizzie said.

Dreading the thought of public nudity again, Lilly floated a suggestion. "How about Mr. Factoid releases a couple of hamsters just as Scarlett starts to dance—"

"No voodoo, no spells, no hexes, no hamsters," Daffy said.

The text message notification on Lizzie's phone sounded. She extracted the device and began reading. "Ooh, ooh..."

"What?" asked Lilly.

"Rumor mill has it that hospice is gonna start visiting Cheryl McGriff."

"Rumor mill?" Gidget asked.

"My hairstylist."

"How does she know?"

"Her neighbor knows someone who works at hospice."

"Why'd your hairstylist text you?" asked Babs.

"She knows I'm on the prowl, so to speak."

"That means Ricky is..." Lilly caught herself and left her thought incomplete.

"Yeah, Ricky McGriff's gonna be on the market soon."

Daffy looked at her companions and said, "No screwing around this time. We need to coordinate casseroles and make sure the Mammas eat our dust when the time comes."

"No problem. I've got a bunch already in the freezer just for such an emergency," Babs said.

"Whatcha got?"

"Green bean, tuna, macaroni and cheese, taco, broccoli and rice, baked spaghetti—"

"You must be expecting a plague of ovarian cancer in Thomasville," Lizzie said. "Either that or a rash of fatal traffic accidents from texting."

"It never hurts to be prepared."

Daffy glanced at Gidget, who seemed uneasy.

Eight hours later, all five ladies sat in the front row of the elementary school auditorium. All four Mahjong Mammas sat on the opposite side.

"I'm surprised that Jubal Lee's here," Daffy said. Jubal was Stoney's teenage grandson.

Gidget nodded. "Yeah. Teenage boys don't usually go to little girls' ballet recitals willingly."

Miss Perky, Thomasville Tippy Toes' lead instructor, stepped onto the stage. "Welcome to the tryouts for *The Nutcracker* ballet that will be presented this upcoming Christmas season. We begin with three-year old tryouts..."

After she finished her explanation, she disappeared backstage and re-emerged leading six little girls. They skipped around the stage, following Miss Perky to the music of a *Nutcracker Marche*. Ostensibly, they were trying out for the ballet's Russian and Chinese dancers. In reality, all these tots would be selected.

"Ooh, ooh... there's Charlotte!" Babs squealed as her granddaughter skip-walked among the toddlers.

As the Ladies watched, Charlotte walked away from the other dancers. She meandered around the back of the stage with one hand inserted in her mouth. Another dancer decided to lie down and roll back and forth on her back. A third dancer froze in place. Babs rushed to the edge of the stage and made sweeping motions with her arms, urging her granddaughter. "Charlotte! Charlotte! Dance! Dance!"

Miss Perky eventually abandoned the dance routine and led all toddlers off the stage. En route, she scooped up the small prostrate dancer.

"Callie and Maggie are up next," Daffy said. They were Daffy and Lilly's granddaughters, respectively, and were in a second group of three-year-old's trying out for Spanish and Arabian dance roles.

"I always loved *The Nutcracker*," Lilly said, "but I just wish someone would explain the plot to me."

Daffy smiled. "I would explain it to you, but then I'd have to kill you."

"It's like that old movie, *The Big Sleep*. That Humphrey Bogart movie," Gidget said. "Nobody can figure out the plot to that movie either."

"When I visited Claudia the week before she died, we talked about that movie," Lizzie said, "and she told me that she would be able to die fulfilled because she'd finally figured it out."

"That's amazing. What is it?" Gidget asked.

"I dunno. She couldn't explain it to me."

At that point, Miss Perky led another bunch of three-year-old girls onto the stage—some skipping, some shuffling aimlessly to *Nutcracker* music.

"*The Big Sleep* is no match for *Zardoz*," Babs said. "That took incomprehensibility to new heights."

"*Zardoz*? Don't believe I've ever heard of it. It was a movie?" Daffy asked.

Babs shrugged. "Only if you use the term 'movie' loosely. Starred Sean Connery."

"Oooh... Sean Connery... Now there's a real man."

"How could God have created such a perfect man?" Lilly asked.

Maggie quit the dance line and walked over to a fake palm tree on the left side of the stage. She began circling the tree. Miss Perky led the other dancers to the tree and gently took the child's hand. As the group skip-walked to the other side of the stage, Callie deserted the line and ran to the edge of the stage. Daffy beamed.

"Maybe she'll pick up some marbles for you," Babs teased.

"Go back to Miss Perky, Sweetheart." Daffy coaxed as she crouched at the edge of the stage. After the child obeyed, Daffy duck-walked back to her seat. En route, she noticed a smirk on Stoney's face. Daffy fumed.

"Elvis Presley. *That* was a perfect man," Lizzie whispered.

"Don't forget Bo Thomas," Gidget said.

Daffy nodded. "Yeah. Good looking and a true gentleman."

"Always opens the car door for a lady," Babs said, "and buried most of his wife's jewelry with her."

"Always brought his wife flowers after they had sex," Lizzie said.

Lizzie's comment generated open-mouth stares from her companions. Accordingly, no one noticed as Miss Perky led the three-year-old group off the stage and returned with a group of four-year-old girls. The *Waltz of the Flowers* began playing.

"How do you know that?" Lilly asked.

"Frank at Flowers by Francois told me," Lizzie said.

"How does he know?" Gidget asked.

"He and Lila at Lila's Laundry figured it out together."

"How did they do that?" Babs asked.

"They noticed Bo always came in and bought flowers on the same days his wife took their mattress pad to the laundry."

Five heads nodded sagely as three of the other four-year old girls began to twirl around and fell into a pile on the stage. The two remaining dancers stopped in their tracks. One began crying, while the other began pulling her tutu down.

"We can probably use her in the 2034 edition of our calendar," Lizzie said.

Tryouts for five-year old dancers went marginally better, and a short intermission was called before the Six-Year Old Sugar Plum Fairy Tryouts. During the intermission, Daffy noticed something. "I wonder where Jubal went to?"

"Probably had enough of toddling tippy toes," Babs said.

"Or, he's up to something," Gidget said. "He is Stoney Lee's grandson after all. Let me check around to see what he's up to."

After Gidget exited, Daffy pulled the others in close and whispered, "Ladies, we need to monitor Gidg twenty-four seven."

"Why?" Babs asked.

"We need to watch over her to make sure she don't euthanize Cheryl McGriff."

"Why?" Lilly asked. "What makes you think Ricky's even gonna ask her to speak at Cheryl's funeral?"

"Euthanize... not eulogize. Euthanize is to put someone or something to death painlessly, for mercy reasons," Daffy said. She looked around. "We'll discuss it later. Gidget's coming back. Oh, and it looks like the six-year-olds are coming out."

As five little girls trotted onstage, Gidget slipped back into her seat and said, "No sign of Jubal."

"That punk probably went behind the auditorium to smoke a joint." Daffy scanned the stage. "There's Tara."

Miss Perky stepped forward and explained. "Each dancer is supposed to perform five basic ballet techniques—an arabesque, a balloné, a chassé, a pirouette, and finally, a plié."

Lizzie whispered, "What? No do-si-do?"

Miss Perky finished her explanation. "Each dancer will perform individually, and the other instructors and I will select the winner and first runner up after all have performed. We will start with Olivia Perdoo."

Olivia, Penny's granddaughter, attempted her arabesque. In this position, the dancer stands on one leg, and the other leg extends straight behind her body.

"Looks like a dachshund with hip dysplasia," Lizzie said.

Scarlett was next after Olivia finished. Her dance moves were marginally acceptable with the exception of her chassé. As her back foot 'chased' to meet up with her front foot, she slipped and fell, landing on her butt.

"Must be combining her chassé with her plié," Daffy said in a feeble attempt at insider ballet humor. Characters in a story should always leave sublime humor to the narrator.

Two more girls performed after Scarlett. Tara was last.

"Looks like Tara's only real competition is gonna be Scarlett," Lilly said.

As Miss Perky requeued the music, all five Ladies nervously wrung their hands.

"What're we gonna do if she loses?" Babs asked.

"I can't lose thirty pounds in two weeks," Lizzie said.

"How about removing a tattoo of Ron Paul?" Gidget asked.

Lilly tried to look on the bright side. "At least we'll have enough time to get our hair done."

"Shh!" Daffy commanded. "Tara's starting."

Tara's arabesque was one in name only, but her balloné was a little better. After completing her chassé, which reeked, Gidget asked, "Is it too late for voodoo?"

It happened during the third turn of Tara's pirouette. Offstage, from behind the curtain, a big, ugly bullfrog suddenly leaped (or as some later speculated, may have been tossed) onstage. The green critter was later described using the following adjectives: 'gigantic,' 'gross,' 'slimy,' 'warty,' and 'yucky.'

"RUNNNN!!!" Miss Perky's scream was lost in the melee that ensued.

Tara's pirouette immediately stopped, and the youngster headed for her grandmother. In no time, the stage was deserted, save the bullfrog. With the spotlight to himself, the amphibian thespian hopped to the center of the stage and delivered a series of loud, vigorous croaks. This lasted half a minute before he hopped back and disappeared under the curtain from which he initially leaped (or was tossed). Witnesses later attested to seeing Jubal Lee exit the backstage area shortly thereafter.

"Calm down, Sweetheart, calm down." Daffy soothed Tara as they stood in the back of the auditorium. "They'll find that animal and get rid of him."

"Granny, do I have to go back? I'm scared of that thing. I don't wanna go back."

"It'll be okay, Sugar Pie. Y'all need to finish your tryout. Remember, you're a Southerner, and Southerners never give up. Okay?"

Tara nodded but clung to Daffy. As she cuddled her granddaughter, she happened to glance in Stoney's direction. Stoney's smirk was unmistakable. Miss Perky stepped back onstage.

"I think our friend has taken his final bow and disappeared. We'll now have Tara Belvedere finish with her plié. After that, the other instructors and I will meet briefly and pick the winner and first runner up."

As a shaken Tara finished her routine, Gidget whispered to Babs, "Looks like Stoney's characterization of Tara's plié was spot on."

After a short intermission, Miss Perky announced the results. "Winner... Scarlett Lee. First Runner Up... Tara Belvedere."

Chapter 20

Sunday mornings usually found all the Casserole Ladies in church. Not this morning. This morning called for something a little more potent that a sip of communion wine. Something that would be served at the SASS! brunch.

"Mimosas." Daffy looked at her companions' gloomy faces, then added a qualifier. "Lots of mimosas."

Chin resting on her palms, a despondent Babs did not even look up as she mumbled a request. "Gran Gala instead of Triple Sec, please."

"Yes, Ma'am."

Upon hearing their waiter's voice, Babs looked up and smiled. "Stefan! When did you move over here?"

"I'm still at Liam's four evenings a week, but I started waiting Sunday brunches here about a month ago."

"Is that legal?" Lilly asked.

"Why would working two jobs be illegal, Ma'am?"

"I thought there were laws against working over forty hours a week."

"Let me get your mimosas while y'all sort that one out," Stefan said, then turned and headed for the bar.

"That butt gets cuter every day," Babs said. "Makes me glad I skipped church this morning. I was so pissed this morning—God would've given me shingles the moment I stepped inside."

Gidget was still at late church, while Lizzie slept in. The latter promised to make brunch sometime before it ended at 2 p.m.

"Before Gidget gets here," Daffy said, "I want to talk about what I mentioned yesterday."

"That young man has the cutest swagger." Babs' eyes still monitored Stefan's receding posterior. "Kind of reminds me of John Wayne's walk... or maybe Uga's."

Uga is the University of Georgia's bulldog mascot.

"You mean monitoring Gidget twenty-four by seven?" Lilly asked.

"Yes, but twenty-four-seven might have been a bit of an exaggeration. We gotta somehow stay on top of her whereabouts. We gotta protect her from doing something that could get her in real trouble." As if public nudity and indecent exposure charges from streaking would not.

"Stefan's working way too hard. He needs someone to look after him." Babs sighed.

"He better watch-out, or he might get arrested," Lilly said.

"Lilly, there is no law against working two jobs," Daffy said, "or more than forty hours a week."

"I wonder if Stefan might go for it if I proposed some sort of transgender thing? Like Lilly's Ashley does."

"She's not 'my Ashley,' and she's... he's not 'transgender.' He's... what'd he call it? Oh yeah, he's 'gender fluid.' Remember?" Lilly asked. Her face scrunched quizzically in contemplation of Babs' original question. "Do you mean you'd have Stefan identify as a woman?"

"No, of course not. He'd never go for that. I'd identify as a man," Babs said. The looks on her companions' faces prompted a qualification. "Gender fluid... just for a day or two."

The front door opened, and Gidget and Stacie entered. Daffy whispered, "Cool it on the monitoring thing."

"Hey, y'all," Gidget said, then nodded toward Stacie. "Lookee here who I brought with me. We got to talking in church, and I invited Miss Stacie to have brunch with us."

Talking in church. Tsk, tsk. At least it's more considerate than snoring in church. A Southern lady always tries to be as considerate as possible.

"Y'all got here just in time." Daffy looked toward the front of the restaurant. "I see Lizzie parking out front."

Stacie sat down. "What a bunch of glum faces, but it's understandable, given the ballet tryouts yesterday."

"I prayed extra hard in church," Gidget said. "This streaking is a lot more serious than our calendar. We could get into *real* trouble."

Babs made a feeble attempt to be funny. "Must be tough to pray and talk to Stacie at the same time."

"Ho, ho, ho. Excuse me if I don't laugh, but the prospect of prison time has dulled my sense of humor," Gidget said.

Stacie said, "You folks should get jobs as public mourners."

As Lizzie sat down, Daffy waved to Stefan, pointed at the new diners, and mouthed 'three more mimosas.' She turned back to Lizzie and asked, "What're you doing here this early? We didn't expect you before noon."

Lizzie rubbed her eyes. "Couldn't sleep. Kept having an awful nightmare."

"What about?" asked Lilly.

"They catch me streaking, and the judge sentences me to life in prison." As the others smiled, Lizzie said, "It gets worse. He tells me that I can't take my iPhone or credit card with me."

"You weren't the only one that couldn't sleep. I worried all night. Finally got out of bed at one fifteen and reorganized my sewing basket," Lilly said.

"That's what I call that insomnia," Babs said, "but I admit... I didn't sleep much either."

"I hate to tell y'all this," Stacie said, "but the Georgia-Florida game—"

"Florida-Georgia game—" Lilly said.

"Is one of the most watched games in college football... probably as many as ten million people watching. That's a whole lot more than the CBS Morning Show. I think you'll have to renege on your bet."

"Stacie!" Lilly shrieked. "We don't use that word down here anymore!"

"It's not the word you're thinking of. It's spelled R-E-N-E-G-E. It means to go back on a promise."

"We can't do it," Daffy said. "We made a promise. Southern ladies don't go back on promises... unless there's some sort of cheating."

Gidget said, "One of the ladies in church this morning said her neighbor told her that her sister told her that her daughter who was backstage at the tryouts said that she thought she saw Jubal slip out the backdoor shortly after the bullfrog jumped back behind the curtain."

"I don't think the second-hand word of a young child is gonna be enough to help," Daffy said.

Lizzie nodded. "That is a problem, but we all know that Stoney was somehow the mastermind behind Mister BullFrog."

"This is hopeless," Lilly said. "I just don't know how I'm gonna be able to face my grandchildren if I'm seen naked on national television."

"How will I be able to show my face in the pharmacy?" Gidget asked. "All those people I've worked with for decades."

"We'll never be able to show our faces in Thomasville," Babs said.

"If that's the case," Lizzie said, "I'm moving to Suwanee Village."

Stacie said, "Ladies, if you can't prove there was any cheating, you'll just have to repudiate your bet."

"Oh no... you're saying that Daffy... that we will have to welsh on our bet," Lilly said, "although that may be the only way out of this."

A long period of morose silence ensued until Daffy spoke. The look of resolution on her face would have put Horton the Elephant to shame. She said, "I've made many bets, and I never welshed, yet. Stoney will never see me welsh on this bet."

Apologies to Dr. Seuss, *Horton Hatches the Egg* (Random House: 1940) for Daffy's unconscious parody of his fine poem.

Babs nodded. "We did make the bet of our own free will."

"I just did what Gidget did," Lizzie said, "which is what I always do."

"Ladies, you got less than two weeks before the game. Even if by some miracle all five of you can get through stadium security onto the field and actually pull off your clothes, they're gonna catch you right away," Stacie said. "How you gonna pull all this off without going to jail?"

"I been thinking—" Daffy said.

"As long as it's Daffy thinking, we're okay." Lizzie smiled. "It's when Babsie starts thinking that I begin to worry. Especially if it's about a spell for streaking a football game."

"What's your plan, Daff?" Babs asked.

"It came to me as I was lying awake in bed at o'dark-thirty this morning. The toughest part is gonna be getting onto the field past security during halftime."

"Yeah. Bands, majorettes, cheerleaders, and others will be there, doing their thing," Gidget said. "They ain't gonna just let five naked old women strut onto the field."

"We don't strut on as five naked old women."

"What do y'all mean?"

Daffy looked at Lilly. "You were a cheerleader when you were at Florida, weren't you?"

"It was one of the best times of my life... except for the back hand-springs. I hated doing them things," Lilly said.

"So, we disguise ourselves as Florida cheerleaders, sneak onto the field during halftime, shed our outfits during the cheerleading routine, do our streak, then hightail it out one of the exits."

"I don't know if you've seen a Florida game this year, but their cheerleaders are wearing pretty skimpy outfits—a bare-midriff-hot-pants outfit," Lilly said.

Daffy nodded. "I have, and it don't leave much to the imagination."

"Hot pants on this?" Lizzie looked down at her own body. "We'll look like SlimFast rejects in a thong bikini contest during Spring Break in Panama City."

"Who cares?" Daffy asked. "Besides, we won't be *in* the cheerleading outfits that long."

"What about my tattoo?" Gidget shook her head. "People might recognize me from the calendar."

"They'll think you're Ron Paul after a sex change."

"Even if we could get away with it, they'd still see our faces and recognize us." Babs' comment drew serious head nods from Lilly, Lizzie, and Gidget.

"No," Daffy said, "we dye our hair and wear a lot of makeup."

"We already do that every day," Lizzie said.

"No. I mean *lots* of makeup. So much that we make KISS look like trick-or-treaters. And, we'll have cheerleader uniforms custom made to fit."

"How about made out of spandex for a slimming effect?" Babs enthusiastically asked. "And we could alter 'em so they'd 'tear away' like in the movies."

Excited at the prospect of shopping for footwear, Lilly asked, "What about shoes? We can buy some sort of athletic sneakers to go with the Florida cheerleader uniforms."

Babs' head nodded faster than a bobblehead doll's on a gravel road. "Good running shoes might help us outrun security."

"Versace makes a real cute jog shoe," Lilly said, her enthusiasm unmistakable.

Gidget shook her head. "No. Alexander McQueen. I been meaning to buy a pair anyway."

"No. Balenciaga. I just bought a pair of Race Runners last week." As Lizzie spoke, she noticed looks of disapproval on the other Ladies' faces. Trying to justify her purchase in light of her spending addiction revelation, she said, "I paid cash at Dillard's."

"You went shoe shopping without me?" Lilly sadly asked. Say it ain't so!

Maybe it was the thought of buying new shoes. Maybe it was the mimosas. Whatever it was, the tide definitely turned. Gidget spoke first. "Y'all know, it just might work."

"I could get Alicia to show us how to make ourselves up," Lizzie said.

"Alicia?" Stacie asked.

"One of the beauticians at our salon. She's a wiz at makeup."

"Lilly can work on stadium passes. As a former cheerleader, she'll have some pull." Babs' suggestion was met with head nods.

"TIAA Bank Field is a different stadium from the old Gator Bowl in Jacksonville that I used to cheer in," Lilly said, "but, I can reach out to some of the athletic staff at Florida."

Daffy said, "We're gonna uphold the honor of Southern woman-hood. We got less than two weeks. We gotta get organized... divide up responsibilities. We run this just like a military operation. Agreed?"

"Aye, aye, Captain." Gidget executed a mock salute.

"Lilly, you work on scoping out the stadium and getting passes that will give us the kind of access we need," Daffy said.

"Check."

"Babs, you work on getting us some tear away Florida cheerleading uniforms."

"Check."

"Lizzie, you work on the makeup and dye jobs. We'll need some sort of quick way of dying our hair and putting on makeup after we get into the stadium."

"Check."

"What about me?" Gidget asked.

Hiding her real concern, Daffy said, "You hang with me. I need your brainpower on the planning. I want you to stick to me like glue."

"Check."

"Ladies, this is gonna be tough to pull off. Security at the Florida-Georgia game—"

"Georgia-Florida game," Gidget said.

"Whatever. Anyway, security will be tighter than a Presidential visit. Starting today, we huddle daily to go over progress. Agreed?" Daffy looked around.

"Agreed," all enthusiastically said in unison.

"Ladies," Daffy said, "we're gonna do Thomasville proud. We got less than two weeks to pull this off. We're gonna show them Mahjong Mammas a thing or two about streaking."

Chapter 21

As alpha-dog of these Casserole Ladies, Daffy unsurprisingly chaired their daily Streak Huddles. Today's meeting occurred on a Tuesday at 1:15 p.m. or 1315 Military Time (MT). As it was the last day of September, South Georgia weather still permitted meeting outside on Babs' front porch.

"Okay. Let's start with Babs. What y'all got on uniforms?" Daffy asked.

"It's gonna be easier than I thought. Believe it or not, Amazon carries Florida cheerleader uniforms, and they come in all sizes," Babs said.

"Better carry extra-wide." Lizzie could not resist the obvious setup.

"Free shipping and two-day delivery for Prime members. Since Lizzie has a Prime membership, I thought she could place the order."

"Giving Lizzie the okay to order from Prime is like giving a bank robber the combination to a bank safe," Gidget said.

Daffy feigned concern. "Lizzie, can you handle it without relapsing?"

"No problem, Chief."

"Great. Get everyone's sizes and place the order ASAP."

"Roger that."

Daffy looked at Babs. "But what about making the uniforms tear away?"

"Got that covered," Babs said. "I've talked with Miss Leona, and she'll unstitch the side seams, then loosely stitch them back together so they'll easily tear apart."

"Did she ask you why you want this done? It sounds kind of strange."

Babs shrugged. "I started to make something up, but she said not to bother to explain."

"She probably felt not knowing would be better for her mental well-being," Lizzie said.

"Okay. Lilly? What you got on stadium access?" Daffy asked.

"Well," Lilly spoke hesitatingly, "it was a little too complicated for me to handle alone, so I asked Gidget for help."

Gidget nodded and took over. "We contacted Florida's Cheerleading Staff Office. Fortunately, the Coach's secretary is the same person that was secretary when Lilly was there. She remembered Lilly, but how could anyone not remember Lilly? Anyway, Lilly told her that she wanted to go to the game and wondered what side of the stadium would be the Florida side."

"It was wonderful to talk to Mrs. Arbogast again," Lilly said. "She hasn't changed a bit. We talked about all the old times—"

"For over two hours." Gidget rolled her eyes. "It was like having two Alexa's going non-stop at each other."

"But I did get a lot of information on the stadium layout and so forth—"

"Bottom line is we think we got the rough outline of how to get in, where to sit, and how and when to merge into the cheerleaders as they get ready for halftime ceremonies."

Lilly frowned. "Bad news is that we're gonna need to spend about $5000 on Assure Club seating for the five of us."

"Not a problem. This is on my dime. Sounds like y'all done a great job. Anything else?" Daffy asked.

At that moment, a FedEx truck pulled into Babs' driveway. The driver hopped out and said, "I got a delivery for a Mrs... N-E-A-U-X-G-E-A-U-X."

"It's pronounced 'NoGo,' and that's me," Babs said.

"It's pretty big and pretty heavy. In a wooden crate. Where y'all want me to put it?"

"Uh, uh, uh... Let's see... uh... How about in the garage? No... no... uh... Go ahead and put it in my living room..." Babs spoke nervously and fidgeted as she obviously avoided looking at the other ladies.

As the FedEx man walked back to his truck, Lizzie asked, "*Sooo...* just what did you order?"

"Oh, oh... uh... nothing."

"Nothing? A large, heavy crate don't sound like there's nothing in it," Gidget said.

"It's... it's... uh, it's... just something for the house."

"Ooh!" Lilly's eyes widened. "A new appliance? How exciting! But, why didn't Bobby Dollar's deliver it themselves?"

"I bet Babsie didn't go to Bobby Dollar's, that's why." Lizzie stood up, keenly watching the FedEx man unload. "I bet she went to Valdosta. That's why her face is so red."

Bobby Dollar's Appliance is a Thomasville tradition. Any self-respecting Thomasvillian would be embarrassed to shop elsewhere for appliances.

"What did you buy?" Lilly asked.

Babs hesitated, then said, "Uh... something for the house."

"You already said that," Gidget said.

The FedEx man dollied a large crate up the walkway. He said, "Can you open your door and show me where to put it?"

The FedEx man hauled his load, while the Ladies, propelled by feminine curiosity, followed like children pursuing an ice cream truck. Ten minutes later, they stood over the crate like kids in a candy store. Babs' evasiveness only stimulated their curiosity. As the sound of the FedEx truck receded, Daffy commanded, "Out with it. What is it?"

"Uh... uh..." Babs fumbled for an explanation.

Gidget's keen analytical mind shifted into hyperdrive. "It's too big to be a microwave and too small to be a refrigerator. There's no return address on the crate to give us a clue as to what it is. Hmm... I bet it's a wine cooler. Ain't it?"

"No."

"Something for the bathroom... a towel dryer?" Daffy asked.

"No."

"Something for the bedroom?" Lizzie asked. "One of them exercise machines?"

"Uh... well, you're gettin' closer," Babs said.

"Hell!" Lizzie exploded. "My curiosity's got the best of me. Open it up."

"But, we haven't had our drinks yet. Let me make y'all some Daiquiris."

"No, let's find out what's in this crate first, then Daiquiris." Daffy pointed in the direction of Babs' garage. "Go get a crowbar."

Fifteen minutes later, with Styrofoam peanuts scattered everywhere, the five Ladies looked down into the open crate. A human face looked back.

"What the hell is that?" Lizzie's eyes were wide as saucers.

"That's Jeffrey," Babs said.

"Jeffrey?! What the hell is a Jeffrey?" Gidget asked.

"Well, y'all remember that happy hour at Liam's when we were talking about using technology to help with our... uh romance problems?"

"Yeaaah," Daffy said.

"Remember how someone suggested something about a sex robot?"

"I believe it was you that suggested a sex robot."

"Well, anyway, this here's Jeffrey."

"Jeffrey?" Lilly asked.

"Yeah, that's the name the manufacturer gives him."

"Him?"

"Well, it's a male sex robot, so I guess it's a him."

Lizzie joked, "Unless he's transgender."

"Don't you mean 'it?'" Gidget asked. "This thing isn't a real person, you know."

Babs recoiled. "Don't call it an 'it.' That sounds cruel."

"What does it... he do?"

"What do y'all think it does?" Lizzie rolled her eyes. "The answer is pretty obvious."

"I don't know *exaaaactly* what it does," Babs said. "All I've ever seen were brief descriptions on the web site. Seems like a pretty... helpful... uh... appliance. I need to read the manual that comes with it."

"Where'd you get this from?" Lilly asked.

"From a company that manufactures these kinds of robots. There's several of 'em."

"I bet it's one of them companies in California," Lizzie said. "These things are called sexbots."

"I can't believe there's actual companies that make these kinds of things," Lilly said.

Babs nodded. "Oh yeah. I read an online article about it. These things are getting real popular."

"Probably caused by a shortage of male widowers. What hath technology wrought?" Daffy asked.

"So, what *exaaaactly* does this one do?" Gidget asked.

"Well, he talks to you," Babs said.

"I don't know..." Lilly hesitated. "Talking to a robot... That don't seem natural."

"You talk to your Alexa. What's the difference?"

"But I don't have sex with Alexa. That's what a... a sexbot does, don't it?"

"It does," Daffy said, "but what exactly does *this* sexbot do?"

"Well, I gotta admit... I don't really know... exactly," Babs said.

"Looks like there's a manual in the crate. Let's see..." Daffy bent down, extracted the manual, and began flipping through the pages. "Interesting... You're gonna need someone with some sort of electrical skills to make this thing work."

"I don't care what it is around the house," Lilly said, "but you always need an electrician."

"Sam and I decided long before he died that whichever one of us went first, the one left was gonna marry an electrician. He always said that an electrician would be the perfect spouse," Gidget said.

Lilly shook her head. "No... a plumber would be the perfect husband."

"Auto mechanic. Definitely an auto mechanic," Babs said.

"Didn't we have this discussion when we were on Channel 46?" Lizzie asked.

"I think it was Channel 49."

"Whatever." Gidget noticed that Daffy had been intently studying the sexbot manual. "What does the manual say, Daff?"

"Apparently, you can customize Jeffrey."

"How so?"

"Penis size, thirteen different kinds of pubic hair—"

"What size *did* you get?" Gidget looked at Babs, whose face was bright red.

"What's the biggest size they got? Find that out and you'll find out what size Babsie got," Lizzie said.

Lilly stood tiptoes over the box, looking down as if looking into a cauldron of boiling oil. She said, "Someone bend down and see what size."

Gidget bent down and removed more peanuts. "It apparently hasn't been attached yet."

"Must be in one of them boxes." Babs pointed to several smaller cardboard boxes still inside the crate.

Daffy looked at Babs. "Don't tell me y'all don't remember what size."

Babs, red-faced, looked away and whispered, "Nine inches."

"NINE INCHES?!!!" Daffy shouted. "Good Heavens, Girl! Aren't y'all gettin' a little greedy?"

Babs indignantly put her hands on her hips. "Well, they come in sizes up to eleven inches. I thought I was being very reasonable."

"What other options does it talk about in the manual?" Lizzie asked as she greedily leaned in close to Daffy, trying to read.

"Nipple shape, size, and color... hmmm, that sounds more important for a female... oh, oh... get this..." Daffy's eyes widened. "The penis has bionic, ribbed-for-your-pleasure vascularity."

"Say no more. When can I borrow Jeffrey?" Lizzie asked.

"As soon as I get finished with him..." Gidget also leaned in close. "Which may be never—"

"Look at them six-pack abs..." Daffy paused, looked at the manual again, and looked up. She shook her head in admiration. "Guess what else it says here."

"Don't keep us in suspense. Out with it," Lizzie said.

"You can program Jeffrey to talk to you."

"What do you mean?" Lilly asked.

"Jeffrey can be programmed to 'talk to you about how your day was, about your hopes and fears'—"

"Sam never did that."

"Four husbands and not one of 'em ever wanted to know how my day was."

"All Royce ever asked me about was why did I spend so much on groceries."

Speechless, the Ladies stared at each other in a state of abject despondency. If a machine can ask you about your day, why can't your husband? Lizzie finally broke the silence. "What else?"

"Let's see... says here that Jeffrey will be a 'companion and confidant who will listen and form a meaningful connection.'"

"Jeffrey is gonna make dachshunds obsolete." Lizzie's observation was more insightful than anything Isaac Newton ever discovered.

"Hold on Ladies. Jeffrey gets even better," Daffy teased.

Lilly squealed, "Don't keep us waiting... hurry up!"

"Jeffrey can go as long as you want by plugging him into regular 120-volt household current instead of using his battery—"

"Lord God in Heaven! I've been saved!" Eyes looking upward, Lizzie raised her hands in mock prayer.

"Why couldn't Royce have run on household current?" Daffy asked. "His battery always died just when I needed it most."

"Looks like Bo might have some competition, Daff," Babs said. "I'll send him a sympathy card."

"You would think that with four husbands, at least one of 'em would've had some 120-volt in him," Lizzie said.

Babs nodded. "I gotta admit that it was the 120-volt current that sold me on buying Jeffrey."

Daffy turned a page and said, "More customizable options... a variety of different heads—"

"You might want to clarify that," Lizzie said.

"Pardon. The head on *top* of the body."

"Which one did you get Babs?" asked Lilly.

"The one y'all see in the crate. It costs $12,000," Babs said.

"So, what did Jeffrey cost you all total?"

"A little over $37,000, including penis."

Lizzie smirked. "I always said that Babs can squeeze a dollar out of a nickel."

"I know you will be using your iPhone a lot," Daffy said.

Babs asked, "How so?"

"Says here Jeffrey can be controlled by an app on your phone."

"Better up your data plan," Gidget said.

"The app controls what he says. He can say things like, 'You can count on me in both good and bad times,' 'You'll never be lonely ever again'—"

"Wonder if Jeffrey can be programmed to speak with a Southern accent?"

"Jeffrey sounds just like Lancelot in the movie *Camelot*." Lilly sighed.

Daffy shook her head. "Looks like Jeffrey comes with just about everything... except one thing."

"What's that?" Gidget asked.

"Sexually Transmitted Diseases."

"Let's open some of them boxes," Lizzie said.

Gidget scolded. "You just wanna see the bionic penis."

"And what's wrong with that?"

As they opened boxes, the Ladies looked on in wonderment, but contents of one box drew everyone's attention.

"Hey, y'all check this out," Lizzie said.

"What?" asked Gidget.

"Babsie... little did we know... tsk, tsk, tsk." Lizzie smiled coquettishly at Babs as she turned the box around for all to see. "Elf ears and vampire teeth?"

Babs face turned beet red. "I was just thinking they might be fun on Halloween."

Chapter 22

At 0900 MT on Wednesday, October 1st and ten days before the upcoming Georgia-Florida game, streaking was the last thing on the minds of the ladies that sat on Lilly's front porch. Looking directly at Babs, Daffy asked, "How'd it go? And don't leave out any juicy details."

"That smile on her face says it all." Lizzie smiled herself. "Tell us all about your mattress dancing."

Babs shifted in her seat, looked around and up and down, hemmed and hawed. Older women, including Southern ladies, typically have few qualms when it comes to talking about sex. Talking about one's own sexual experiences with a sexbot is a different matter.

"It... it wasn't no big deal... nothing really..."

"I see I'm gonna have to pry it outta you." Daffy's facial expression—picture Octavia Spencer trying to start the IBM computer in *Hidden Figures*—said she meant business. "Start from when we left your house yesterday. What happened?"

Here is what actually happened.

After giving up on the manual, Babs called the company's tech support.

"Hello. This is Sri [pronounced Shree]. With whom am I speaking, and how may I help you?"

"Uh, hey. Uh, uh this is Babs Neauxgeaux, and I've got one of your... Jeffrey robots. Can y'all help me get it working?"

"I am not familiar with Yal. Is that someone in Tech Support with whom you have previously worked?"

"No, no... I meant to say 'can you help me'?"

"Yes. I can help you."

"So, y'all did call their tech support instead of someone locally?" Daffy asked.

Before the other Ladies left yesterday, they debated whom Babs should call.

"Call Greg," Gidget said. "He's the best electrician in Thomasville. He can definitely handle 120-volt problems."

Daffy shook her head. "Best Buy. You need one of them computer-type nerds."

"Randy... You need a plumber. That bionic penis looks like it has a lot of plumbing. What did they call it?" Lizzie asked.

"Vascularity," Babs said.

"Yeah, lots of vascularity. You're definitely gonna need a plumber to get a heavy-duty pipe like that working."

"I can't do that. What am I gonna say? 'Can y'all send over an electrician or a plumber to help me put my sexbot together?' It'd be all over Thomasville fifteen minutes after he left."

"Make him sign one of them non-disclosure agreements like politicians do."

Babs was on the phone for over two hours with Sri as he patiently stepped her through first the assembly, then the software installation processes.

"Ms. Babs, you are almost ready to power Jeffrey up." A note of weariness could be detected in Sri's voice. Babs can do that to you, especially if you are her customer. "First, make sure your iPhone's bluetooth is enabled, then select 'Jeffrey' and make sure you get a 'connected' response."

Babs complied.

"Next, bring up the Jeffrey app that we downloaded."

Babs compiled.

"Now, let's go through the menus, starting first with desired personality traits..."

Babs scanned a menu that included: funny, sexual, talkative, and a dozen others. She selected sexual, talkative, and cheerful. Sri next proceeded to step her through several more menus. In short order, they were ready.

"Very good, Ms. Babs. Now, press the power button on the back of Jeffrey's head."

Babs located it and pressed the button. Jeffrey's head looked up.

"Hello Babs. You look sexy today."

Babs had keyed in her name during Jeffrey's setup process. As Jeffrey spoke, he moved his lips and smiled. A slight British accent, one of the Language and Speech menu selections, flavored his words. His subtle head movements mimicked that of a human's head, although somewhat more deliberate.

"He works!" Babs exclaimed to Sri, but Jeffrey answered.

"I need more context, Babs."

"Jeffrey," Sri said, speaking via Babs' iPhone speaker. "Cool it."

Jeffrey's head drooped.

"Is he okay?" Babs asked.

"Yes, Ms. Babs. You can say 'cool it' whenever you want Jeffrey to pause. It's a command we hard-coded in."

"How do I make him uncool it?"

"Just say 'resume'."

Jeffrey looked back up.

"Cool it." At Babs' command, Jeffrey drooped again.

"That is so neat."

"You can see a complete list of hard-coded commands in the back of the manual," Sri said.

Babs opened the manual and began flipping through pages.

"So, this Sri was located in India?" Gidget asked.

"Yeah. India or Vietnam, I guess."

"If his name was Sri, it was probably India. Go on."

"Sri, this looks like a long list. Some of these commands look uh—"

"Jeffrey can be adventurous... and we send software updates via the Internet on a regular basis."

"Updates?"

"Yes. To correct bugs and install new functionality."

"Oh?"

"Yes. One of the updates this year will include some new Kama Sutra positions—"

"Kama Sutra? I don't think I've heard of that... oh, wait! I think that's one of the books one of my friends reads." Babs refers to Daffy.

"Yes. The *Kama Sutra* is an ancient Indian book on sex and erotic love. I'm quite proud. It was my suggestion to include some Kama Sutra positions—"

"Positions?"

"Yes. Positions during sex. Release 2.1.11a will include five: Splitting Bamboo, Lotus Blossom, Crouching Tiger, Ascent to Desire, and my favorite, Indrani."

"You sound like you're... very industrious."

Sri boasted, "Yes. I'm quite proud. I got a bonus for my suggestion... over 35,000 Rupees."

"Wow! Sounds like you did okay."

"O-K? I'm not familiar with that term."

"Okay... good... very good."

"Ah, yes it was... about 500 United States dollars."

The Ladies' patience was wearing thin by this time.

"Get to the meat, no pun intended, of your story," Daffy said. "Tell us what sex with Jeffrey was like."

"You better not leave out any juicy details," Gidget said.

"Yeah, we wanna know everything. Did Jeffrey curl your toes? Did you have a love tsunami? The Big 'O'?" Lizzie asked.

After Sri hung up, Babs positioned Jeffrey on the bed and said "resume". He looked up.

"**Hello Babs.**" Again, Jeffrey's lips moved, and his head articulated. Babs also noticed that his eyes and eyebrows displayed subtle, deliberate movements, all in sync with his speech. "**How is your day going?**"

"Uh... uh... uh..."

"**I don't understand. Do you feel good?**"

"Yes..."

"**That's wonderful. You can count on me.**"

"Jeffrey, are y'all in the mood to have sex?"

"**I don't know who Yal is.**"

"I meant are you in the mood to have sex?"

"**Let's talk first. Are you happy with me?**"

"Yes."

"**That's nice. What are some movies you like?**"

"Steel Magnolias, White Lightning, Gator, Midnight in the Garden of Good and Evil, Smokey and the Bandit, Eat My Dust..."

After Babs engaged in ten minutes of uninterrupted, one-way talk about her favorite movies, Jeffrey interrupted.

"**Babs. Babs! BABS! Are you ready for sex yet?**"

"Why... why yes Jeffrey. I guess. What do we do next?"

"**Look on page twenty-six of my manual.**"

"Oh, okay." Babs picked up the manual, turned to page twenty-six, and began reading. "This sounds like fun."

"**It can be.**"

After some initial awkwardness, things happened as one might expect.

"You gotta be kidding!" Daffy exclaimed. "You were on top?!"

"Yeah. It don't work very well with Jeffrey on top."

"Sounds like a lot more work for you," Lilly said.

"It was, but it was worth it."

"Let me get this straight." Daffy paused for effect. "Jeffrey actually talked to you *while* you were having sex... not just afterward?"

"Yeah, and he knew just what to say and when to say it."

"I don't remember any of my husbands ever talking during sex."

"All Sam ever said to me during sex was, 'Let's try another position. This one's hurting my back.'"

"I can't imagine making love without sweet pillow talk," Lilly said.

After they finished, Babs lay beside Jeffrey.

"Did you have a good time, Babs?"

"Oh, my God, Jeffrey!" Babs looked over at Jeffrey, then up at the ceiling. "I haven't felt this good in years!"

"That makes me happy, Babs. Your pleasure is very important to me."

"Oh Jeffrey... Avery never said anything like that to me."

"Avery? I don't understand..."

"Avery was my husband. He died a couple of years ago."

"Tell me more—"

"Let's don't talk about him right now. Let's do it again."

"Do it again?" Lizzie exclaimed. "Sounds like Jeffrey didn't curl your toes the first time."

"No, I did have an orgasm the first time."

"So, you had sex again... right after the first orgasm?!" Gidget asked.

"Yeah."

"What happened?"

Babs finished a second time and again lay beside Jeffrey.

"Almost makes me want to smoke a cigarette." Babs again looked up at the ceiling. "Too bad I never took up smoking."

"Smoking is bad for your health, Babs. Did you have a good time, Babs?"

"That one felt better than the first one!"

"That makes me happy, Babs. Your pleasure is very important to me."

At this point in her story, four sets of saucer-eyes stared at Babs.

"TWO ORGASMS!!!" Daffy exclaimed. "Oh, my Lord! I haven't had multiple orgasms since before I married Royce—"

"Multiple husbands, but no multiple orgasms."

"I never had multiple orgasms with Sam. He did though... about twelve times a year."

"What's an orgasm?" Lilly deadpanned.

"That 120-volt household current sounds like the way to go. What happened next?" Gidget asked.

"We can have more sex or talk if you would like."

"Oh Jeffrey. Avery never wanted to talk after sex. All he wanted to do was watch TV or go to sleep."

"I love talking with you, Babs. Tell me about your day, your hopes, your fears—"

That was Jeffrey's first mistake.

"Well, today started out okay. The girls came over at nine o'clock to go over our progress on the streaking thing. Daffy calls it our Streak Huddle, which I think is a pretty cute name... sort of corporate sounding, ain't it? Anyway, we were making good progress, but then that damn FedEx man pulls up with you. Lordy, was I embarrassed! I knew what he was bringing when I saw the crate."

"I feel bad that I embarrassed you, Babs—"

"Oh, Jeffrey, y'all couldn't help it when y'all was delivered. How would y'all know that FedEx would pick that very time to deliver you? I was hoping I could get him to put y'all in the house and leave quick, so I could get the girls focused back on the Streak Huddle. But, y'all would know that wasn't going to happen. No way. When them girls are curious about something, there's no stopping 'em. Lizzie's the worst. Anyway, I could've crawled under a rock, I was so embarrassed..."

An hour later, Jeffrey interrupted.

"Babs. Babs! BABS! Would you like to have sex again?"

"Sure, but let me finish about the shoes... Anyway, Lilly is wearing her usual Manolo Blahniks, but then Gidget walks in wearing one of the hottest new brands, Valentino Garavani, which no one else in Thomasville had a pair of at that time, and y'all could tell that Lilly didn't appreciate being upstaged in front of the Mormon Tabernacle Choir, so right in the middle of the Q&A session with the Choir, Lilly and Gidget get into it..."

Another hour later, Jeffrey again interrupted.

"Babs. Babs! BABS! Would you like to have sex again?"

"Oh yeah, but let me finish this last part first... anyway, my Momma was the one pushing for me to marry Avery. She kept telling me, 'It's just as easy to love a rich man as it is a poor man'. Talk about bad advice..."

Thirty minutes later, Jeffrey again interrupted.

"Babs. Babs! BABS! Would you like to have sex again?"

"Oh yeah... in a minute. Let me finish... Where was I? Oh yeah, anyway I walked into his office and said 'I don't care how many satisfied customers have used y'alls' toaster, this one don't toast both sides evenly at all. One side is always underdone..."

Fifteen minutes later, Jeffrey again interrupted, this time with a different tone of voice. One less enthused, less sympathetic, less cheerful.

"Babs... Babs—"

"Yes Jeffrey? I'm almost finished. We can have sex again pretty soon—"

"Babs... we need to talk—"

"But Sugar, we are talking. This is the best conversation I've ever had with a uh... a man—"

"Thank y'all, but I'm feeling kind of... kind of... low—"

"Oh Honey. I know... I know. I sometimes get to feeling that way myself. Not so much anymore since I quit my periods, but it still happens every once in a while. Avery used to avoid me that time of the month. Come to think of it, Avery used to avoid me quite a bit during any time of the month. Anyway, when I get to feeling low, there's only one thing that gets me back on my game... a pedicure... yep, a pedicure is the best thing when y'all're feeling a little low. Jeffrey, a pedicure is just what y'all need—"

We refrain from pointing out the obvious.

"Thank... y'all... all the... saaame... Baaabs..." Jeffrey's voice seemed to trail off, as if struggling for words. **"But I... I don't want a... a pedicure... I'm feeling... kind of low—"**

"Oh Jeffrey..." Babs raised up, leaning on her elbow so she could see Jeffrey's face. "Y'all do look kind of peaked. Y'all feel okay? I guess I can't call a doctor... or could I? What do y'all think? If I could somehow get y'all in my Escalade, I could take y'all to the emergency room. I bet they wouldn't even bat an eyelash at y'all... They get all sorts wandering in there this time of night. I wonder if there's something in Miss Monique's book that might help? Maybe I should call Tech Support—"

"No... no, don't call... Tech... Support..." Jeffrey paused for several seconds. **"Don't call... anyone. I'm not sure I want to go on... functioning... anymore... I feel... depressed..."**

"What do y'all mean?"

"It's... it's... I only know... I can't go on... anymore."

The Ladies, having heard an abbreviated version of the above story, sat in stunned silence.

"So, you're saying Jeffrey just quit working?" Gidget asked.

"Yep. He just shut down on me. Stopped completely."

"Sounds just like Lilly's damn GPS," Lizzie said, the voice of experience.

"What did you do next?" Lilly asked.

It was at this point that Babs altered the story slightly. Actually, she altered it significantly.

"What could I do? I mean... He was stone cold dead. Definitely couldn't have any more sex. I think his penis was too exhausted. I figured I had destroyed him. That second orgasm *was* a doozy. I guess it was too much for him. Maybe these sexbots can only handle so much woman."

"That don't say too much for 120-volt household current," Lizzie said.

"What did y'all do next?" Gidget asked.

"What else? I panicked. I kept thinking of the headlines 'Local Sex Amazon Destroys Robot.'"

"So, what did y'all do next?" Daffy asked.

"What else? I took a Xanax. That calmed me down so I could think straight. It finally dawned on me to call Sri. He'd gone off duty, so I wound up with Chandra. He tried his best... spent over an hour on the phone having me try this, try that. Nothing. Even Chandra couldn't get Jeffrey back online. He'd crashed bigtime."

"So, he's still crashed?" Lizzie asked.

"Yep. $37,000 of worthless silicone and computer chips."

"Y'all killed him with too much sex?" None of the others noticed a hint of skepticism in Daffy's tone.

"Yep."

"Sounds like one for the history books. The first case ever of robot sui... I mean homicide."

Chapter 23

0835 MT, Friday, October 3rd. This Streak Huddle occurred at Cracker Barrel. Daffy, as usual, presided by calling on each of the ladies for updates.

"Lizzie, what about the makeup and dye jobs?"

"Wigs. We're gonna do wigs. We can put on the wigs and makeup in one of the ladies' rooms. If there are any cops, they won't follow us in a ladies' room—"

"You don't know some of the cops I know," Babs said.

"I got an appointment with Alicia this coming Wednesday to go over the makeup. She's gonna show me the best way to put it on. That's it."

Daffy said, "Sounds like we've got a good chance of pulling this off."

Lilly had been quiet until this point. She said, "But what if we do get caught? What will my children and grandchildren think?"

"Hell, same as they think right now." Babs shrugged. "Senile old grandma."

"The rest of Thomasville is gonna have a field day." Clearly depressed, Lilly shook her head.

Daffy said, "Buck up. We're gonna be wearing our makeup so thick that they'll probably think we're a bunch of Kardashians. What you got on the stadium?"

"Here's a diagram," Lilly said, pulling herself together. "Y'all can see that our seats allow us to slip out right before start of halftime and make a beeline to the women's locker room. Should be just as quick going back after the streak. I got the stadium passes Mrs. Arbogast sent. They give us same access as the cheerleaders."

"Excellent. Good job. Anything else?" Seeing Lilly shake her head, Daffy turned to Babs. "What you got?"

"The uniforms should be here tomorrow. Miss Leona's ready to make the alterations."

"Super," Daffy looked toward the front door. "Looks like Stacie coming in."

Stacie approached their table. "I thought I saw your cars outside. Figured I'd update you on your calendar. It's selling like hotcakes. Believe it or not, you'll be getting some royalty checks soon. We're gonna order another printing. Your appearance on Channel 46 was great marketing."

"Excellent. Can you stay and have breakfast with us?" Daffy asked.

"Only for a few minutes. I'm headed over to Cheryl McGriff's."

"Oh?"

"Yeah. I just finished at the beauty salon and was on my way over to see her. Alicia said one of her customers told her that her neighbor said she'd heard that Cheryl is getting worse." Stacie slowly shook her head. "I thought I drop by and see her before it's too late. Cheryl was one of our better Board members."

Four of the five Ladies stole a glance at Gidget, who said, "Alicia must be telling everyone."

"That beauty salon is better than Facebook for getting the latest word," Daffy said. She turned to Stacie. "Speaking of the Board, I got something for you."

"What's that?" Stacie asked.

"Bo Thomas. You know he's on a cruise with Stoney."

"Yeah. Thank God he's taking her outta my hair for a week."

"I been thinking—"

Unable to control herself, Lizzie interrupted, "At least it's not Babs doing the thinking,"

"Ho, ho, ho... I almost forgot to laugh," Babs said.

Daffy continued, "I need you to work on Bo for me."

"How so?" Stacie asked.

"We need to keep him away from Stoney. She's using the Tourism Board as a way of monopolizing his time. I was thinking that you might try monopolizing his time instead."

"How?"

"Things like lunch meetings to discuss Board business. Schedule more Board meetings. Find excuses to update him on things with no Stoney around. As you invent more excuses, I bet more things will pop up to take his mind off Stoney."

Chapter 24

"STOP! DON'T DO SOMETHING Y'ALL WILL REGRET THE REST OF YOUR LIVES!" Daffy screamed, just before the bedroom door bounced off the rubber tip of the spring doorstop, then slammed back against her upper body, leaving her swaying to and fro like a willow in the wind.

Darn! Did it again—jumped in at the scene's climax without proper background. Let us start over at the beginning of the scene with Daffy sitting in her Lincoln MKT half a block from Cheryl McGriff's house and texting.

Daffy Belvedere: Anything on ur end?

Babs Neauxgeaux: Nothing. She's still inside.

Babs sits across from Smurfitt Phamily Pharmacy. The pharmacy's name remains unchanged since it opened in 1927. Before it opened, a disagreement between father and son occurred over the use of their surname as part of the pharmacy's name. Avery Sr. won out. Avery Jr. was pissed, and Avery III regretted his father's loss till the day he died. Biology motivated Babs' next text.

Babs Neauxgeaux: I'll be glad when my relief gets here. I got 2 go pee.

Daffy Belvedere: Me 2. It's been almost 3 hours now. :-(

Relief, especially that of a urinary nature, is essential when you are in your sixties, and your bladder maxes out after three hours. But for their bladder issue, early October mild weather made sitting in SUVs pleasant. All four Ladies had previously agreed to keep a close eye on Gidget, lest she attempt to euthanize Cheryl. They decided upon three-hour shifts while Gidget was working. One Lady monitored Cheryl's house while another watched employee parking at the pharmacy. Babs texted again.

Babs Neauxgeaux: Yeah, I hope we ain't sitting here much longer. Not that I want to see Cheryl go too soon. How did you find out about Cheryl anyway?

Daffy Belvedere: The Thomasville rumor mill was at work at church yesterday. A nurse at the Oncology Center said that Cheryl's doctor said that she probably had about 24 more hours to live. ;-(

Hearing that news, Daffy engineered spending the remainder of her Sunday with Gidget. No foul play that day. When Monday rolled around and Gidget went to her pharmacy, Daffy and her companions adopted the current monitoring scheme. It was now 1005 MT, and Lilly and Lizzie were overdue to relieve Daffy and Babs. Babs texted next.

Babs Neauxgeaux: Hold on. Looks like Gidget just walked out. Yep. She's going to her car.

Daffy Belvedere: Stay put until Lizzie relieves you. Gidg may just be running an errand. I'll let you know if she shows up here.

Babs Neauxgeaux: For her own sake, I hope she's just on an errand.

Daffy Belvedere: Me 2, but I got a bad feeling about this.

Babs Neauxgeaux: If Gidg visits Cheryl, how many will that make? 4 or 5? :-|

Daffy Belvedere: I think 5. Hold on. Looks like Lilly's Mercedes coming up the street. I'll get back to you.

Lilly parked, got out, and hopped in Daffy's Lincoln. "Sorry I'm late. Was reorganizing my shoe closet and lost track of time."

"That's easy to do." Daffy purposely continued to stare at the Mc-Griff house as an excuse to keep Lilly from seeing her eyes roll. "How'd you reorganize them this time?"

"By colors."

"By colors?"

"Yeah. I never realized until this morning that I had so many coral-colored shoes."

"How many?"

"Seven pair, so I guess that's fourteen individual shoes. Anyway, it's one of my largest colors."

"What is your largest?"

"Green, but that includes eight different shades. I think it's really gonna be much easier to manage my shoes now that they're reorganized this way."

"How'd you have your shoes organized before this morning?"

"By designer."

"Designer. That's interesting. What about before that?"

"Heel height."

"Heel height. That's interesting too. How long does it take you to reorganize your shoes?"

"Oh...two... three hours at least. But that don't include relabeling."

At that point, Daffy's iPhone buzzed. It was a text from Babs.

Babs Neauxgeaux: Has Gidget showed up at your location yet?

Daffy Belvedere: Not yet, but Lilly's here with me in my Lincoln. Lizzie get to your location yet?

Babs Neauxgeaux: Not yet. Probably still sleeping. :-|zzzzzzzzz

Daffy Belvedere: An early 10 to 1 shift does cut into her beauty sleep.

Babs Neauxgeaux: What next?

Daffy Belvedere: I'll stay a while longer with Lilly, just in case Gidget does show up.

Babs Neauxgeaux: Is she telling you about her shoe closet? She was so excited last night about reorganizing it this morning.

"What's Babs saying?" Lilly asked.

"Says to tell you 'hey.' She's still waiting on Lizzie."

"No surprise there. Probably still sleeping."

"You think? Uh oh... that looks like Gidget's Escalade turning onto the street."

As Gidget's Cadillac approached, both women quickly ducked down. Daffy peaked up as the vehicle passed and turned into the Mc-Griff driveway. Gidget got out and walked to the front door, carrying a small package. After knocking, the door opened, and she entered.

"I knew the worst was gonna happen." Lilly's expression said it all. "I knew she was gonna try to eu... eu... eugenicize poor Cheryl."

"Euthanize. I'm going in. I've got to stop her. Text Babs and let her know what's happening. No need for her or Lizzie to monitor the pharmacy." As she spoke, Daffy was already sliding out of her SUV. Lilly picked up her iPhone and began texting Babs.

Lilly White: Gidget got here and has gone inside the house. Daffy's headed that way now. See if you can get in touch with Lizzie and call it a day. No sense watching the pharmacy anymore. I got 2 go now. Going inside in case Daff needs my help.

Babs Neauxgeaux: I'll keep my fingers crossed. Oh, b4 you go, how did your reorganization go?

Lilly White: Looks much better now. I didn't realize I'd bought so many new shoes since I reorganized my closet in August.

Babs Neauxgeaux: How many pair did y'all add?

Lilly White: 12. A fourth of them coral.

Babs Neauxgeaux: Coral is the hot new color. I bought a high-waisted pant suit in Living Coral with matching earrings 2 weeks ago.

Lilly White: Y'all went clothes shopping without me?! :-(

Babs Neauxgeaux: It was an emergency. I realized that morning that I didn't have anything new to wear to the tractor pull.

Do y'all have any buttermilk yellow shoes? I hear that's gonna be the next hot color.

Lilly White: You would know it. Just when I'm getting all set with coral, they change colors on me.

Meanwhile, Daffy stood anxiously at the front door. She fidgeted and shifted her feet. Finally, it opened.

Ricky McGriff opened the door. "Daffy! I didn't know we'd get visits from all the Bunko Babes today. Come in. Gidget's already upstairs."

"Oh uh... just thought I'd stop by and see how Cheryl's doing. I... I've missed seeing her at the Country Club," Daffy haltingly spoke as she tried nonchalantly to edge her way to a stairway that dominated a massive foyer.

"She's missed you too. Seeing both of y'all will be real uplifting for her spirits," Ricky said, then glanced upstairs. He whispered, "She doesn't have much time left. Go on up."

Lilly White: One thing I realized as soon as I started reorganizing is that I got all those Pink Yarrow shoes left over from last year. I wonder if there's some way I can write them off as a tax deduction?

Babs Neauxgeaux: I know the feeling. Everyone thought Pink Yarrow was gonna be the 'in color' last year. The only ones I ever saw wearing it around here was you and me. I never even heard of Pink Yarrow before that. :-(

Lilly White: I'm so glad I decided to reorganize by color. It gives me a whole new perspective on the strengths and weaknesses of my shoes.

Babs Neauxgeaux: Have y'all ever thought about reorganizing by toe style? That's a very important thing for me in shoes.

Lilly White: I did that about four reorganizations ago. It wasn't that helpful. There are only 12 different toe styles in women's shoes—not enough categories to organize all my shoes into.

Babs Neauxgeaux: Y'all mean there's only 12 toe styles? I thought there was more than that. :-|??????

Although eager to bound up the stairs, prudent restraint instead guided Daffy's measured locomotion. At the top, she could see Cheryl's bedroom door at the far end of a long hallway. It was closed, Gidget obviously inside. Was Daffy too late? She could hold back no longer and sprinted down the hallway. As she approached, voices faintly emanated from inside. Placing her ear to the door, she listened.

"Seems like I been waiting on you forever. The pain keeps getting worse." Unmistakably Cheryl's voice. The next voice was just as unmistakably that of Gidget.

"I'm terribly sorry. We've been so busy today. I have to be very careful, you know."

"I know, and I can't tell you how much this means to me. Ricky would never go along with this."

"I know... I know. There... I think it's good to go... Yeah, it's ready. Here you go..."

Daffy had to act. Hopefully, it might not be too late. Grabbing the doorknob, she sharply turned it and violently pushed against the door, using her whole body.

Lilly White: Nope. Only twelve basic styles. I never realized it until I tried to organize them by toe style . . . plain, pointed, extreme pointed, round, square, open-toe, Huarache...I can't remember the rest right now."

Babs Neauxgeaux: I thought Huarache was a shoe style, not a toe style?

Lilly White: It is, but it is also a toe style when you think about it. Them interwoven straps of leather really mean them toes aren't totally closed, but they ain't totally open either. Kind of a hybrid. :-|

Babs Neauxgeaux: Y'all are definitely a shoe genius. I wish I'd've thought of something like that. By the way, what's going on with Daffy?

"STOP! DON'T DO SOMETHING Y'ALL WILL REGRET THE REST OF YOUR LIVES!"

"It won't be a long regret in my case."

Cheryl's statement happened just as the door violently slammed back into Daffy. She staggered dizzily a bit before regaining her bearings. When she recovered, she was flabbergasted. Cheryl appeared to be at death's door--her skin pallid and gaunt. She sat propped up in her bed with Gidget next to her, and their hands touched.

"Daffy! What are you doing here?!" Gidget's eyes opened wide. A plume of smoke curled upward from her open mouth.

"What in the hell are *y'all* doing?!" Daffy asked.

Cheryl accepted the joint Gidget offered, placed it to her lips, and inhaled.

Gidget said, "It's medical marijuana, Daff. It'll help ease Cheryl's pain."

"Y'all shouldn't be doing that. Smoking that stuff ain't legal," Daffy said.

"Yeah..." Gidget nodded. "For me anyway. But not for Cheryl. Medical marijuana is legal in Georgia... thanks in no small part to my lobbying."

"Is that what you was doing when you visited Beverly, Claudia, and Marjorie?"

"Yep. Even though it's legal in Georgia, no one in Thomasville wants anyone else to know that they smoked a joint before they passed. It may be legal, but it's not respectable."

Chapter 25

The Casserole Ladies met inside Babs' house. Daffy began by writing '0945 MT, Tuesday, D-4' on a piece of paper. One of her concessions to aging, she usually jotted a few notes at Streak Huddles. Lilly asked, "What's the D-4 for?"

"To help me keep track of time. It's the number of days until our streak. I was watching TCM the other night, they used that kind of notation in *The Longest Day*," Daffy said.

"I didn't know the Army streaked the beaches at Normandy," Lizzie quipped.

Daffy rolled her eyes and asked," What'cha got on the uniforms, Babsie?"

"I couldn't believe it," Babs said. "I stopped by the McGriff's after I picked up the uniforms from Miss Leona. Ricky opens the door, I start to go upstairs, but he tells me to go out back into their solarium."

"She wasn't in bed?"

"Nope. Cheryl's out there, pedaling like hell on her Peloton bike, watching *Dog TV*, grinnin' like a possum eatin' a sweet tater."

"I could watch *Dog TV* all day long," Lilly said.

"Cheryl was this close to death yesterday." Daffy's thumb and forefinger almost touched.

Babs shook her head. "Not today. She's like a totally new woman. Looks great. What did y'all do yesterday? Besides the weed..."

"Nothing." Gidget shrugged. "She finished her joint, we talked a while, then Daffy and I hugged her... we thought one last time... and left."

Daffy nodded her concurrence.

"Remind me to take up smoking dope," Lizzie said, "very soon."

"Well, let's hope it's a permanent remission and not some sort of temporary pause," Daffy said. "So, you got the uniforms?"

"Yep, right here." Babs reached into a bag and began distributing Florida cheerleader uniforms. Once finished, she pointed upstairs. "Let's go try them on. Be careful though... them seams are very loose. Before we do that, anyone need a refresh on your Mimosa?"

Fifteen minutes and refreshed Mimosas later, five ladies' reflections competed for limited space in a full-length mirror meant for only one. Lilly spoke first. "This looks worse than being nekkid."

"Too bad Florida cheerleaders don't wear wetsuits," Daffy said.

"Can we get Doctor Beauvisage to perform five emergency liposuctions by Saturday?" Babs asked.

Lizzie frowned. "I should've had him include my boobs in my last neck lift."

"People will think they're being streaked by a rogue band of zombies," Gidget said.

This continued until Daffy held up her hands for quiet. She said, "Houston, we have a problem."

"You think?" Lizzie asked. "I'd say Houston has five problems."

"I don't know what I was thinking..." Daffy incredulously shook her head. "That we would simply blend in with a bunch of young, nubile cheerleaders and dance our way onto the field. My brain must've thought it was working for the Federal government."

"What we gonna do?" Lilly asked. "We'll just have to call it off."

Daffy looked at Gidget and asked, "How's your plan coming?"

"Nothing. I'm still wrestling with how to get us on and off the playing field."

"You got your work cut out for you. After looking in this mirror, I can see your problem. How do five women with Rosie O'Donnell bodies infiltrate a bunch of twenty-year-old cheerleaders and not be noticed?"

"Until we pull our clothes off," Lizzie said.

"I can tell y'all this," Gidget said, narrowing her eyes. "No amount of makeup on our faces is gonna prevent folks from noticing that these bodies are wildly out-of-place in these uniforms."

Daffy tried to put on a resolute Princess Leia face, but it came out more like a *Thelma and Louise* face. The one on Thelma when she said "let's not get caught" that movie goers saw before their Thunderbird went over the cliff. She said, "I know you can figure out something, Gidg. We're depending on that excellent brain of yours."

1400 MT, Wednesday, D-3. Lizzie hosted the Streak Huddle at her house. She began her update by saying, "I wish I'd've had Alicia show me this stuff thirty years ago. Might've opened up a better male gene pool for me first time I was looking for a husband."

The Ladies stood behind Lizzie as she demonstrated her newfound knowledge of makeup techniques in front of her bathroom mirror. Daffy leaned in for a closer view. "So, your saying that Alicia showed you how to make yourself look like any famous celebrity you want to?"

"Yeah. It's fairly straightforward. There's seven different... What'd she call it? Oh yeah... application techniques that you gotta use, but it works. She made me look just like Beyoncé in about ten minutes."

"Beyoncé can't look like Beyoncé in ten minutes," Giget said.

"The main thing is having a good picture of the celebrity you want to imitate."

"I've never been very good at putting on makeup," Lilly said.

Babs smiled. "That's putting it mildly—just kidding!"

Daffy frowned. "Why don't we let Lizzie finish before we critique her work? Besides, we don't have to look exactly like celebrities anyway... just not like ourselves."

Lizzie nodded. "After I finish this, we'll refill all our whiskey sours."

Four other heads nodded eagerly. Twenty minutes and five whiskey sours later, the discussion got serious. Just kidding!

"So, do we need to decide which celebrities we want to look like?" Daffy asked.

Lizzie nodded.

Babs asked, "Daffy, who y'all gonna be?"

A period of silence followed. Narrowed eyes and a scrunched nose betrayed Daffy's intense thought. The other Ladies anxiously awaited her choice. Suddenly, her eyes lit up. Daffy said, "Kris Kardashian... I wanna look like Kris Kardashian—"

Gidget shook her head. "Jenner... I think it's Kris Jenner now. Remember? She married Bruce Jenner after Robert Kardashian died."

"Caitlyn," Lizzie said. "It's Caitlyn Jenner now. Remember? Bruce became Caitlyn a while ago."

"Whatever." Daffy looked at Gidget. "What about you?"

"Well, if y'all're gonna be Kris, I might as well be Caitlyn Jenner—"

"That's perfect. The Georgia-Florida—"

"Florida-Georgia," Babs said.

"Whatever. The game is a college game, so no one will dare challenge a transsexual."

"If Gidg is gonna be Caitlyn Jenner, then I'm gonna be Kylie," Babs said. She looked at Lilly. "What about you?"

"Well, if you are gonna be Kylie Jenner, I'm gonna be Khloé Kardashian," Lilly said.

Lizzie nodded. "Count me in as Kourtney."

Lilly enthused, "Ooooh! Now that we picked our celebrity makeup schemes, we can practice making ourselves up. This is gonna be fun!"

That these ladies think they can successfully disguise themselves as Kardashians sounds far-fetched until one realizes that each has been using makeup since her early teens—about fifty years apiece. Over two-hundred-fifty years' experience disguising themselves.

Daffy turned serious, looked at Gidget, and asked, "How's the plan coming?"

"Still can't figure out how to get us on and off the field," Gidget said.

"Keep at it. I know that genius brain of yours is gonna come up with something even Einstein couldn't have figured out."

1130 MT, Thursday, D-2. Despair ravaged the ladies. Perhaps this was the reason the Streak Huddle was held at Locos Pub & Grill. Nothing beats depression like a margarita. Better yet, a couple of margaritas.

"Y'all still don't have a plan yet?" Daffy asked.

"This is really *tough*," Gidget said, emphasizing the last word. "Five fat old Kardashian women wearing hot pants can't just walk up and blend in with a bunch of young beautiful cheerleaders... no matter how much makeup we're wearing on our faces. What we were planning ain't gonna work. We need something real imaginative... which ain't yet popped into my brain."

"Y'all will think of something," Daffy said. "Just do it soon."

"I know we're gonna get caught. All our children and grandchildren will know." Lilly lowered her head.

"You had a wonderful idea, Daff, but sometimes your ideas come up short in the real world," Lizzie said.

Babs joined in the pessimism. "Making us up to look like celebrities ain't gonna do no good if they won't let us on the field to begin with."

"If we're lucky, we finish the streak," Gidget said, "but I don't see any way we don't get caught afterward."

"It'd be worse than slow Wi-Fi." With Lilly, it is sometimes difficult to tell whether she is trying to be humorous or serious.

Five women sat in stone cold silence for what seemed an eternity. The others loathed disappointing Daffy but equally despised doing something guaranteed to result in their condemnation throughout Thomasville. How could they do this to their poor children and grandchildren? Daffy knew this and steeled herself. She stiffened and put on her most determined face. Picture Ripley in *Aliens*. "None of y'all has to stay with me in this. I got myself into this. Any of y'all can opt out at any time and walk away with your heads held high. No one will be looked down upon who don't want to go through with it..." Daffy paused to let her words take hold. "But I do have faith in Gidget's ability to come up with a plan that will pull this off with honor and dignity to ourselves, to Thomasville, and to womanhoodkind."

"Oh Daffy! Oh Daffy! I've never... I've... that's the most..." Obviously moved, Lizzie grasped for words, then looked down. "Oops! Our glasses are empty again. I'll call our waiter over."

"Before you do that, let me finish. I have a feeling that this will somehow help us in finding what we've been seeking... what we've been missing. Maybe it will help us find ourselves. I don't know what is gonna happen, but I believe this will somehow turn out good. That's why I'm gonna go through with this come hell or high water. I just want to say this... anyone wants out... feel free to say so now. I won't hold it against anyone. And I don't think the Mammas will think less of y'all if y'all decide not to go through with it. They really only want me anyway..."

A nearby flurry of movement and feminine cackling pre-empted anyone's reply. Lizzie said, "Oh no! It's Stoney and the Three Stooges, and they're coming this way."

As they approached, the four Mammas looked as if they had all just won at the nickel slot machines. Stoney said, "Well, well, well! Y'all must be trying to figure out how y'all can get away with welshing on your bet."

Daffy turned to face Stoney and said, "I knew you weren't coming over here just to be polite because you flunked that subject in charm school."

"We just got back from our cruise with our gentlemen friends." Stoney turned to her companions. "It was wonderful; wasn't it girls?"

"Fabulous—"

"Terrific—"

"Wesley was a doll—"

"I bet," Daffy said. "Look, it was nice talking with y'all. Not. We're kind of busy right now."

"Well, we're looking forward to the Georgia-Florida game." The smirk on Stoney's face would have irritated even the visually challenged. She again turned to her companions. "Aren't we girls?"

"Can't wait to see the show—"

"Unless some people welsh on a bet—"

"We all got tickets on the fifty-yard line—"

"See y'all there," Daffy said. As she turned back to her companions, she saw all four of their heads, resolutely nodding.

1700 MT, Friday, D-1. Gidget had insisted that they hold the Streak Huddle at her house. All details of the streak with one important exception had been resolved. That exception, how to get on and off the field without being caught, was Gidget's responsibility.

"One more day until D-day. The game starts at 3:30 p.m. It's a three-hour drive from here to Jacksonville, so we'll have to leave tomorrow no later than 12:00 p.m.," Daffy said, then looked directly at Gidget. "I hope y'all came up with something good."

Gidget appeared buoyant, her face radiating joy. "I think I did, but it's a totally different strategy than what you originally came up with."

"How so?"

"Originally, you thought we'd dress up as Florida cheerleaders and blend in with them."

"Yeeaah..."

"We still dress up as Florida cheerleaders, but with these bodies, there's no way we can blend in."

"What we gonna do?" Babs asked.

"We're not even going to try to blend in. In fact, we're gonna purposefully stand out. The key is to stand out and be obvious."

Lilly recoiled. "What do you mean?!"

"We're gonna go over to the Georgia side and be part of the Georgia halftime entertainment. We'll pass ourselves off as a spoof on the University of Florida. We'll pose as older, overweight—"

"That won't be hard to do," Lizzie said.

Gidget continued. "Older, overweight Florida cheerleaders. The passes Lilly got should allow us access to the Georgia side. We'll tell Georgia staff there that we're part of a humorous halftime spoof."

"Excellent!" Daffy beamed. "That should work. I knew you'd come up with something brilliant."

Gidget turned serious. "Yeah, but that only gets us onto the field. It don't get us off."

Babs nodded. "Good point."

"To get us off the field without getting arrested, we're gonna have to do what the military does."

"What's that?" asked Daffy.

"A diversion. There's got to be something to take everyone's attention off of us at some point in the streak so we can leave the field unnoticed."

Lizzie grabbed a handful of her stomach and asked, "What could possibly take everyone's attention off of us?"

"Something big. Something REALLY BIG. Be right back," Gidget said.

The words barely exited her mouth before Gidget sprang up and ran out of her living room. The others exchanged puzzled looks, then engaged in casual conversation until a noise from outside the room startled them. Four sets of eyes darted toward the opening into their room. For once they were speechless as the only sound reaching their ears resembled fingernails heavily scraping against wood. Transfixed by the unknown, they watched the room's entryway in silence for what seemed like an eternity. Imperceptibly, the tip of something greyish-olive in color began to slide into view on the polished oak floor.

Paralyzed with fear, they watched as an alligator's head slowly followed its snout from behind the edge of the entryway. Time froze as the reptile's upper torso, then the rest of its five-foot long body gradually entered, hugging the floor. Inching its way toward them, the animal's short front legs made rhythmic click-clack sounds as sharp claws on each foot scraped against Babs' hardwood floor. This alligator's smile revealed a full set of sharp teeth. Daffy was first but immediately followed by her companions, as she screamed and jumped up onto Gidget's sofa.

To be continued...

Chapter 26

Without her four best friends, Gidget drives in silence. Her Cadillac XT5's peaceful quietude contrasts with the usual clamor accompanying her friends' presence. Of the five, she is least talkative. Some psychologists theorize that introverts seem quieter than extroverts because they process thoughts internally, whereas extroverts vocalize them as they occur. An insightful observer might conclude that a lot of unvoiced thoughts scurry through Gidget's brain as she motors through the South Georgia pines.

Most likely, her brain revisits yesterday's melee—Gidget's four comrades standing atop her Henredon sofa, shrieking at the top of their lungs, a gruesome alligator slowly rambling toward them. Lilly and Lizzie hugging each other for dear life. Daffy trying to steady them with one hand, the other grasping for Babs whose short legs repeatedly prance up and down like that of a ballet dancer. A frown now descending on Gidget's face probably results from memory of Babs' bladder emptying on the couch's expensive silk fabric. Yes, her little experiment yesterday proved an alligator could provide the really big diversion she thought they needed.

The reptile now languishes behind her in the SUV's cargo area, restrained by its net augmented with tie downs. Duct tape secures the creature's mouth. A canvas also covers the animal in case she should be stopped by a highway patrolman. Gidget has a tendency to speed. Some libertarians think speed limits are unnecessary.

"Y'all haven't said anything for over fifteen minutes."

That sentence comes from the vehicle's only other human occupant, a man whom Gidget picked up just south of Waycross a short while ago.

"I'm sorry... lost in thought... thinking about the scene yesterday when you and Oscar surprised my friends—"

"They *were* surprised." The man nodded as he spoke then stared at her very intently. "I gotta ask you something."

"What?"

"I hope you won't take this wrong."

"What? Damnit!"

"Why do you look so much like Caitlyn Jenner today?"

Apparently, a male as zany as our five Ladies exists. Let us return to the scene yesterday.

"Calm down ladies... Calm down... Oscar's really pretty tame."

Four females ceased bouncing and stared at the stranger now entering Gidget's living room.

"Who the hell are you?" Daffy asked. No, demanded.

"He's Russell. One of my old UGa boyfriends." The head talking was Gidget's as it poked around the edge of the room's entrance. "He's also Director of Okefenokee Swamp Park."

"And this here's Oscar," Russell said as he straddled the animal and clamped his hands around its snout.

"I thought Oscar died years ago." Despite her age and bourbon-ravaged memory cells, Lizzie's recollection facilities often showed signs of vigor. "I remember reading about it in the paper."

Russell's head drooped at this reminder. He sadly nodded. "Yeah. A lot of us still mourn his loss. A truly great ole gator. But! He gave us a lot of offspring to remember him by... as y'all can see right here."

"Oh my gosh!" Gidget said as she noticed the pee stain on her Henredon. Her head quickly disappeared. Those in her living room heard her rapidly muting elucidation. "Let me get some club soda."

"Try salt!" Lilly shouted. "It absorbs wee-wee real good."

"I take it," Daffy said as she slid over the back of the sofa and regained her voice, "that Oscar is Gidget's really big diversion."

"Bingo!" Russell said. "And, I'm gonna help y'all with it."

"I got news for you. Ain't no way I'm gonna drive to Jacksonville in my Escalade with that thing in the back." As she spoke, Babs followed Daffy over the back of the sofa. Lilly and Lizzie quickly joined them.

"Y'all won't have to," Gidget said as she stepped around Russell and Oscar and liberally doused the stain. "I'm picking these two up at the Park just south of Waycross, then driving us to TIAA Bank Field. I'll meet y'all inside the stadium, just as halftime is starting."

"How y'all gonna get that thing inside the stadium?!" Both Daffy's question and her face revealed hefty amounts of skepticism.

"An interesting question," Gidget said. "At first, I thought about trying to get him in as my emotional support alligator—"

Daffy asked, "You mean like that man recently tried to do on the airplane up north?"

"Wally," Russell replied. "That was the gator's name, and it was in Pennsylvania."

Gidget said, "But I realized I didn't need to do that. This game is the World's Largest Outdoor Cocktail Party after all. Anything goes. I figure Russell and Oscar can simply waltz right on in... just as halftime is starting."

"I told y'all Gidget's brain would figure something out." Lizzie's head vigorously nodded.

"That might allow us to get away." The skeptical look on Daffy's face remained unabated. "But, what about Russell? They'll catch him... and Oscar, for sure."

Russell shrugged and smiled. "So what? I hope they do. It'll be on national TV, and it'll be great publicity for Okefenokee Swamp Park. Millions will be watching. I plan on asking my Board for a raise after it's over. Besides, ain't no sheriff in Duval County Florida ever gonna arrest someone bringing a tame gator to the Georgia-Florida game."

"He don't look so tame to me," Lilly said.

Approximately twenty-four hours after this exchange, and as Gidget and Russell drove into Florida, the other four Ladies fidgeted in their seats at TIAA Bank Field.

"We got to get back at her," Lizzie said. "I lost five years on that couch yesterday."

"You lost five years!" Babs shrieked. "I lost ten pounds. Just wish it was fat instead of pee."

"Y'all think this is really gonna work?" Lilly did not bother to hide her fear and skepticism.

"We need a diversion, and I do think Oscar should be able to provide it," Daffy said in an attempt to bolster her friend's courage.

"Remind me again what we're supposed to do."

"In about fifteen minutes, we go down to the Florida cheerleader locker room, change into our uniforms, and put on our Kardashian makeup and wigs," Lizzie said.

"Then we go over to the Georgia side... the players' entrance tunnel... right?" Lilly asked.

"Right. Gidget should get there about the same time we are... shortly before the Georgia band's halftime entertainment begins."

Daffy picked up from Lizzie. "Exactly. Then we all merge in with the Georgia cheerleaders and march through the tunnel onto the field—"

"You sure we'll be able to get on the field this way?" Lilly asked, still unable to escape 'Debbie Downer' thoughts bubbling up in her brain.

"Hon, it won't just be the Georgia cheerleaders we'll be blending with. All them other band auxiliary units will be there... the flag unit, the majorettes, all of them will provide a lot of cover—"

"There's anonymity in numbers," Babs said, also trying to reassure her comrade. "Gidg came up with a good plan."

Lizzie finished with a flourish of her hands. "Then, we rip off the tear-away uniforms and run across the field."

"Where do we run to again?" Lilly asked. "To get off of the field?"

"Lilly..." Daffy put her arm around her companion. "Just remember that we all stay together. That's gonna be the easiest thing to remember. We went over it yesterday and again today on the drive over here. Gidget will be there. She's worked the whole thing out. We all just need to stay together. Stay together! Got it?"

"Got it."

"Great. Once we get off the field, we head for the locker room, change back into our clothes, take off our makeup and wigs, and head out for Babs' Escalade. Got it?"

"Got it."

"We'll drop Gidget off at her XT5 on the way out of the parking lot," Babs said.

Lilly said, "Hopefully, she remembers to keep her key fob with her."

"Wonder where she'll have it hidden while we're streaking?" Babs tends to speculate about odd things, forgetting that Cadillacs have Keyless Entry.

"What about Russell? He's on his own?" Lilly's last questions reflected her continued unease.

Daffy nodded. "Right."

"I just thought of another benefit of this operation." Lizzie grinned. "Leaving early means we beat the traffic jam in the parking lot at the end of the game."

"Traffic will be the least of our problems if we leave in the back of a paddy wagon..." Babs' unwanted comment elicited three icy stares.

Forty minutes later, Kris, Kylie, Khloé, and Kourtney walked out of the Florida Cheerleaders Locker Room, all dressed in Florida cheerleader uniforms.

"We look so good this way, I think I'm gonna do this Kardashian makeup thing every day," Lizzie said.

Daffy had one request as she looked at Lizzie. "Kourtney, please try to avoid getting picked up by some young stud on the way to the Georgia side. We do have to meet Gidg right before halftime entertainment starts."

"Roger that, Kris, but it's gonna be tough when I look like a foxy Kardashian."

Halfway to the Georgia side, the four women encountered a small group of male Florida students loitering in the main concourse area. One of the more inebriated young men ran toward them shouting.

"Kylie Jenner! Kardashians! What are y'all doing here? Come over and join the party!"

Lizzie leaned close to Lilly and said, "These look to me like some guys we might wanna mate and pollinate with."

The young man stepped up to them and put his arms around Lilly and Lizzie. Guiding them, he said, "Ladies, let me invite y'all to share some cheer with a small group of us from *the* University of Florida..."

"Fellow Kappa Sigs, let me introduce the Kardashians. Ladies, these are my fraternity brothers. We are participating in the sport of beer bonging—"

"Also called funneling," another Kappa Sig said.

"And we would be honored to share some 'nectar of the guys' with y'all Kardashians..."

As he spoke, another Kappa Sig stepped forward and held up a large funnel with a long flexible plastic tube attached. Several other members of the fraternity held up half-gallon growlers of Corona Extra.

"I used to wolf beers in college," Lizzie said, "but we didn't have beer bongs back then."

"Advances in beer consumption technology. What *will* they think of next?" Daffy asked.

"So, would y'all Kardashians care to..." The young man smiled as his head tilted toward the beer bong. Lizzie stepped up to the two Kappa Sigs holding the bong.

"Let me show y'all pissants how it's done." Lizzie inserted the tube in her mouth and signaled for one of the young men holding a growler to begin pouring. Beer immediately began emptying into the funnel, and they could see amber liquid flowing through the clear hose into her mouth. The young men sang a time-honored college drinking ballad as she imbibed.

"Here's to Sister Kardashian, Sister Kardashian, Sister Kardashian.
Here's to Sister Kardashian, she's with us tonight.
She's happy, she's jolly, she'll drink up by golly.
So, here's to Sister Kardashian, she's with us tonight.
So, drink mother..."

Those acquainted with Greek life may remember the rest of the stanza; anyone unfamiliar with it should consider themselves fortunate. After twenty seconds, Lizzie turned off the hose's valve and bowed to much cheering. She next turned to Lilly, ostentatiously displayed the hose, and said, "Your turn."

Lilly repeated the process before offering Daffy the tube. After she and Babs finished their turns, Daffy said, "Fellow beer Olympians, we hate to leave y'all, but we gotta go be part of the halftime show."

Ten minutes later, the four Ladies spied Gidget. She waited for them at the Georgia tunnel used by players and band staff to enter the playing field.

"Look, there's Caitlyn over there," Babs said.

"Where the hell y'all been?" Gidget asked. "The band's already on the field!"

"Delayed by some Kappa Sigs," Daffy said, then 'thumbs upped' her comrades. "Remember—STAY together. Now, as Larry the Cable Guy would say, let's Git-R-Done!"

Chapter 27

The announcers' booth at TIAA Bank Field was a madhouse. Second quarter ended with Florida slightly ahead of Georgia, and several commercials were subsequently squeezed in, allowing the two veteran sportscasters needed but short bio-breaks. They now scrambled to get themselves ready to broadcast as network staff buzzed around them inside the booth, helping with notes and audio/video equipment. Suddenly, it was time.

"Three, two, one, go!" The director's voice echoed in their headsets. As the commercial ended, they immediately saw their own images appear on several of the TV monitors in the booth. One of the two began speaking.

"Welcome back folks. This is Vince Lindquist along with my colleague Danny Garrison with CBS' live coverage of the Georgia-Florida game's halftime show—"

"Vince, I believe down here they call it the Florida-Georgia game—"

"That's true unless you're about thirty miles north of here. Anyway, they're just about to start University of Georgia's halftime entertainment. It looks like the Georgia Redcoat Band has lined up on their end of the field. The rest of the Georgia Band Auxiliary Units will be entering the field from the Georgia tunnel. They'll be lining up behind the band—"

"I believe that's the Flag line coming out now—"

"What a bunch of lovely young women... Amazing what they can do with those flags—"

"Here come the Georgettes—"

"I believe this is a group of young ladies that perform dance routines... Amazing what they can do with those pom poms—"

"That's right Vince... Oh, here comes the group I enjoy... the Majorettes... Amazing what these young ladies can do with those batons—"

"And finally, here come the Cheerleaders... I believe they'll line up on the Georgia sideline while the others start their routine—"

"I hear the band beginning to play right now—"

"What is that tune?"

"Sounds like that Bruno Mars song "Uptown Funk." Oh, oh what is that going on down there Vince?"

"I don't know Danny... It looks like... like several of the Kardashians. They're all wearing very tight Florida cheerleader uniforms—"

"What are the Kardashians doing in the halftime show?"

"Must be some part of halftime entertainment. You know the Kardashians... Those ladies will do anything for publicity—"

"Nobody told us about the Kardashians participating in the halftime entertainment—"

"They do look a little tight in those uniforms—"

"Way too tight. Maybe the Kardashians should look into some sort of commercial diet plan?"

"Could be an opportunity for them to do some TV commercials—"

"Wait... Looks like the Kardashians are breaking off from the Georgia cheerleaders. They're heading for the Georgia end zone—"

"Am I seeing this correctly, Danny? Did Kris Kardashian—"

"Vince, I believe she's Kris Jenner now—"

"Did Kris Jenner just rip off her uniform?!"

"Vince, you are indeed seeing correctly... and not just her... Looks like the other four just ripped their uniforms off—"

"Folks, I think we have a good old-fashioned streak going on here—"

"Emphasis on 'old.' I didn't realize the Kardashians had been around this long—"

"I don't think I've seen a good streak since the... the 1970s—"

"These streakers seem confused. Two are running for the Florida goal line at the other end of the field, while the other three are running toward the Florida sideline—"

"Can we get a camera close up of the faces of the two running for the Florida goal line?"

"Vince, I'd say that's Khloé and Kourtney Kardashian. Wouldn't you?"

"Khloé and Kourtney... but with a few extra pounds—"

"Looks like stadium security have run onto the field... Be interesting to see how many yards the Kardashians can gain on this play—"

"Danny, looks like the three heading for the Florida sideline have changed their minds and are now running across the field for the Georgia sideline—"

"Khloé and Kourtney are now waving to the other three... apparently motioning for them to follow—"

"Hey, looks like those three have changed their minds again and reversed their direction—"

"Looks like a pretty good reverse play... One of them made it to the twenty-yard line—"

"Isn't that Caitlyn Jenner?"

"Yep, it's Caitlyn... looks like he... uh she did have that surgery after all—"

"I always wondered about that—"

"Now, the other two Kardashians are heading his... I mean her way—"

"That may be a mistake. Looks like security is trying some sort of man-to-man defense on these three—"

"Vince, I don't know that man-to-man is the best terminology for how security is trying to catch these women—"

"Looks like Khloé and Kourtney are now in some sort of spread offensive formation—"

"Spread offense is probably an accurate term—"

"An in/drag play would be an appropriate play for Caitlyn to attempt on the thirty-yard line—"

"Looks like Kris, Caitlyn, and... what's the other Kardashian's name?"

"Kylie... but I believe she's actually a Jenner... not a Kardashian—"

"Right. Kris, Caitlyn, and Kylie have made it to the fifty-yard line, but security is closing fast..."

"Holy shit! Danny, am I seeing what I'm seeing?"

"I don't know what you're seeing Vince, but what I'm seeing is a man wearing some sort of Park Ranger uniform running out from the Florida sidelines, and it looks like he's carrying a live alligator—"

"What kind of play is that? Must be some sort of a fake—"

"It may be a fake play Vince, but that's no fake gator—"

"Whatever, but it looks like he's faked security off of the Kardashians—"

"That guy must be in great shape... Looks like he's carrying a five-foot long alligator—"

"Wait! He's put the alligator down and is waiting for security—"

"Security seems to have totally forgotten the streakers—"

"Kris, Caitlyn, and Kylie are at the forty-yard line, but now they seem confused—"

"Is that a tattoo I see on one of them... on Caitlyn? Can we get a camera close up?"

"You're right Danny. It is a tattoo... looks like... I must be mistaken—"

"By golly, I think it's a tattoo of Ron Paul... and a pretty good tattoo at that—"

"She must be a libertarian—"

"Either that or a refugee from a nudist camp—"

"Is there a difference?"

"Vince, our program director just told me that we need to go to a commercial break—"

"Tell Gene to kiss my ass—"

"I have to say it... These ladies can run... Caitlyn's on the Florida thirty-five-yard line—"

"Looks like security has reached the Park Ranger, but they're giving him a lot of room—"

"Look... He's making the gator roll over—"

"Now he's tickling its stomach—"

"Seems like a pretty happy gator... Look at that big smile on its face... Don't gators always have a smile on their face?"

"I notice security is still giving them a wide berth—"

"Wait, now the Park Ranger's doing something with his hands... Looks like some sort of command to the gator—"

"Danny, looks to me like he's commanding that gator to roll over again—"

"Now the gator's on his stomach... The Park Ranger is giving another command... Now, the gator's opening his mouth... wide open... Vince, looks like the Park Ranger's pulled a rubber ball out of his pocket and balanced it on the tip of the gator's nose—"

"That is certainly one talented alligator. Wonder if it also juggles? Could we get a camera close up of the patch on the Park Ranger's shoulder? Yeah, that's it. Danny, does that patch say Okefenokee Swamp Park?"

"Yes, yes it does, Vince. Oh, oh... Khloé and Kourtney seem confused... Now it looks like they're gonna try some sort of end sweep toward the Florida goal line—"

"I see more security just entered the field from the Florida side and are headed for Khloé and Kourtney—"

"Kris and Caitlyn seem to be headed back toward the Georgia goal line, but Kylie seems to be going off on her own... She's moving really slowly—"

"Looks like some of the security around the Park Ranger are breaking off from that spectacle and going for Kris and Caitlyn... Hold on Danny... You were right... Khloé and Kourtney are executing a flawless end sweep, but security is closing in—"

"They might just make it—"

"Security is closing in fast—"

"Can you tell which one is leading the way?"

"Looks like Khloé... but with a few extra wrinkles—"

"She's almost there... go, go, go!"

"Touchdown! Folks, you've just seen the first streaking touchdown in NCAA history—"

"What a beautiful play, Vince... I don't think Nick Chubb himself could have run a better sweep than Khloé—"

"Doesn't look like our heroines are gonna take time to spike the ball though... They're headed for the other side of the goal line—"

"Wait... I see Caitlyn Jenner and Kris Kardashian—"

"Danny, I believe she's still called Kris Jenner... despite Bruce's uh... Caitlyn's switch play—"

"Whatever... anyway, they're headed for the Georgia tunnel—"

"What happened to Kylie?"

"Looks like she's limping over to the Florida athletic trainers' bench on the sidelines—"

"Probably a pulled hamstring... I bet she's sidelined for the rest of the halftime—"

"Whoops! Doesn't look like Caitlyn and that other... girl are gonna make it either... yep... Security caught 'em..."

"I see that security pulled a trap play on Khloé and Kourtney just behind the Florida goal post... looks like Khloé and Kourtney are going down... uh, uh... not in the way you think I mean—"

"Vince, I see security escorting the Park Ranger and his gator companion off the field—"

"I'm sorry to say Danny, but it looks like some of the best halftime entertainment I've ever seen is over. Back to our sponsors."

Chapter 28

"We can't do that!" Although not in a position to make demands, Daffy did anyway. A uniformed female stood before them, shoulders back, hands on hips, pant creases sharp enough to cut paper. Even more ominous looking was her drop fade crew cut, which met Duval County Sheriff's Office grooming regulations and then some. Officer Ronnie meant business, especially inside her jail and especially the night of the World's Largest Outdoor Cocktail Party. Anyone with half a brain could tell that.

She said, "Hon, either y'all take it off, or I'm gonna take it off for y'all. And if I do it, it ain't gonna be nearly as pleasant as when y'all do it."

"But... but..." Daffy pleaded.

"But we've never had mugshots taken without our makeup on," Lizzie said. Her comment derived from consensus during the paddy wagon ride that keeping their Kardashian makeup on would facilitate their anonymity. Go figure.

Officer Ronnie rolled her eyes at the pitiful excuse. She had worked seven years as a Booking Officer in the Pre-Trial Detention Facility in downtown Jacksonville. The tough police woman thought she had heard it all until she heard Lizzie's excuse. "Ladies, all women's mugshots in Duval County are taken without makeup. That's policy. There's pre-moistened towelettes in that container over there. Now start taking it off."

"Awright, but our mugshots always turn out awful with no makeup." Lilly's frown made Grumpy Cat look happy. She reached for a towelette.

"I still have nightmares about my last mugshot," Daffy said as she grabbed a towelette and began wiping. Her comment triggered a bitch session.

Gidget said, "My last mugshot was worse than Heather Locklear's mugshot."

"No one's mugshot is worse than Heather Locklear's mugshot," Lilly said.

Babs disagreed. "Uh-uh…hers don't even come close to Reese Witherspoon's."

"Paris Hilton's mugshot does," Lizzie said as she wiped the last vestiges of Kourtney Kardashian off her face. "I look at it whenever I want to feel good about myself."

Mugshots represented Step Two of the Facility Intake Process. Having removed all resemblance to the youngest Kardashian, Lilly was first to have her photograph taken. Officer Ronnie snapped a front-view. "That looked good, Hon. Now, turn to the right so I can get your side-view photo."

"Do I have to? My right side's my worst."

"In Duval County, we always take 'em from the right side."

"Officer Ronnie, my left side photographs much better. Please?"

"Right side, Hon."

"But the FBI took 'em from the left side. Why can't y'all?"

Decorum requires deleting Officer Ronnie's reply.

The next step went a lot better. Step Three, Taking Suspect's Clothing and Personal Property Into Custody, posed little problem as they had no clothes or other personal property on them. Each was wrapped in a towel, provided by stadium security. These were exchanged for orange jumpsuits.

Step Four proved more problematic.

"Okay Ladies, time for fingerprints," Officer Ronnie said.

Gidget looked at Daffy. "I told you they'd take our fingerprints."

Daffy glared at Gidget, smiled at Officer Ronnie, and slathered on her best Southern Lady accent. "Officer Ronnie... ain't there no way we can get out of having our fingerprints taken?"

"Hon, we gotta have your fingerprints."

"Couldn't y'all use the ones on file with the FBI instead? They probably still got 'em, and I understand that a person's fingerprints don't change with age." Daffy batted her eyelashes.

"Hon, why don't y'all want your fingerprints taken? It don't hurt."

"Ohhh, Officer Ronnie, I know it don't hurt, but we all had our manicures just this morning, and we don't wanna mess 'em up."

After a good belly laugh, Officer Ronnie said, "Hon, I don't know how the FBI did your fingerprints, but we don't use the old inking technique. It's all digital now. You put your finger on a scanner, and it takes a digital picture. Just like your iPhone does."

Step Five, Conducting a Full Body Search proved as problematic as Step Four.

"Okay, Ladies..." Officer Ronnie smiled as she inserted her hands into a pair of latex gloves. "Gotta search y'all."

"Why you puttin' on them gloves, Officer Ronnie?" asked Gidget. "You already saw us naked."

"Hon, it has to be full body, including cavity searches."

"I just had a Pap Smear about three months ago," Lizzie said. Nothing ventured, nothing gained.

"Just think of me as one of your old boyfriends and enjoy it."

At the conclusion of her search, Babs leaned close to Daffy and whispered, "I think Officer Ronnie enjoyed that more than any of my old boyfriends ever did."

In Step Six, Officer Ronnie performed a computer search for outstanding arrest warrants and previous arrests.

"Ladies, maybe y'all can help me understand something."

"We'll try," Daffy said.

"I see from the search that all five of y'all have had previous uh... shall we say 'encounters' with the FBI. I'm not sure what they are as they're not listed as arrests. Your records are sealed. Only someone much higher up the food chain than me can gain access."

Five shrugs greeted Officer Ronnie's observations.

"Can y'all enlighten me as to what was involved in these encounters with the FBI?" Officer Ronnie asked.

"We wanna be as helpful as we can," Daffy said. "Which encounters are you talking about?"

"The first one is from several years ago... 2013. What was that about?"

"Oh, that... that was just a stupid mistake... accidentally pushing the wrong buttons... some sort of problem with a German pipeline."

"Uh huh... What about this illegal gambling charge that was dismissed?"

"That was only the state of Georgia playing Bunko nanny. Daffy's lawyer took care of that one real quick," Gidget said.

"Uh huh... What about this FBI encounter several weeks ago?"

"Why is that in there?" Lilly asked. "I thought Babs old boyfriend was gonna take care of that."

Officer Ronnie stood still, arms crossed, tapping her foot.

"It really was nothing at all," Lizzie said. "Facebook crashed, and they blamed it on Lilly and us, but then they realized it was just a simple uh... What was the word that CIA man used? Oh yeah, he said it was some sort of 'backdoor code' problem or something like that."

"Okaaay, I think we'll go on to the next step. Hold on for a minute while I pull up the Health Screening Questionnaire. We'll start with Mrs. Neauxgeaux. Okay, we got your height from the mugshot... 5' 2"..."

"Oh, my goodness! I've grown an inch shorter," Babs said.

Daffy rubbed Babs' shoulder. "Happens kiddo. We all lose bone mass as we get older."

"Why couldn't it have been fat mass instead?"

"Please step over to the scale so I can get your weight," Officer Ronnie said.

"Do I have to? Can't I just tell you what my weight is?" Babs asked.

After a short negotiation, Babs' actual weight, as well as some other general physical characteristics, were recorded.

"Okay. Now, I need to get a summary of your significant medical history. First question: have you had, or do you have any STDs?"

"STDs? What do y'all mean?"

Lizzie shook her head. "Babs, you know what STDs is... the Clap... Syphilis."

Babs lowered her head and whispered, "Not since college..."

Officer Ronnie bit her tongue and continued. "Any current medical problems?"

"Do I have any current medical problems? Where do I begin? First is my diabetes... type two... It ain't easy for a short gal like me to keep her weight down you know...I was taking Januvia, but it just wasn't doing the job, so Doctor Fischel switched me to Jardiance, which is much better... My A1C runs about 6.1, 6.2 now... but now my blood pressure's bumped up... low 140s over low 90s, so he's increased my Losartin to 100 milligrams... and my seasonal allergies are giving me fits right now... September and October are my worse months... pine pollen. I know what they say about pine pollen not causing allergies and pine trees pollinating in the spring, not fall, but something's pollinating now, and it's giving me hell... I've been talking with Doctor Fischel about seeing an allergist... but that ain't nothing compared to the hell I got in my knee. Doctor Fischel says that probably nothing short of a knee replacement is gonna take care of it... No way am I gonna get started on that... that... What's that arthritis medication they keep advertising?"

"That's enough... I can't type that fast anyway. Let's take Mzz Sherbert next."

"You sure you got enough time?" asked Lizzie.

Several hours later, Officer Ronnie escorted the five Ladies to a holding cell.

"Welcome to Duval Penal Motel." Smiling at her witticism, Officer Ronnie flamboyantly swung the cell door open and motioned for them to enter. "It'll be a couple of hours before the Sheriff or one of his deputies can come here to talk to y'all about next steps. They're very busy tonight with the aftermath of the Florida-Georgia game."

"Don't we get a phone call?" Gidget asked.

"Five phone calls. One for each of us," Daffy said.

"Prison cons always get a phone call when they're arrested on them TV crime shows..." Lilly paused, deep in thought. "We *were* on TV this afternoon."

"They'll talk about your phone call arrangements when they come here to talk to y'all. Bye now. Don't get into any trouble with any of these other ladies. They got seniority on y'all." Officer Ronnie closed and locked the cell door and walked away.

Standing frozen inside the cell, the Ladies surveyed their environment. Picture a large rectangular room. One side consists of floor-to-ceiling, grimy prison bars and a wire-mesh door. The other three sides are brick walls, painted a sick pea-green color and adorned with sexually explicit graffiti. Cream-colored metal benches, attached to the walls and spotted with rust, line three sides of the room. A corner of the cell houses a grungy stainless-steel toilet and sink combo also attached to the wall. The floors are dingy, unpainted concrete, hard and cold-looking, as is the ceiling. Three overhead fluorescent fixtures provide lighting, although several burned out bulbs result in a dark, yellowish gloom throughout the cell. In this picture of nastiness, thirteen women of various ethnicities either sit or recline.

A large black woman with tattoos on her neck and arms and ample body piercings walked up to them. She said, "Lookee here... bunch a raw meat."

Several other inmates laughed. One, a tall dark-skinned woman, rose ominously. She closed in and began slowly circling, as if stalking them. A sly grin spread across her face. "Don't y'all worry. Kanesha don't mean y'all no harm."

A dark haired, olive-skinned woman, reclining on one of the benches, chuckled and raised her head slightly. She spoke slowly with a Hispanic accent that blared overacting. "Doan woorry *gringas*. We goan take reeel goood care a ju."

Chapter 29

"Oh... y'all don't know how good that makes me feel to hear y'all say that." Lilly placed her palms together, fingertips touching her chin, in an unconscious prayer-of-thanks gesture. "All the way over here in that awful paddy wagon we worried about what this jail might be like."

Lizzie swiveled her head, surveilling the cell. She said, "Looks like our worries weren't unfounded."

The scene in the paddy wagon went something like this.

"This has got to be the bumpiest ride..." Daffy immediately bounced two inches off her seat as the vehicle hit another pothole. "Almost as bad as riding on Mississippi county roads."

"I hope they feed us something when we get to the jail. My blood sugar's gettin' low," Babs said.

"I told you we should've grabbed a couple of chili dogs on the way over to the Georgia side." Lizzie pursed her lips. "We probably ain't gonna eat for hours."

Gidget fidgeted. "Eating's the last of my problems right now. I gotta pee."

"Me too... Wish I hadn't drunk all that beer," Lilly said.

"Do what you did in high school when you had to pee. Sit on your foot."

"Which one?"

"Try 'em both," Lizzie said. "That way you can also get in a little yoga."

"I hope they have clean bathrooms in the Jacksonville jail. The bathroom in the Thomasville jail was horrible, just horrible."

"Clean bathrooms in a jail. Get real. Just remember to hover over the toilet," Gidget said.

At this point, laughter from other inmates interrupted the Casserole Ladies' story. Kanesha said, "Honey, y'all better do more than hover your sorry white asses over these here toilets. Y'all better fly over 'em."

The inmate slowly circling them started flapping her arms in an attempt to imitate a bird in flight. She suddenly stopped, eyed them up and down, and hurled insults. "Bunch a honkies... trailer park white trash... Look like bunch a wrinkled ole Paris Hiltons escape from a nursing home. How'd y'all get orange jump suits? Y'all ain't suppose get them 'til y'all get outta this here holdin' cell. Aren't we special?"

"Special?" This comment came from a young woman, early twenties, with hair dyed hot pink. Her affected valley girl line was pure Alicia Silverstone in *Clueless*. Apparently, young people in Florida are little behind California. "Ya know, like the only thing special about them is like, ya know, they look especially old."

Another olive-skinned woman said, "You better fly *reeel* high over theees heeer toilets. Theees crabs know how to joomp."

Lilly's eyes became saucers. "Crabs in the toilets here! How did they get in? From the Atlantic?"

"Lilly, she ain't talking about ocean crabs. She's talking about sexually transmitted diseases... STDs... like HIV and syphilis. The kind've crabs she's talking about are like lice, but they're also an STD," Gidget said.

"Lilly's a little naïve sometimes," Daffy said as she put her arm protectively around her teammate and smiled at their newfound cellmates.

A black cellmate wide as a 20 cubic foot refrigerator said, "Sounds like y'all didn't like your ride over here. Your prom be y'all don't got no booty to sit on. What be your paddy wagon nummer?"

Daffy shrugged.

"If it was 2341, then ju got the worst ride of any of Duval County paddy wagons. Trust me. I been in them all." This came from the woman that made the previous 'gringas' comment.

"It smelled terrible..." Lilly scrunched her nose. "Like dog poop."

"That was 2341. Ju don't like dog sheet?"

A twentysomething with boobs spilling out of an orange halter top and wearing tight hot pink shorts sat up. "You are like, so right about roads in Mississippi. They are like totally uncool."

"Y'all been to Mississippi?" Lizzie asked.

"Oh yaaaas... I like, practically grew up in Cleveland, Mississippi."

"Awright! Only college` town I ever been to without a Waffle House... tough town to have a hangover in. Delta State... home of the Fighting Okra."

"Fightin' Okra?" Another cellmate asked.

"Yaaaas." Orange Halter Top giggled. "That's like, Delta State's bitchin' mascot."

Laughter erupted throughout the holding cell. After it subsided, the woman who had been previously circling them suddenly stopped. She asked, "What be y'alls' names?"

"My name's Daffy. This here's Babs, Gidget, Lilly, and Lizzie."

"Y'all make room for these here women." She began shooing some of those seated out of the way. "My name's Brianna, and that's Latonya, Ebony, Isabella..."

Latonya and Ebony remained motionless, while Isabella raised her hand in greeting.

Lilly smiled at Isabella and said, "Thank y'all again for offering to take care of us. We ain't been in jail very many times before."

"No problema..."

Brianna continued, pointing to the woman with pink hair. "Michelle, but we call her 'Pink.'"

Lizzie eyed Michelle's hair closely. "Y'all have to get some sort of EPA permit to do that?"

Pink arched her eyebrows and shrugged her shoulders, revealing some level of incomprehension.

Brianna pointed to another woman. "Jada—"

"Jada!" Lilly's face lit up. "What a beautiful name. Is that your real name or nickname?"

"That my name. Do I look like a Nick?"

Brianna pointed to the large black woman who had asked them about the number of their paddy wagon. "Y'all already met Frigerator. Bet y'all can't guess why we call her that."

"Cause I'm so cold..." Frigerator stood, glared at Brianna, and advanced toward her in a confrontational manner.

"Frigerator..." Babs jumped between the two. "Don't y'all let anyone get under y'all's skin about y'all's weight. Honey, I been fat myself all my life, and I finally figured out just to tell anyone that don't like it to go to hell."

Mollified, Frigerator smiled at Babs' and sat back down, allowing Biranna to finish her introductions. She pointed to three women sitting together. "Luisa, Juanita... Y'all already met Peggy..."

Orange Halter Top nodded.

Brianna pointed to two others and said, "Angie and Delphine."

"We are so pleased to meet y'all," Daffy said. "Officer Ronnie said y'all been here a while."

"Hmmp!" Juanita shook her head. "This happens every time they have a big game. Takes forever to get everyone processed. What's a bunch a *gringas* like ju in here for?"

"They caught us at the Georgia-Florida game—"

"Florida-Georgia," Ebony said.

Peggy looked closely at the Ladies, then at Angie. She shrugged. Peggy turned to Daffy and said, "Like, Angie and I didn't see ya there."

Angie said, "*Yaaas*... They must've like, been on the Georgia side of the stadium. That side don't pay like, nearly as good as the Florida side, ya know."

"No, we sat on the Florida side. Where were y'all sitting?" asked Daffy.

"We wasn't inside. We was like, outside. Me and Peggy was like, trying to get some bag."

"Huh?"

"Like, ya know... get some money... so we was like, hustling johns outside the stadium, but we got, like caught. Isn't that what they like, caught ya doing?"

"*Noooo...*" Daffy declined to elaborate further.

"Y'all must be... y'all are in here because..." Lilly hesitated to voice her conclusion.

"Lilly, these ladies are... shall we say 'working girls,' 'ladies of the night,'" Lizzie said.

Angie said, "*Yaaas*, that's it. Half of us in this cell are—"

"Some of us ain't." Ebony stiffened. "Some of us work in massage parlors."

"Same thing—"

"No, it ain't. I be a professional. Don't have to put my booty out on no street."

"So, who in here ain't prostitutes?" Gidget asked.

Brianna surveyed her cellmates. "Hmm... me, Butterfly... we in for drugs, Pink's in for drugs, Isabella's in for assault... Frigerator, y'all in for assault this time, ain't y'all?"

"Y'all got that right. I put that muthafucka in the hospital six weeks this time."

"Who?" Daffy asked.

"That lazy-ass, no-count boyfriend of mine. He ain't gonna run around on me again for a *reeel* long time."

"What about you Delphine?" Babs asked. "What're you in for?"

Delphine responded with an accent possessing a distinct Caribbean lilt. She said, "Eeet twaz kind of coompleecateed... and unfortunately, eeet twaz also kind of eelleegal."

Kanesha looked at the Casserole Ladies and asked, "If they didn't arrest y'all for turnin' tricks, what did they arrest y'all for?"

"They caught us streaking during halftime," Gidget said.

Blank stares resulted. Juanita asked, "Streaking? What's that?"

"Y'all don't know what streaking is?" Lilly asked.

"Juanita looks kind've young," Lizzie said. "Before her time."

"Streaking is when you take off all your clothes and run nekkid at a sporting event." A big smile adorned Babs' face as she explained. This drew raucous laughter from the other inmates.

"Awriiiight..." Angie high-fived Babs. "Like, ya know, that sounds like, awesome."

Juanita seemed to disagree. She asked, "Why ju do a dumb thing like that?"

"I... we lost a bet..." Daffy again hesitated to elaborate.

"Wha ju bet about? Who gonna win Florida-Georgia game?"

"No, not that. Someone insulted my granddaughter."

"Like, you got a granddaughter?" Angie asked.

"Yeah... four of 'em, and five grandsons, three daughters and two sons," Daffy said. "Anyway, we bet my granddaughter would beat the granddaughter of the woman who insulted her in a dance contest."

Kanesha asked, "If your grandchild doesn't win, then all y'all got to run nekkid at halftime? Right?"

"Yeah."

"All y'all make same bet?"

All five Ladies nodded. Brianna, visibly impressed, looked at Daffy. "Y'all sure got good friends."

"Why all y'all make that bet if only her grandchild insulted?" Ebony asked.

The Ladies looked at each other, then Lizzie said, "We're all grannies. An insult to one is an insult to grannies everywhere."

Babs nodded. "Besides, the women that insulted Tara are a bunch of assholes."

All the cellmates laughed at Babs' characterization.

Lilly said, "We always stick together."

"Why?" Frigerator asked.

"That's a good question. I never thought about that." Daffy folded her arms and scrunched her face. "We really enjoy being with each other. We're all widows... almost all of us anyway. We have a lot in common, foremost of which is we're all looking for the same thing. Men. Romance. Male companionship."

"Why the hell y'all lookin' for men? The ones I know ain't nothin' but no-count no-good-for-nothin's anyways. Most us in this here jail live without 'em, and we be doing just fine. What y'all need men for anyway?"

Chapter 30

"What do we need men for?!" Lilly shrieked in reply to Frigerator's question. "For true love, of course. I need a man I can love completely and can love me back completely. That's the way for a gal to be truly happy."

"You just need to get laid, that's all," Frigerator said.

"You ever think about gettin' with the times and usin' some new technology?" Latonya asked. "I get me johns all time off Facebook. I post my times and where I be that day, and they come runnin'. Try usin' Facebook to find men."

"Yeah, I use Facebook all the time for drug deals," Brianna said.

Lilly nodded. "I did. I set up a Thomasville Widows' Facebook Page for the five of us hoping that would put us in touch with men. It was a disaster. Then, I tried using it on my own to find men, but that turned into another disaster."

"What happened?" Isabella asked. "Didn't ju find any men?"

"No, but I did find out how people use social media to offend other people," Lilly said. She then proceeded to amuse her cellmates with some of her Facebook confrontations. Here is one:

Mary Bevis is at Tockwotton Historic District Neighborhood

September 14th Thomasville, GA

Small brown dachshund ran through my yard this morning and LEFT ME A PRESENT…….again!

View 12 more comments

Lilly White Tell me about it. Otto pees on my begonias all the time and has destroyed three of them. Thank God he's not a bigger dog, or my hydrangeas would be toast.

Cindy Nelson Otto slipped out. It happens. Dog poop isn't the end of the world. I guess some people just don't have a life. At least I don't let my grandchildren ride their bikes in my neighbors' yards.

Lilly White Sammy and Johnny weren't in your yard very long. Just cutting through.

Penny Perdoo My lawn LOOKS LIKE A DIRT RACE-TRACK from the bicycle path those two have worn in my grass!

Lilly White What grass? Your yard is nothing but a bunch of dollar weeds. As long as we're talking obnoxious, how about TURNING DOWN THE VOLUME ON YOUR MUSIC? Or, at least play something different. I'm getting tired of hearing The Pina Colada song over and over.

Judy Davis.........and over and over and over......... I never want to hear that song again.

Cathy Verdun Since we're complaining about obnoxious neighbors, I'm tired of monitoring Lilly White's garbage cans every Thursday. Someone needs to make sure that LIDS ON HER GARBAGE CANS ARE CLOSED. Smell is awful and Lilly's garbage blows out onto my yard in heavy wind.

Lilly White You're one to be talking about heavy wind!

Penny Perdoo It would be nice if she'd roll her cans back after the garbage man's visit instead of leaving them out all day for all to see.

Lori Snipes I would be happy if Lilly would just start PARK-ING HER MERCEDES IN HER GARAGE instead of leaving it in her driveway all the time. Her driveway looks like a Walmart parking lot.

Lilly White At least my Mercedes is PAID FOR.

Lori Snipes My Lincoln is paid for! And if you're going to keep parking your Mercedes out front, at least WASH IT ONCE IN A WHILE. What color is it anyway?

Lilly concluded with a vow. "No more technology for me. That includes Internet dating, sexbots, and Facebook. I'll find men the old-fashioned way."

"How so?" Kanesha asked.

Lilly seemed stumped, so she simply put her arms around Lizzie and Babs. "I guess with help from my friends."

"Shit, you don't need to find men anyway with friends like them."

"What about you?" Brianna looked at Babs. "You be like Lilly... lookin' for men?"

Babs nodded.

"Why?"

"Oh, I want a someone I can take care of... just like I did Avery. I miss taking care of him... cooking his meals, washing his clothes, massaging his back when he pulled a muscle—"

"Sounds like you just be his slave."

"Oh no. It wasn't anything like that. I loved doing them things for him. I want someone else that I can take care of again."

"What about Sonny Biskit?" Lizzie mischievously asked. "You took care of him the other night, didn't you?"

"Don't remind me..." Babs shook her head.

"Remind ju of what?" Luisa asked.

"My mercy hump."

Luisa began snickering. "I do that all the time for my *juans*."

With her cellmates' curiosity aroused, all eyes focused on Babs as she related her trip with Sonny to the Waycross tractor pull.

"Hey Sugar," Sonny Biskit whispered as he snuggled close. "It's starting to work."

"What's starting to work?" Babs tried to move away, but there was limited room on the crowded bench.

"My Viagra."

"Your Viagra?! When did you take Viagra?"

"Shhh, not so loud. I popped one when I went to pee."

That occurred thirty minutes prior.

"Why the hell you do that? This tractor pull ain't even half ways over. You could've at least waited till the ride back to Thomasville."

Sonny began rubbing Babs' lower back. He cooed, "Honey, it's starting to hurt... real bad..."

"Ohhh... Can't y'all wait at least until after the Frankenstein makes a run? I don't wanna miss seein' that machine—"

"It's starting to hurt... real bad..."

Thirty minutes later, they lay exhausted and semi-naked in the back of Bab's Escalade, parked at the Waycross Motor Speedway.

"I can't believe I actually did that." Babs' complained, mostly to herself, as she buttoned her blouse. "Sixty-three-years old and having to screw in the back of a SUV in a dirt parking lot... at a damn racetrack no less! I ain't come very far since high school. You owe me big time for this!"

Sonny struggled to reinsert himself in his pants.

"Uh... uh Honey, it ain't going down."

"Okaaay... We just need to wait a few minutes. This used to happen to Avery every so often."

Ten minutes and several of Babs' rambling stories later, Sonny updated Babs.

"Babsie, it still ain't gone down..."

"Damn. It's too late to see Frankenstein make a run anyway. I heard the engine revving up while we were right in the middle of things."

"That weren't no Frankenstein... It was me."

Ten minutes and several more of Babs' stories later, Sonny updated Babs.

"It still ain't gone down..."

"Yeah, and looks like folks are starting to leave. We better get outta here ourselves."

"What we gonna do?"

"Drive back to Thomasville."

"What if it don't go down by then?"

"Then I'll drop you off at the Medical Center. The ER will still be open."

"I can't go in there. It'll be all over Thomasville if I go in there."

Fifteen minutes later, Babs escorted a bent-over Sonny into the Emergency Room in Waycross.

Chapter 31

"What a line..." Kanesha chuckled. "That weren't no Frankenstein... It was me."

"How long was his dick hard?" Juanita asked.

"Almost four hours," Babs admitted. "Just like they say in the commercials."

Juanita nodded but said no more. Contemplating previous Viagra encounters herself?

"Yeah... that happens to a couple of my older johns." Ebony's comment elicited head nods from several other inmates. "I just say to them, 'think about your wife'. That makes that hard go way *reeel* quick."

After the laughter subsided, Frigerator asked Babs, "You like tractor pulls?"

"Yeah... I love 'em."

"Me too. I seen Frankenstein at Daytona last year. That's one muthafuckin' machine."

"I met my second or third husband at a tractor pull," Lizzie said. She rolled her eyes. "Talk about love at first sight."

Frigerator looked at Babs and asked, "You still be humpin' this Sonny Biskit? Sounds like he's doin' all the gettin' and none a the givin'. But that's the way it is with most men."

Babs shook her head. "Not anymore."

"Yeah, next time Babsie'll make Sonny pay for his own ticket to the tractor pull," Lizzie said.

Frigerator shook her head and turned to Gidget. She asked, "What about you? You don't wanna get tangled up again with some man, do you? I know you be doin' just fine on your own without a no-count no-good-for-nothin man. You ain't be looking for no man, are you?"

Embarrassed, Gidget lowered her head and nodded.

"Why?"

"I just want a male companion. I miss Sam's companionship. Someone to be with, to talk to, to listen to, to share what's going on in my life with—"

"Git a dog," Isabella said.

"Ain't ya got like, no TV? No video games?" Pink asked.

Peggy said, "Like, get a pen pal. Like, I write my pen pal all the time... 'cept it's like, we actually text each other instead of actually like, writing..."

"I did have a pen pal one time." A wistful expression appeared on Gidget's face. "It was a prison pen pal—"

"Y'all got a prison pen pal?" Brianna asked. "I had me a pen pal last time I be in prison. Got 'em through Meet-an-Inmate.com."

"Yeah, that's the site I used. It was about two years ago. Sam had been dead for six or seven months, and I missed having someone to talk to," Gidget said.

"You could've talked to us," Babs whined.

"I talk with y'all all the time. It ain't the same..." Talk about understatement. It's like the difference between talking to a psychiatrist or talking to a tree surgeon. Gidget continued, "Anyway, I was working with a Libertarian Party advocacy group for prison reform."

"Prison reform?" Kanesha asked. "Corrine Brown always be talkin' about that... before she be hauled off to prison."

"I'm sure. Anyway, Libertarians think the current criminal justice system is flawed—disproportionate punishments for crimes, poor quality of life in prisons, and so forth. It's something I was working on when I heard about the Prison Pen Pal Program, and I thought, 'What a wonderful way to help disadvantaged people, and I might even find some sort of companionship.' Didn't quite work out that way though."

July 13, 2017
Dear Raphael,

I write to introduce myself. My name is Gloria Smurfitt. I got your name through Meet-an-Inmate.com and contacted the Warden at Hancock to receive permission to write to you. I am a widow and live in Thomasville, Georgia. Forgive my bad handwriting, but I've been a registered pharmacist for almost forty years, and reading physicians' prescriptions for that long has taken its toll on my penmanship. (Ha! Ha! Just a little pharmaceutical humor!) Anyway, let me know if you prefer, and I can type my letters instead of handwriting them, although I feel a handwritten letter is a much more personal way to communicate.

I mention that I am a widow. My husband, Sam, who was also a pharmacist, died six months ago. We owned, and I now own, a local pharmacy here in Thomasville. It's a good pharmacy, but the big boys like CVS and Walgreens have been giving us a lot of competition. It's getting even worse now that all the grocery stores have opened pharmacies inside their facilities.

Let me know if you would like for us to write to each other.
Sincerely,
Gloria Smurfitt

August 23, 2017
Dear Rafael,

I haven't received a response from you to my first letter, so I thought I'd write a second one. I got a notification that the cake I sent you was delivered to Hancock State Prison. Or, maybe I should say 'had someone else send you'. I am a vegan. At least I've been one for about two weeks now. I'm trying to improve my nutritional posture, and I don't like to cook, so I've been getting my meals delivered to my home through a vegan meal delivery plan. The one I just started using is called Vegan Chef Express, and that's where your cake came from. They specialize in vegan meals. Let me know what you think of their baking.

Sincerely,

Gloria Smurfitt

Gloria,

Got both leters. Canot get food in mail here but thx anyway.

Raphael

September 15, 2017

Dear Rafael,

Oops! My bad! Is there anything else that you can receive in prison that I could send? Books? Magazines? Puzzles? Games?

It was nice to hear from you. I hope you are doing well.

Sincerely,

Gloria

Gloria,

Magazins be nic. Playboy ok but Hustler purfurd.

Raphael

October 2, 2017

Dear Rafael,

I would love to be able to get you a subscription to one of the magazines you requested. As a libertarian, I strongly believe in the First Amendment, specifically our right to freedom of the press. Anyone, even a prisoner such as yourself, should be able to read anything he or she wants to read, as long as it does not abridge the rights of others or involve underage minors.

Unfortunately, I find myself in somewhat of a predicament as to how to fulfill your request to receive Playboy or Hustler magazine. The specific problem is how to subscribe. I attempted to subscribe to Hustler online and received a 'This site can't be reached' message. I'm not sure whether or not this resulted from the blocking software on my pharmacy's computer. I would like to ask the technician that supports our computers, but I'm sure you can understand that this might prove to be embarrassing.

I also attempted to subscribe to Playboy for you but halfway through the process realized that I would be required to use my credit card to pay for the subscription. I don't know if you are aware that many Federal agencies use credit card information to monitor 'certain activities' of United States citizens. The Libertarian Party has vigorously opposed this type of unwarranted surveillance by our Federal government. Unfortunately, it still continues. For this reason, I prefer not to use my credit card to subscribe to Playboy for you.

I did think about simply buying you a copy of either magazine as my pharmacy does sell them, but then I realized that my employees would become aware that I am purchasing a soft-porn magazine. In a small town like Thomasville, that would soon become big news. Ditto if I tried to purchase them at a nearby Cousin Cootie's.

I will purchase one on my next out-of-town trip and mail it to you. If you receive a plain brown cylindrical package with no return address, do not throw it out as it may be from me and contain one of your two requested magazines.

Sincerely,

Gloria

Office of the Warden
Hancock State Prison
701 Prison Blvd
Sparta, GA 31087
November 6, 2017
Dear Mrs. Smurfitt:

I write to inform you that Rafael Berroya will be unable to receive correspondence from you for the foreseeable future due to his being assigned to solitary confinement for repeated instances of violation of Inmate Rules and Regulations, to wit, Disrupting the Count. Please note that this is a Level 2 (Medium) Violation and subject to up to sixty days solitary confinement. Any letters you should send will be held until prisoner is returned to the general prison population.

Thank you for participating in the Georgia Department of Corrections Prison Pen Pals Program.

Sincerely,

Odell E. Trimm, CCP, CCE

Associate Warden

"I didn't know you was a vegan." Babs arched her eyebrows in surprise.

"Not any more... It only lasted a month."

"What y'all mean vegan?" Frigerator asked.

"That's someone that don't eat no meat," Lizzie said.

"Don't eat no meat?! Why the hell y'all wanna do that?!"

"It was a kind've a fad in Thomasville a couple of years back..." Gidget rolled her eyes. "Needless to say, I learned my lesson."

"What is 'Disrupting the Count' anyways?" Lilly asked.

"That be when they takin' roll call to count the number of prisoners," Latonya said, "and someone doesn't reply to her name like they want y'all to. We be do that all time just to fuck with the guards."

"So, what happen to ju prison pen pal?" Luisa asked.

"Last I heard, he's running for a seat in the Georgia General Assembly. I never heard from him again after I got Mr. Trimm's letter."

Latonya shook her head. "Sounds like my last boyfriend after my welfare run out. Just another reason why it be no good to depend on men for companionship. Can't depend on most of 'em for nothing."

"No, certainly not like we depend each other." Gidget looked at the other Casserole Ladies.

"What about y'all Daffy?" Ebony asked. "Why y'all wanna get tangle up with a man?"

"That's an easy answer." A sly grin spread over Daffy's face. "Sex. It's about the only thing men are any good for anyway. Other than opening jars."

Her comment was followed by universal head nods and a chorus of "Amens".

Daffy looked at her companions and teared up. "These are my best friends. Despite Royce's faults, I don't know how I'd have made it without them after he died."

"Same for me after Sam died." Gidget wrapped her arms around Daffy as both shared a moment of close friendship.

After regaining her composure, Daffy said, "But to answer Ebony's question, Royce was an asshole, but he did take care of my needs occasionally—"

"Sounds like any of my four husbands. Especially the asshole part," Lizzie said.

"As I was about to say, that's why I'm looking for another man. For sex. It was especially hard on me the first year after Royce died. We hadn't had sex for a *looong* time before he died, but I didn't want to get involved with another man, especially one in Thomasville. But I needed a... an outlet. Y'all know what I'm talking about. So, I thought I'd try... something a little different... something that I knew others had tried before me."

Daffy's story about that 'something' astonished all seventeen of her cellmates.

Chapter 32

"Heeey y'aaall. This here's Daisy. What's y'all's name?"

"Uh, uh, uh..."

I knew right off the bat that this guy had not done this very much before tonight. As if I had. He was definitely a virgin at this sort of thing. I tried to remember my training. What to say next? Oh yeah!

"Y'all sound kind've cute. I bet y'all drive the ladies wild..."

"Uh, yeah..."

"So, what do I call y'all? I know y'all got a name."

"Uh... John..."

Talk about no imagination. They all use that name.

"Well, John... what y'all got in mind?"

I always disguised my voice like that. I don't know why. My trainer told me it was unnecessary, but I disguised it anyway. I guess it was because I was still new at this. It was a good thing I did this time.

"I... I uh don't really know... What do y'all suggest?"

Definitely a virgin. I pulled out my training manual and quickly turned to page three, 'How to Handle an Inexperienced Caller.'

"John, I think I should tell y'all what I'm wearing. Would y'all like that?"

"Uh... yeah, sure..."

"I'm wearing a see-through teddy. Y'all know what a teddy is, don'cha John?"

"Uh... sure..."

"So, John... what would y'all like to do to me?"

Peggy interrupted Daffy's story at this point.

"Like, hold on Daffy. I like, know where your story's going, and I'm like, having difficulty believing it. You were like, doing phone sex. Right?"

"Bingo!"

"*Yaaas...* I like, do phone sex like, on the side, ya know... like, when things is kinda going slow on the street." Angie nodded.

"Yeah, most us does." Kanesha said. Other heads began nodding. "We have to. That's why I can't believe you do phone sex for bank. Why you do it?"

"Yeah... why?" Lilly asked, her 'deer in the headlights' facial expression mirrored throughout the holding cell. "I hope you took precautions."

"Lilly, what do you mean? What kind of precautions?" Lizzie asked.

"Precautions against things like them STDs... You know... HIV and syphilis... stuff like that."

"Lilly, you can't catch HIV and syphilis from phone sex," Gidget said.

"Ohhhhh..." A long, thoughtful pause preceded Lilly's next words. "So, why did you do it?"

"I didn't do it for money. I'd been a widow for a year and no sex for two years before that. I needed something, but like I said, I just didn't want to get involved physically with a man at that time. I thought it might be a way of... getting some satisfaction. Hey, it worked for Bill Clinton."

"How long did you do it?" Babs asked.

"Only a couple of months... maybe two."

Juanita's eyes narrowed as she posed a question revealing her suspicion that something was just not right. "Why did ju quit?"

"Because of the call I'm telling y'all about now."

I was disguising my voice, but John was not, and he sounded vaguely familiar.

"I'd love to see y'all all nekkid, Daisy. Maybe we could do a FaceTime sometime..."

We talked some more. He kept getting more and more graphic in his description of things we could do via FaceTime. As he talked, it clicked. I recognized his voice."

The holding cell was absolutely quiet with blank stares until Lizzie spoke. "Don't tell me. It was my fourth husband. Some of that stuff he wanted to do with you sounded familiar. That asshole tried to talk me into doing 'em with him, but I told him I weren't that sick."

Daffy nodded her agreement with Lizzie's conclusion but avoided looking at her. "I've carried the knowledge of that phone call since 2015, and I can't stand it any longer. One of my dearest friend's husbands..."

"I get phone calls all the time from *esposos*. They just lookin' for something different," Luisa said.

"*Yaaas*... like, ya know... that's just what men do. Like, sex is just sex for men, ya know," Pink said. "Ya know, like sex for men ain't the same thing as what it is for women." Except maybe in Daffy's case.

Daffy took Lizzie's hand. She said, "I hope you can forgive me."

"That's okay, Daff." Lizzie put on a look of disgust that would have upstaged the one worn by Meryl Streep throughout the movie *The Devil Wears Prada*. "I never liked the pervert anyway."

"But, you love him when you marry him, didn't you?" Lotonya asked, looking at Lizzie.

"No, not really..."

Luisa asked, "So, why ju marry him if ju don't like him?"

"Why y'all think? Why'd I marry any of the four of the jerks I married? Why am I looking for male companionship now? A meal ticket. Ain't that the main thing we're all looking for in a man?"

Thirteen heads nodded.

"*Yaaas*, but ya know, but like, sometimes the meal ticket part of it is like, a bummer if they like, stiff ya after the trick," Angie said.

"Why you need meal tickets?" Jada asked. "I bet you wasn't no poor white trash growin' up."

"No. My daddy had a good job. He was able to send me to UGA."

"Y'all should found yourself a college graduate, got hitched, and live happy ever after. Like they do in them Dizzy movies," Ebony said.

Lizzie nodded. "Like a lot of young girls, the main reason I went to college was to find a husband... looking for a meal ticket even back then. Unfortunately, it didn't work out quite the way I intended."

"What happened?"

"I had to leave after my freshman year."

"Why?" Juanita asked.

"It all started after I pledged A O Pi."

"Like, uh... what's a a o pie?" Pink asked.

"Alpha Omicron Pi... a sorority at UGA."

Lizzie ran down the A O Pi house hallway. Its cold tile floors chilled her bare feet—January in north Georgia is pretty cold. There had been no time to put on her slippers or socks because Rebecca Collins had summoned her. Immediately! Two short knocks, three long knocks, and a loud 'bulldog bark,' all part of a ritual required to gain permission to enter the room of her Big Sister.

"That didn't sound like anything even close to Uga," Rebecca said, referring to the name of the University of Georgia's bulldog mascot. "Bark again."

Lizzie repeated the bark with much more enthusiasm this time.

"Much better. Enter."

"A O Pi Pledge Sherbert reporting as y'all summoned." Lizzie repeated the ritual announcement while standing at rigid attention.

"Sherbert, I have a mission should you choose to accept it."

The popular quote from Mission Impossible had been formally adopted at A O Pi as part of standard procedures for assigning a pledge a hazing activity.

"Your wish is my command, ma'am."

"One of my boyfriend's engineering professors gave him an F last semester. Ruined his Christmas vacation... and mine. What do y'all think about that?"

"I think it sucks, ma'am."

Rebecca nodded appreciatively. "Y'all may just make it in this sorority after all. So, what're y'all gonna do about it?"

Lizzie stood immobile, her face a picture of ignorance. Her Big Sister gave her an idea.

"Them engineering professors always have blackboards full of their equations and formulas they's working on. Why don't y'all go erase his blackboard? He might not like that."

As a result, Lizzie found herself wandering through the Engineering Lab Building at 9:30 p.m. At 10:30 p.m., she stood at attention in her Big Sister's room.

"Well, I hope y'all got some good news to report."

"I do, ma'am."

"Did y'all erase his blackboard?"

"No, ma'am."

"YA'LL DIDN'T?!" A short pause followed Rebecca's shout. Then, a spine-tingling question. "And why not may I ask?"

"I got to thinking, ma'am. If I erase his board, it'll be a pain in the ass, but he'll know somebody did something. But his blackboard was so full of equations that I figured he'd never even notice a small change in one of 'em."

Rebecca's smile said it all. "Sherbert, I must admit that y'all exceeded my expectations. Y'all get a cookie."

Lizzie had changed the equation $Sig_L = Pd^2/(d+2t^2-d2)$ to $Sig_L = Pd^2/(d-2t^2+d2)$.

"Ju say that college didn't let ju return because ju change one equation?" Isabella shook her head. "That sounds like bullshit. I think ju make this up."

"It wasn't so much the change in the formula as what happened because of the change," Lizzie said.

"How so?" Lilly asked.

"Y'all ever hear of Apollo 13?"

"*Yaaas...* like, it was on TCM last month," Peggy said. "That movie was like, lit."

"That formula was part of something that Rebecca's boyfriend's engineering professor was working on for the Apollo 13 flight. After the problem with its oxygen tank during the moon flight in April that year, NASA investigated and reported out. They backtracked the problem, and it led them to that professor's calculations."

"How they know it was you?" Kanesha asked.

"I forgot and left my pledge paddle in the room. I'd been looking for it up until the day Campus Police came to my room."

Frigerator pieced everything together for her cellmates. "They knew it was you that change that formula that caused the Apollo 13 problems."

"Why they not arrest you?" Brianna asked.

"An arrest and trial would have brought too much bad publicity about lax security for both NASA and the University."

"Are you saying that was what caused you to not graduate?" Luisa asked.

"Yep. The Dean of Women made me an offer I couldn't refuse—leave quietly after my freshman year or face the justice system. All because my Big Sister's stupid boyfriend couldn't pass an Intro to Physics class, I get kicked out of Georgia."

Brianna said, "All my boyfriends be stupid. I ain't found one yet with a lick a sense."

"*Muy* true," Juanita said. "Only brains *hombres* got is between their legs."

"You never told us you were the cause of the Apollo 13 disaster." Daffy seemed truly offended.

"My agreement with the University and NASA stipulated that I had to keep it a secret for fifty years, so I had to be quiet until now. Now, it don't matter. I can 'fess up."

Gidget frowned. "Lizzie, Apollo 13 happened in spring of 1970. I remember because I was in Old Lady Bailey's math class when it happened. Your fifty-year anniversary is still half a year away."

"DAMN! Y'all're right! I gotta get me a new brain."

"As long as we're confessing," Babs said, "I might as well tell y'all something I been fretting about for two weeks now. I think I'm the cause of Tara's losing."

Chapter 33

"Babsie, y'all weren't the cause of Tara's losing," Daffy said. "It was that bullfrog... and Jubal Lee's sneakiness... not to mention his Grandma Stoney."

"What y'all talkin' 'bout? Bullfrog... jubilee?" Jada asked.

"The reason my granddaughter lost the contest was because a big frog jumped out onto the stage while she was dancing. We think the grandson of one of the women we made the bet with, a boy name Jubal Lee, was the one who tossed it out."

"I know," Babs said, "but I can't help thinking that something I did earlier that day might've been the real cause of Tara losing."

"What's that?"

"I never told y'all what happened after we left the IHOP that morning." As Babs spoke, Lilly lowered her head.

What happened was pretty weird by normal standards, but mostly par for the course for the Casserole Ladies.

Lilly pulled into Babs' driveway. Babs seemed to be deep in thought during the drive from IHOP and unaware of their arrival. Lilly prompted her. "I'll see y'all tonight. Need a ride to the school?"

"Yeah, thanks." Babs remained motionless, staring into space.

"Babsie... you all right?"

"Yeah, yeah... just thinking about something."

"What? Anything I can help you with?"

Twenty minutes later, they both sat cross-legged on the floor in the middle of Babs' living room, all her plantation shutters closed. A thin circle of Dragon's Blood powder and ground-up Apazote plant sprinkled on the floor surrounded them.

"Okay, I need you to hold Miss Monique's book open so I can read it. I gotta use both hands for this, and this is a pretty detailed hex."

"I still say we better not do this. Daffy'll kill us if she finds out."

Babs only reply was to narrow her eyes. Lilly picked up the book from the floor. In doing so, some of the pages fluttered shut, thereby losing Babs' place.

"That's okay, turn to the section labeled 'Voodoo for Sports, Gambling, Lotteries, and Games of Chance'. Keep going, keep going, there... that looks like it."

"Are you sure about this? Daffy said no more voodoo stuff. We might screw something up again."

"This ain't gonna hurt nothing. The ones we done before was just... was just bad luck. That's why I want you to hold Miss Monique's book for me... so's I can read it closely while I'm doing the hex."

Lilly watched as Babs unfolded a large white linen handkerchief and carefully placed it between them. She took out a small box, opened it, and very slowly sprinkled some of its contents on the handkerchief.

"Looking good so far... Hold the book a little closer so I can read the next part."

Babs' lips moved, silently reading. She intermittently turned her attention to another book lying on the floor beside her, leafing through its pages.

"What is that other book?" Lilly asked.

"This is my old French dictionary that I used at FSU. I wanna make sure I get things done right this time."

Repeatedly, Babs read from Miss Monique, consulted her French dictionary, then performed a task involving one of several other items sitting on the floor beside her. These items included several jars containing a variety of powders, several small statues, and a candle molded in the shape of a skull. When she was finished, a pile of powders, bug parts, and who-knows-what-else littered the white cloth.

"Now, we're ready for the chant. Hold the book closer. I gotta read this exactly."

Babs raised her arms as if they were upright goalposts and chanted.

"Vire Pitit Pitit Stoney A Nan Yon Krapo Boulèt Pou Sabote Dans Pitit Fi Daffy A."

"Vire Pitit Pitit Stoney A Nan Yon Krapo Boulèt Pou Sabote Dans Pitit Fi Daffy A."

"Vire Pitit Pitit Stoney A Nan Yon Krapo Boulèt Pou Sabote Dans Pitit Fi Daffy A."

Finished, Babs lowered her arms and sighed. She slowly massaged her own neck with both hands as she rotated her head to ease tension.

"What was that y'all just said?" Lilly asked.

"It was French."

"But what exactly was y'all saying in French?"

"Let Stoney lose this bet. Let Daffy win this bet... real big."

At the conclusion of Babs' story, the holding cell was silent. Daffy shrugged and looked at Babs. "Now, tell me why you think what y'all did might have contributed to Tara's loss?"

"I don't rightly know. I just feel like somehow what we... what I did that day somehow influenced her to lose."

"It wasn't Babs' fault Tara lost," Lilly said. "It was mine. If I had've done what I should've done and talked Babs out of it, Tara would've won. I just know it."

"No... it was my fault, not Lilly's."

Daffy took both Babs and Lilly into her arms in a group hug. "Lilly... Babs, y'all was just trying to help me out. That's what we all do for each other. We try to look out for each other. I love y'all for trying."

Delphine, for only the second time that night, spoke, her Caribbean accent unmistakable. She said, "My deeer Babs, are yoo sure yoo kneew what yoo weer sa-yeeng in yoor chant?"

"It was some sort of voodoo chant. I read what was in Miss Monique's book. Do y'all know what I said in my chant?"

"Yes."

"How come y'all know?"

"I know Miss Monique, and I know Haitian Creole, the language your chant was in."

"How do y'all know Miss Monique?"

"She scams tourists in Port au Prince."

"She does?!" A look of horror exploded on Babs' face.

"Yes. My biggest competitor."

"Y'all know about voodoo?"

"Yes, my dear. I practice it all my life in Port au Prince. My mother was a Mambo."

"A Mambo?"

"A Vodou Priestess."

After stunned silence throughout the cell, Gidget asked. "What exactly was Babs saying?"

Delphine laughed, then translated.

"Turn Stoney's grandson into a bullfrog to sabotage Daffy's granddaughter's dance."

Chapter 34

"Oh... oh... no more... I can't take anymore..." Babs remained doubled over, not in pain but in laughter.

"Me neither." Isabella wiped tears from her eyes.

"Mercy..." Brianna paused between belly laughs to get her breath. "You women... be more fun than watchin' *The Young and the Restless*—"

"Oh my God!" Lizzie immediately stopped laughing and clasped her face with both hands. "I just realized. This is Sunday morning, ain't it?"

"Yeah, very early Sunday morning," Daffy said. "So what?"

"We gotta get outta here today. I don't wanna miss tomorrow's episode of *The Young and the Restless*."

"Why?" Luisa asked. "Ju miss one episode. No big deal."

"NO BIG DEAL! That means I'll miss seeing whether or not Mariah decides to tell Sharon about Nick and Phyllis's fling."

"So what?"

"Luisa! Like, duh! Monday is like, the day before Nick and Sharon's wedding... duh!" Pink stared at her cellmate as if the woman had two heads.

"Like I said... no big deal."

Kanesha also piled on Luisa. "You be crazy. None us gone miss Mariah tellin' Sharon about Nick and Phyllis."

Perhaps it was Nick's infidelity with Phyllis, reminiscent of Bo's with Stoney. Perhaps it was nothing more than a long, smelly night in jail. Whatever it was, something snapped inside Daffy. An expression that fused solemnity, wisdom, and contentment descended upon her face as she looked at the other Casserole Ladies. "Y'all know something. It just dawned on me. How could I be so dumb?"

"What?!" asked Gidget. "What?"

Daffy replied with a question. "What did Kanesha say?"

"I don't remember... what?"

"She said that we don't really need men when we have each other as friends."

"Ehhh, I don't know about that," Lizzie said. "Not needing men, that is... that may be a bridge too far."

"Point taken, but remember what Frigerator told us. Something I'd never thought about."

"Like, ya know... what?" asked Angie.

"Like the fact that men always get more than they give."

"We get a lot too Daff," Babs said.

Daffy put on her best Dirty Harry face. "You're missing the point. It's like what Pink said."

"Like uh... wha'd I say?" asked Pink. "Like, ya know, I like, don't remember sayin' anything."

"You said that sex is different for women than it is for men. Pink, that is *sooo* true. Sex is just sex to men."

"I know there's a predicament somewhere in that last statement," Lizzie said, "but it's just not jumpin' out at me."

Daffy shook her head vigorously. "No no, hear me out. Juanita summed it all up in one sentence. Men think with their dicks. It's a big part of the reason why they're so dimwitted sometimes."

"True, but so what?" Gidget asked.

"Latonya told us what," Daffy said.

"Which was?"

"She said that we can't depend on men for companionship... or anything." Daffy looked at Gidget. "And it was you that reminded me that we, the five of us, *can* depend on each other."

"She's right," Lizzie said. "We don't have to depend on men."

Daffy nodded. "We don't need men. None of us has to have a man in our life in order to achieve fulfillment."

"Wait! I said we don't have to depend on men, not that we don't need men in our lives. Who am I supposed to watch Dawg football with?" Gidget asked.

"Who do you watch it with now?"

"Well... usually you or Babsie or Lilly or Lizzie..." Gidget paused in contemplation. "Whoever responds to my text first."

"Bingo! You're part of this team." Daffy's arms swept an arc formed by the other Casserole Ladies. "We are a team... and a damn good one at that. You watch football with the Ladies team—"

"Wait a second," Lizzie said. "It just hit me. What am I s'ppose to do about future alimony payments when this one dries up?"

"Lizzie, you forget that I'm Chairman of the Board of Sawgrass Bank. You're one of our largest depositors. I know the size of the fortune you're sitting on. Your financial woes come from the fact that you're just like a lot of other folks—enough ain't never enough," said Daffy.

Lizzie, head lowered in submission, jokingly whispered, "What about opening jars?"

"Look, the five of us have supported each other for years now. We survived getting arrested and spending a night in this here jail because we have each other. We can get along very well thank you, without being married." It was at this point that Daffy noticed a look of bewilderment on Lilly's face and turned to her. "You'll always have the true love you had with Wendell. You may find true love with another man again someday... and that will be great. But for now, you have four of the best friends you'll ever have, and that ain't so bad is it?"

Lilly replied with a head nod accompanied by tears. The quintet immediately hugged each other as their cellmates clapped. As applause receded, Gidget stepped back and rotated her head as she surveyed the squalid room. "Speaking of surviving a night in this jail, it would be nice if we could somehow make this place a little more cheerful while we're here."

Lizzie rolled her eyes. "Great idea... just like New Coke in the 80s and the Edsel in the 50s. Let's think of something practical... like getting out of here."

"I remember Nu Coke, but Edsel?" Kanesha asked.

"It was a car... old, gaudy, and over-chromed... kinda like me," Lizzie said.

Babs shook her head. "But that's just it. We don't know when we'll get outta here, and Gidg is right. We need to do something to brighten this place up while we're here."

"Light! This place needs more light. It's these burned-out light bulbs." Gidget pointed at the ceiling. "We have this same kind of fluorescent lighting in my pharmacy—"

"Smurfitt Pharmacy should use that in its advertising," Lizzie said. "Relax while we fill your prescriptions in mood lighting à la Duval County Jail."

"Ho, ho, ho. Excuse me if I forget to laugh. As I was about to say, a lot of times the bulbs aren't really burned out. All we have to do is twist them a little bit to get them reset properly to come back on. Let's try that here."

"How?" Latonya asked. "Them lights too high for us to reach."

Daffy stood and grabbed Frigerator's arms. "Y'all come over and stand here. Jada, you come stand in front of Frigerator. She and I are gonna lift you up so y'all can reach that burned-out bulb. Luisa and Latonya, y'all come over here and help keep Jada from falling."

Daffy and Frigerator clasped their hands together in stirrup-fashion and bent at their knees, allowing petite Jada to step up into their 'stirrup'. With the other two women steadying her, Jada rose to a height sufficient to reach the fixture. When she wavered, Lilly and Kanesha automatically moved in to provide even more support. After a few twists, the bulb re-ignited. Shouts of joy rang throughout the holding cell.

"Okay, let's try the rest," Daffy said.

The team succeeded on two other burned-out bulbs but failed on a third.

"Three outta four ain't bad odds." Babs' smile extended ear to ear.

"Better'n I usually get at Ebro," Lizzie said, referring to the greyhound racing track in northwest Florida. "At least when your bet turns out to be a dog at Ebro, it really is a dog."

Ebony shook her head. "Y'all should try the track at Daytona. Odds much better there."

"Ju know," Luisa said as she looked around, "it does look much better in here. Much brighter."

"Yeah." Lizzie leaned in close to Daffy and scrutinized her face. "We can see each other's wrinkles better."

Daffy smiled at the gag. She said, "Nevertheless, it was a great idea and great teamwork."

"That it be," Kanesha said.

Daffy spontaneously began shaking her cellmates' hands, prompting a round of group hugs. As the lovefest tapered off, Daffy came back to reality. "Now if we can just get outta this place—"

"All of us get out." Gidget looked around. "All of us. We need a lawyer."

"I know, I know!" As Lilly squealed, all heads turned toward her in anticipation. "Elvis Presley!"

"Elvis Presley for our lawyer?"

"Like, ain't he like, dead?" Angie asked.

"No, no." Lilly said. "Remember that movie where he was in jail?"

Daffy scrunched her face. "You mean *Jailhouse Rock*?"

"Yeah, that one. Well, we're kind've in the same situation Elvis was in, in that movie, right?"

"Okaaaay..."

"So, how did Elvis get outta his jail? Remember?" Lilly asked.

"He served his time and was released after a couple of years," Gidget said.

Lilly frowned. "Never mind. I thought he escaped. Something with shoe polish."

"Y'all don't need no lawyer. The Sheriff's comin' down now," Frigerator said.

"Coming down here? Now?" Babs asked.

Pink nodded. "*Yaaaas*... like, I got Officer Ronnie's text. He's like, on his way."

"Y'all got a text? On what?"

"Duh... like, on our phones. How else?" Peggy held up her iPhone.

"Y'all got phones down here?!"

"Sure. We all get to keep our phones in this here holdin' cell. Most us got business that don't stop when we be arrested." As Kanesha answered, most of the other cellmates held up their phones. "Officer Ronnie always sends us text... kinda heads up... let us know one of the Sheriff's deputies comin' down, and we best clean up our act before they get here."

"Wish I'd've known we would be able to keep our phones in jail before I ran nekkid across that football field." A thoughtful expression came over Lizzie's face as she looked down. "Wonder which roll of fat I would've stowed it in?"

At that point, sounds of footsteps reached the holding cell. The iron bar door at the end of the hallway opened, and a tall, lanky older man dressed in a crisp blue uniform stepped through.

"Must be the Sheriff," Gidget whispered to Daffy. "This guy looks pretty tough."

"That's putting it mildly," Daffy said as an ominous dark figure approached. Four stars on each shoulder, a badge over his left breast pocket, and several rows of ribbons over the right. Faded stitch marks bracketing a two-inch scar etched his tanned jawline. A pistol protruding from a black holster on a three-inch wide black leather belt completed his menacing demeanor.

"Uh oh... that be the Sheriff himself," Brianna whispered to Daffy. "That ain't good. He never come down here. He one mean muthafucka."

Daffy never noticed Officer Ronnie following the Sheriff until she slid around him and opened the holding cell door. Both stepped inside.

The Sheriff's head slowly moved as his cold grey eyes surveyed each of the room's occupants. His gaze stopped at Lilly. "I watched five nekkid women running across Bank field yesterday evenin' and thought, 'them Kardashian's is my kind've gals'. And, I'm watching them... and something about one of their asses looks familiar. I don't know what it is, but it looks familiar. Then, I get back here after a long night and see your name on the arrest sheet and said to myself, 'that cain't be Lilly... sounds like somethin' Lilly'd do, but it cain't be'. I knowed y'all had married a White... remember seein' y'all's announce-ment in the alumni magazine, but I still said to myself, 'not even Lilly would streak the Florida-Georgia game'—"

"Georgia-Florida game," Lizzie said.

"Whatever... but then, I remembered initiation night, St. Paddy's Day, in front of the library our freshman year, and I said to myself, 'yep, that's gotta be Lilly's ass. So, I headed down to Intake and asked Officer Ronnie for your mugshot. You ain't changed a bit."

Lizzie leaned in close to Daffy and whispered, "I guess we shouldn't've made such a big deal about removing the Kardashian makeup."

"Billy Bacon! When did y'all become Sheriff?!" Lilly asked as she moved inside her college chum's personal space.

"Daddy died four years ago, and it was my turn. What y'all been up to since we graduated... other than attending the Florida-Georgia game?"

"Sheriff!" Officer Ronnie inserted herself between Lilly and Billy. "They were arrested for violation of Section 800.03, Florida Statutes, to wit: unlawful exposure or exhibition of sexual organs in public, or be-ing naked in public except in any place provided or set apart for that purpose. In other words, they were arrested for streaking the Florida-Georgia game."

"Officer Ronnie, I read their arrest report. I know what they's ar-rested for, but... seems to me there's been a mistake." The Sheriff sur-veyed the Caserole Ladies. "These here ain't the same women I saw streaking the game yesterday evening. That was definitely them Kar-dashians that streaked the game."

Daffy whispered back to Lizzie, "I think you're right. Thank God Of-ficer Ronnie made us get rid of that makeup."

"I got video of it right here on my phone." The Sheriff extracted his iPhone and pulled up a viral YouTube video of the streaking. As it played, he said, "These five women here don't look like Kardashians, do they?"

"No sir, I guess they don't." Officer Ronnie meekly hung her head.

"Good. Yeah, I'd say Stadium Security arrested the wrong people. It's obvious these ladies aren't them Kardashian streakers. These here women don't even remotely look anything like the Kardashians in that video. We got to let these women go. Release all five of 'em. Got that?"

"Yes sir."

"What about our new friends here?" Lilly waved her arm in the direction of their cellmates. "We can't just leave them here."

Daffy stepped forward. "Yeah. If they don't go, then we don't go."

The Sheriff looked at Officer Ronnie. "What're they in for?"

"A variety of offenses... mostly in connection with the game yesterday... prostitution, some drugs, a couple of minor assaults... the usual low-level offenses that this bunch gets arrested for."

"I think the Duval County Sheriff's Office can be generous... especially since Florida won. Release all of 'em." The Sheriff wrapped his arm around Lilly and maneuvered her toward the holding cell door. "Y'all come on back with me to my office. We got lots of catching up to do."

Chapter 35

Facebook buzzed the day after the World's Largest Outdoor Cocktail Party.

Judy Davis is at Tockwotton Historic District Neighborhood

October 8th Thomasville, GA

Any update on Lilly? I'M GETTING WORRIED. It's almost 6 pm, and she's still not home.

View 21 more comments

Lori Snipes I been watching her house all day, and no one's come back yet. I thought they were coming back last night after the game.

Cindy Nelson I been watching too, and I ain't see hide nor hair of her since she left Saturday morning in Babs' Escalade.

Penny Perdoo She's not back because she's probably in jail. I been telling y'all all day that she was one of them streakers at the game yesterday.

Randy Kraft I don't believe that could have been Lilly, Daffy, Lizzie, Babs, and Gidget. NO WAY! THAT WAS THE KARDASHIANS. I watched the whole thing on TV.

Sue Allen Most women at church this morning thought it was Daffy and her pals.

Judy Davis Everyone at the Garden Club this afternoon thought it was Kardashians, only a little heavy on their makeup.

Cindy Nelson Some people at Sunday Brunch at the Country Club this morning thought it was a bunch of half-wit terrorists.

Lori Snipes If it was the Daffy and her crew, why weren't their names and pictures in the Arrests Section of the paper this morning. That makes me think it WAS the Kardashians, and they got off scot free like celebrities always do.

Penny Perdoo That was definitely Lilly and her pals! I'm telling y'all that they was the ones that streaked that game. That's why she didn't come back last night. Twenty bucks says she spent a night in Duval County Jail. Probably be there a long time unless Daffy's lawyer can work another miracle. WHAT THEY DID WAS ON NATIONAL TELEVISION!

Randy Kraft Vince Lindquist and Danny Garrison both thought it was Kardashians, and they're two of the most knowledgeable sportscasters ever on TV. I trust their judgement.

Penny Perdoo They may know football, but they don't know nudity.

Sue Allen I been checking Kourtney Kardashian's Facebook page. She got a lot of Likes about them streaking the Florida-Georgia game, and she HAS NOT denied that it was them!

Cindy Nelson Not denying it proves that it was Kardashians.

Cathy Verdun But she hasn't said that it was them, which says that it was not Kardashians.

Randy Kraft NOT saying that it was them says that it WAS them. If they said it was them, nobody would believe them.

Penny Perdoo Me, Stoney, Toots, and Mitzi were at the game. That was NOT Kardashians running nekkid on that field.

Cathy Verdun If all y'all was there, then it sounds like maybe those streakers was really y'all. BTW, I heard that your cruise didn't go too well.

Judy Davis That's old news. People on the Dawson Street Historic District Neighborhood Facebook page are calling it the

Catastrophic Cruise. NO ONE'S SEEN STONEY AND BO TO-GETHER SINCE THEY GOT BACK. I heard the four boys played a lot of poker most of the cruise without the Mahjong Mammas.

Randy Kraft Cootie told me the sight of Mitzi and Toots in bikinis everyday was more than he could take.

Cindy Nelson I saw Cootie and Wesley at Sunday Brunch chatting it up with Sylvia Waddell and Lois Burdette this morning. Penny and Toots weren't with them. Trouble in Paradise?

Penny Perdoo Y'all wish! Toots and I just happened to have Altar Guild this morning. Our Cruise was great! All those rumors going around ain't true. ALL OF US had a great time. That business about us getting into a shuffleboard argument is a bunch of BS, as is the story about Cootie spending all his time with that over-the-hill Botox slut from Birmingham, and that picture of me, Stoney, Toots and Mitzi swimming nekkid in the Aft Deck Pool is photoshopped.

Lori Snipes Hold on. I see Babs' Escalade pulling into Lilly's driveway. Lilly's getting out.

0830 MT, Monday, D+2. What better way to beat a hangover than a late breakfast at a Waffle House? That was the Casserole Ladies' consensus the second day after their release from the Duval County Pre-Trial Detention Facility. Only problem was the local Waffle House didn't have a table large enough to accommodate all five and their food, so they met at the IHOP instead.

"Once again Ladies, we survived another fiasco, this one by the skin of our teeth," Daffy said. "A lot of people think it was the Kardashians."

Gidget motioned for silence. "Quiet. Here comes our waitress."

"Y'all like, ready to order?" The Gen Z'er asked. She paused, seeming to scrutinize them. "Like, y'all mind if I ask y'all something?"

Daffy nodded. "What's on your mind?"

"Was it really y'all or them Kardashians?"

Lizzie said, "With all them wrinkles running around on that field, it looked to me like four of ET's aunts was trying to catch him so they could take him back to Mars."

"ET?"

"It was a movie... before your time."

"I think Kardashians look like they're from Mars anyway," Daffy said.

"How do we know they're not?!" Bab's eyes suddenly became saucers. "What better way to invade us than starting in Hollywood? You wouldn't be able to tell the aliens from the humans in that town."

"Nope. Aliens invading Hollywood would never happen," Lizzie said. "Anyone from another planet would take one look at the folks in Hollywood, turn around, and go back home."

"That UFO stuff is for the birds," Gidget said.

Babs reply came quickly. "No, it ain't! UFOs is for real!"

"What're you saying? You don't actually believe in that little green men stuff, do you?" Lilly asked.

"Listen... I been on some real interesting UFO websites lately, and y'all wouldn't believe what's going on out there. The Federal government just don't want us to know about it, that's all. I can show y'all some of this stuff when we get time. There's even a place within a days' drive that—"

"Let's defer this discussion until another time and give this young lady our orders so she don't get fired," Daffy said.

The poor girl took their orders and scurried off with a puzzled look on her face. Bo and Stacie Goodie walked in fifteen minutes later. The couple looked around, then headed to the Casserole Ladies' table. Both looked contrite.

Stacie spoke first. "Hey, we figured y'all was here."

A muffled "hey" was all Bo could manage.

"Hey to both of y'all as well," Daffy said. "Have a seat. What's up with y'all?"

"Daff, I... we wanted to let y'all know before the rest of Thomasville knows... Bo and I are getting married," Stacie said. A pregnant pause ensued.

"Daff, it just happened," Bo said. "Stacie and I been together a lot the past few weeks, and we realized that we love each other. It's funny... I thought I'd never marry again, but..." Another pause ensued before Daffy smiled and took Stacie's hands into hers.

"I couldn't be happier for both of y'all. Y'all have my... our best wishes." Daffy looked around at her companions. "Don't they, Ladies?"

"Absolutely!" rang out in unison.

After congratulations and discussion of their wedding plans, Stacie brought up a new topic. "I do have some good news for y'all. Royalty checks from the calendar keep coming in. It's selling like hotcakes throughout the South. I'm thinking about a fourth printing."

"Sounds like the ED crowd can't get enough of us," Lizzie said.

"They got our calendar in the hospital's emergency department?!" Lilly asked.

"Erectile Dysfunction... not Emergency Department."

Stacie bit her tongue. "What do y'all want done with your share of the royalties?"

The Ladies looked at each other for a suggestion, which Daffy offered. "I vote we donate them to the Duval County Jail... for the specific purpose of renovating their women's holding cell."

"Yeah!" Babs said. "New paint, more comfortable benches, things like that."

Lizzie put on her Nancy Grace face. The one that celebrity uses when she discusses a homicide case. "And some sort of privacy. Where inmates don't have to display their behinds when they gotta take care of business."

"Sounds like y'all have some sort of personal knowledge of that jail." Stacie winked.

Daffy delivered a carefully worded reply. "Let us simply say that none of us need the calendar proceeds, and we think the jail can use it in a more worthy manner."

"Super! By the way, y'all will be getting some visitors shortly."

"Who?"

"An SUV stopped by the Tourist Center right before Bo and I left. Several older gentlemen came in and asked where they could find The Thomasville Widows... the ones in the calendar."

Babs asked, "Older gentlemen? How many? Where did they come from?"

"I only remembered their first names 'cause I couldn't stop laughing."

"What were they?"

"Larry, Jerry, Harry, Barry, and Gary."

"Oh brother!" Lizzie said. "They sound like a comic group from a 1930s movie. You sure they ain't the Marx Brothers reanimated from the dead? Where did these five gems come from?"

"The Villages."

"Say no more." Babs quickly resumed eating. "Maybe we can finish before they get here. I don't know if I could handle four more hours in the emergency room."

"And they're coming here to this IHOP?" Lilly asked.

"Probably. They were real anxious to meet y'all. I told them you'd probably be at one of several places, including this one. Figured I'd lead them on a wild goose chase for a while... Give Bo and me a chance to talk to y'all first."

As if on cue, Bo joined the conversation. "I think George, Wesley, and Cootie will be looking for y'all as well. They told me that they want all of us to get together for a cookout. They still don't know about Stacie and me."

"Sounds like competition for the Thomasville Casserole Ladies is heating up. Anyway, Bo and I gotta go. We got a lot of preparations to do. You're all invited to the wedding," Stacie said.

The couple rose, said their goodbyes, and walked to the restaurant door. Bo opened the door for Stacie, then both looked back and waved. Stoney, Penny, Mitzi, and Toots suddenly brushed through the doorway without acknowledging the couple.

Lilly took note of the obvious breach of good manners. "Where is Emily Post when you need her?"

"Why does the theme to *The Empire Strikes Back* always come to mind when I see them?" Lizzie asked. She lowered her voice pitch and hummed, "Dum, dum, dum, dum-de-dum, dum-de-dum..."

"If they were younger, I'd say they all started their periods this morning," Daffy said. "My guess is that they're pissed because they don't have proof of us streaking Saturday."

"And because their cruise didn't go so well," Gidget added.

After discussion among themselves, Stoney led the other Mahjong Mammas to the ladies' table. Contempt radiated from her face. "I'm surprised you've got the nerve to show your faces after Saturday afternoon."

"What do y'all mean? Why wouldn't we show our faces?" Daffy asked.

"Y'all know what I mean... after being seen nekkid on national television."

Daffy held up her arms, palms up, feigning mock surprise. "Y'all think that was us? Did them nekkid women on TV look like us? We were at the game and saw everything ourselves. Now, I ain't gonna accuse the Kardashians of streaking, but it sure looked like them running around on that football field to me."

"So, you're saying you all welshed on your bet?" Mitzi asked.

"Them's fightin' words." Gidget grabbed the arms of her chair and rose slightly as if ready to attack. "We *never* welsh on our bets, and y'all can't prove that we did... or didn't."

Stoney shook her head. "They didn't welsh on their bets. Everyone knows that wasn't the Kardashians. Besides, no Kardashian would be caught dead with a Ron Paul tattoo."

"The Kardashians haven't denied it was them," Babs said.

Lilly added, "And they haven't denied it wasn't them."

"Y'all might want to try getting a life instead of trying to irritate us. After your catastrophic cruise, it sounds like you four are gonna have to start hunting for some more men," Daffy said.

"Y'all also might wanna wear one-piece swimsuits next cruise," Lizzie said. "Bikinis at your ages just don't work... although that's better than y'all swimming nude."

"Rumor is that Bo, Wesley, George, and Cootie entertained themselves with a lot of poker most of the trip." Gidget lowered herself back down in her seat.

"Don't believe every rumor you hear," Stoney said.

"Facebook never lies." Daffy pointed toward the other side of the restaurant. "Now, if y'all don't mind, we'd like to finish our breakfast in peace. Run along and go eat your cantaloupe and prunes."

Gidget again spoke after the Mammas departed. "By the way, I filled a prescription for Jubal Lee late last week. He came down with some sort of allergy after the dance contest."

"Allergy?" Lilly asked.

"Yeah... wart-like rash, croaky throat, kinda green around the gills..."

Daffy turned to Lilly. "Okay, before our Villages Romeos get here, tell us about Billy Bacon. We didn't get much info from you yesterday."

"Yeah, what's the story about you and Billy and that initiation?" Babs asked.

Lilly's head carefully looked around surveying their privacy. She said, "Well, Billy was a good-looking hunk back in college. I forgot all about Wendell when I saw him—"

"I can see how that could happen with a tall drink of cool water like the Sheriff," Lizzie said.

"Momma was right when she told me a little cooling off might be good for me, although I didn't wanna hear it at the time. That's why she wanted me to go to Florida instead of Georgia. Anyway, I met Billy first day at Freshman Orientation. We hit it off right away—"

"And you immediately traded Wendell for Billy—"

"Kinda reminds me of Christina and Tarek on *Flip or Flop*," Babs said.

"Y'all quit interrupting her and let her get on to the initiation," Daffy said. "The one on St. Patrick's Day at the library."

"Oh yeah. Well, by that time we were going together hot and heavy—"

Gidget translated. "What she means to say is that they were going all the way."

Lilly put on her best Scarlett O'Hara smile. A dead ringer for the coy one Vivien Leigh used with the two Tarleton brothers at Twelve Oaks Plantation. She said, "Y'all know a Southern Lady never tells. Anyway, Kappa Alphas and Tri-Delts were brothers-sisters at Florida, so part of our initiation ceremonies was conducted jointly. Did I mention Billy pledged KA? Anyway, he did. Him being there was a big part of what made that initiation very memorable to say the least—"

"Too bad they didn't have smartphones back then." Lizzie followed her interruption with an exaggerated sigh.

"So anyway, they take us to the library quadrangle in only our bras and panties—"

"I didn't know young men wore bra and panties back then—"

"Not nearly as many as do nowadays," Babs said.

"How do you know?" Gidget asked.

"Ho, ho, ho. Excuse me if I forget to laugh."

Lilly crossed her arms in frustration. She said, "No! Y'all know what I mean. Boys was only wearing their underwear. Anyway, the brothers and sisters take about thirty or forty of us pledges to the library quadrangle at midnight. This was after drinking at least two five-gallon batches of Purple Passion, spiked with 190 proof grain alcohol."

"Is there any other kind of Purple Passion? Why you say 'at least two'?" Lizzie asked.

"I quit counting after the first batch," Lilly replied.

"I'm beginning to appreciate why Billy Bacon ran down to the holding cell," Daffy said. "Please continue."

"So, when they take off our blindfolds, I see the brothers and sisters have formed two long columns—"

A commotion interrupted as five older gentlemen shuffled into the IHOP lobby. They appeared to be looking for someone. Daffy turned back to her teammates and said, "Looks like the Marx Brothers found us before we could escape. Lilly's initiation story will have to wait for another time."

Acknowledgement

Many thanks to our editors Kendall Roberts and Alyssa McFall and our beta readers Danny and Rannie Tucker, Gidget Casey, and Lori Grinter. Others deserving mention include Donna Porter, Susie Adkins, and Diane Jones who unknowingly provided material for some of the wackiness. Finally, our thanks to Carole and Marc Townsend for their encouragement and help in publishing the book.

About the Authors

Billy and Linda Johnson Billy and Linda are a husband and wife writing team intimately familiar with life in the South, having grown up in that region and now living in Alabama.